"It's [...]
when Jo [...]
as the four other men raised their voices in agreement.

Suddenly, the door swept open and Mrs. Surratt rushed in. "Wilkes!" she said excitedly. "There was a man in the hall—listening!"

The men ran to the window. "There he is," Booth shouted, "running across the yard!"

"This could get us all hanged, Booth," Lewis Powell said.

"Make them leave," Mason Butler, the War Department clerk, said to the actor. "I can take care of this, but I won't say a word with them here."

Grumbling, the four men descended the stairs. When they were gone, Booth said, "You know the man, Mason?"

"Yes, I do, and I'll remove him for one thousand dollars."

"All right," Booth agreed.

"There's one more thing," Butler said. "I've given heart and soul in the service of my government, and gotten nothing in return. When you tell the world about these dead tyrants of government, I want you to convince them that certain men of quality have been cheated out of their rightful public offices by Seward and Stanton and Lincoln. Men like Mason Butler."

Booth said through clenched teeth, "Do you really expect me to cheapen my greatest moment with an advertisement for you?"

"If you expect me to commit murder to save your plot," Butler said. "Now, what's your answer? Do I kill him or not?"

"Yes, damn it!" John Wilkes Booth cried out. "Kill him! Kill him!"

## The Making of America Series

# THE
# ASSASSINS

**Lee Davis Willoughby**

A DELL/JAMES A. BRYANS BOOK

Published by
Dell Publishing Co., Inc.
1 Dag Hammarskjold Plaza
New York, New York 10017

Dell TM 681510, Dell Publishing Co., Inc.

ISBN: 0-440-00332-6

Printed in the United States of America

First printing—January 1984

# Chapter 1

The loud, frantic pounding on the front door downstairs sounded like the end of the world to Stephen Bedford. In the master bedroom of the Arlington family mansion, the young Confederate captain flipped the white linen coverlet off his bare chest, raised himself up, and groggily swung his legs over the side of the mattress.

"All right, all right," he muttered, more to himself than to the intruder. He fumbled a white phosphorous match out of the box next to the bed, struck it, touched the fire to the wick of the oil lamp, and strained to look at his watch. It was 11:46. What was all the noise about? The war was over now, with Lee's surrender at Appomattox two days ago, on April 9, 1865. Why on earth would anyone be rousing him out of bed at this time of night?

Annoyed by the constant banging on the door, he hurriedly slipped his arms into the satin dressing gown his father had owned and yanked the sash tight around his waist. A tall and slender man of twenty-five, Stephen possessed what the women in the Bedford family of Virginia called "dark good looks": the traditional Bedford black hair, the strong chin, the deep-set hazel eyes and finely chiseled features. Even though he was still clean-shaven and hence a good deal more youthful-looking than most Confederate officers, he had gained the respect of practically every surviving man in Lee's Army of Northern Virginia with a daring bravery combined with a natural good sense.

"Captain Bedford!" a voice muffled by two inches of solid oak called out to him. "Wake up!"

"All right, I'm awake!" he yelled back. "I'm coming!"

Stephen tugged on his military boots, snatched up the lamp, and headed out of the bedroom into the hallway on the second floor. The familiar voice behind the door was making his blood rush excitedly through his veins. It belonged to Patrick O'Connor, the big Irishman he had dragged unconscious out of a storm of gunfire at Antietam in '62. He knew this man would never impose on him for any reason short of a crisis over life and death.

Downstairs, in the spacious marble foyer where his parents had once greeted Southern dignitaries like Jefferson Davis, Robert E. Lee, and Alexander Stephens, Bedford grabbed the black leather holster and belt off the wall rack and slid the blue steel Colt revolver out of the scabbard. Pressing the pistol firmly against his right thigh, he swung open the massive door.

"What is it, Paddy—"

"Captain—" O'Connor interrupted. The huge bearded

man was gripping his left biceps with his right hand. Blood was trickling out of his gray Confederate jacket and through his fingers. "We got trouble here."

"Damn, look at you!" Stephen jerked open the screen door. "What's happened?"

"Never mind me, Captain." He gestured with his head toward the front lawn. "I'm all right. This lad here's asking for you."

Bedford's eyes shifted from Paddy to the grass in front of the stone steps. In the glow of a single flaming torch stuck in the soft ground, he could see a blond man, no more than twenty. He lay curled in the arms of Dr. Ellis Madison, the old physician from Alexandria who had attended Stephen's mother the night she died of the fever. Bedford leaped down from the porch and sank to his knees beside the young man.

"Private Massey!" he exclaimed. "Who did this to you?"

"He might not hear you, son," the white-haired doctor told him. "He's pretty far gone."

Bedford ignored him. "Massey, say something, man!"

"The boy's got a bullet in his back, Stephen," Madison informed him. "He's bleeding to death. He won't last another five minutes."

Bedford felt his anger rising. "Why would anybody do this!" he growled. "Don't they know the war is over!"

"Maybe they don't know," the doctor offered. "Some of these Union soldiers don't know how to quit."

"Begging your pardon, sir," O'Connor chimed in, "but I can tell you for sure, that was no Union soldier I saw riding high-tail out of here. This lad was dressed in city clothes, with a black coat and a tall silk hat."

Stephen felt the young man's fingers groping along his

arm. Suddenly, as he clutched his wrist, Massey's eyes fluttered, then opened. "Cap . . . tain . . ." He struggled to speak.

"I'm here, Private. Take it easy."

"Captain . ., . Gettysburg."

"I know," Bedford touched the other man's hand. Gettysburg wasn't something he would ever forget. The images of human carnage were burned into his memory. He had been a lieutenant in the cavalry then, and Massey no more than an eighteen-year-old recruit under his command. They had stood together and braced themselves as Pickett's crazed men came charging wildly down Seminary Ridge, and then, later, they had staggered side by side off the body-littered field, in a bloody train of Southern men. There had been so many of them: 10,000 dead or missing, 18,000 wounded . . .

"Captain," Massey whispered, "Save . . ."

Bedford lowered his ear to Massey's lips. "Save who, Private?" he asked.

After a few strained moments of silence, the boy mumbled, "Gettysburg," in a low, choking voice.

"Massey," said Stephen, trying to stay calm. "Listen to me. Gettysburg is over. Do you understand me? Gettysburg is dead and gone. Now, tell me who you are talking about. Who is in danger?" He saw the boy's eyelids droop, then close. "Massey!" he shouted. "Wake up, damn it! Massey—can you hear me? Talk to me!"

"It's no use, Stephen," the doctor said.

"But he can't die—not like this."

"He's already dead, son. He's in the hands of God now." With those words, he lowered the body gently to the grass.

Bedford stared blankly at the pale, gaunt face of Donald

Massey. Another dead man. How many had it been now? How many men had he seen buckling under a barrage of cannon fire, how many sprawling on the grass or snow, choking on their own spit and blood? A thousand? Ten thousand? Somewhere around the Battle of the Wilderness in May of '64, he had stopped counting. He sucked in a deep breath and rose to his feet.

"What a damned useless way to die," he rasped through clenched teeth. He watched old Dr. Madison shed his coat and drape it slowly over the body. He had hoped this familiar feeling of total frustration would end with the war, but here he was again—standing helplessly over a boy's body, unable to do a thing to save him. "Useless," he repeated.

"The lad died easy, though," O'Connor noted. "It didn't take long. And finding you helped some."

The sentiment didn't help Stephen any. "Did he say anything to you?" he asked Paddy.

O'Connor scratched his tawny beard. "All he told me was, he saw the man's boots. He said they shined like glass."

"Glassy boots." Bedford frowned. "Not much to go on, is it?"

"No, sir," Paddy agreed. "It ain't."

"Doctor—" Bedford turned to Madison, "go through his pockets. Maybe that will tell us something."

While the physician lifted the coat and began digging dutifully into Massey's pockets, Stephen stole a look at his friend Paddy O'Connor. The Irishman was massive and powerful enough to lift a cow or break a man's back like a dry twig; but under all that brawn was a soft heart. Although Paddy was embarrassed by any show of emotion,

Stephen had more than once seen a tear come to his eye, as was the case now in the presence of Donald Massey.

Bedford couldn't help but note that he and his friend were so different in their outlooks. While Bedford had long ago reconciled his mind to the realities of civil war, to fighting against men of his own country, O'Connor hadn't. To this Irish immigrant, men were men, no matter what color coat they wore. He had proven himself a faithful Confederate, but Paddy owned a loyalty only to men of his own native country—and to the one man who had saved his life, Stephen D. Bedford.

"This was all the boy had, Stephen," the doctor noted as he handed him a stack of objects from the Massey's pockets. "It's not much for a lifetime."

Bedford took the items and glanced through them: a receipt for $25.60 from the General Land Office, a rusty bone-handle pocketknife, two ten-dollar bills, a latchkey to Room 103 of the Capitol Park Hotel, and a torn, blood-stained playbill. The advertisement for the play interested him the most. He stepped closer to the torch to read it. Most of the letters of the words in the notice had been ripped away:

> -----------centric comedy,
> ----performed by her upwards of
> -----------Nights,
> -------------------tled
> ------------merican
> ---------*USIN*
> ---enchard. . . . Miss Laura Keene

On the back of the wrinkled page was a series of letters written in pencil. At first, they made no more sense to him than the printed ones: $g\ w\ l\ t\ q\ k\ j\ i\ j—14—c\ e\ l\ a—q\ w\ x.$ But then, suddenly, it occurred to him that the sequence had an underlying meaning.

"There's a message here, Paddy," he announced. "It looks like the Vicksburg Code." That was the Confederate designation for the Vigenère Tableau, the substitution cipher used by Jeb Stuart's spy rings during the war. Stuart had learned it from Major Albert Myer, a Unionist who was appointed the first commanding officer of the Army Signal Corps when it was created in 1863. Stephen had used the code once himself, in a message he sent to Colonel Jubal Early on the deployment of Union troops at Chancellorsville.

O'Connor scratched his beard thoughtfully. "Now why do you suppose this brave little lad would be carrying such a thing as a coded message, Captain?" he wondered aloud.

"He must have been bringing it to me," Bedford answered quickly. "That's why he was killed." He looked at the physician. "Dr. Madison, would you take care of Massey? I've got some business in the house."

"Don't worry, Stephen; I'll see to him," the doctor assured him. "I'll get old Samuel to help me."

"Thank you."

"Now wait a minute there, Captain," Paddy spoke up. "You ain't going off without telling me what you're up to, are you?"

"And while you're at it, do something about Sergeant O'Connor's wound," Bedford said to the doctor. "The pain in his arm is making him nosey."

"I'd remember the war is over if I were you, Captain," O'Connor pointed out. "It's possible you'd be better off leaving that message just as it is."

But Stephen Bedford was in no mood to be cautious.

Paying no attention to O'Connor's words, he left the two men, dashed into the house, slid open the library doors, and lit the oil lamps on the hand-carved cherry desk in the center of the room. Then, whipping out a sheet of stationery from the middle drawer, he dipped the desk pen in the inkwell and scribbled out a quick tableau for the code. It consisted of a square pattern of letters made by meshing the alphabet written twenty-seven times vertically and twenty-seven times horizontally.

Now, in order to make the substitution, he needed to know the secret key phrase Massey had used to create the coded message from his tableau. He tried several combinations that had been used in the Army recently: Davis is in Richmond; In God we trust; River Queen; and Torpedoes. But none of them worked.

After a moment of frustration, he leaned back in the leather chair, drew in a deep breath, and tried to think calmly and clearly. If Private Massey had come to Arlington to deliver him the message, he reasoned, then the man would have done everything he could to reveal the key phrase to him before he died. He recalled the scene with Massey on the lawn. The only word he had repeated was *Gettysburg*. Now he understood—Massey had been talking about the code, not the battle! Stephen instantly scratched the letters of that word beneath the nonsense letters of the code, and checked the columns of the tableau. Like a locked door opening, the procedure worked.

"Captain?" O'Connor appeared in the doorway in his shirt sleeves, with his arm bandaged. He was holding his Sharps breechloader by the end of the barrel and casually resting the walnut stock on the floor.

"Just a minute." Stephen held up his left hand while he continued to write with the other. "I've almost got it.

Three more letters.'' A minute later, as the Irishman drew close to the desk, he snapped up the paper. ''This is it, Paddy,'' he said. ''Listen: ASSASSINS. FOURTEEN. WASH. SEW—'' He popped the paper with the back of his hand and stood up. ''An assassination in Washington City. Probably the fourteenth of this month. That's three days from now. It isn't much time.''

''Much time for what, Captain?'' He leaned his rifle against the desk and picked up the playbill.

Stephen began pacing the floor and running his fingers nervously through his black hair. ''If the word *assassins* is correct,'' he said excitedly, ''there could be more than one attempt in Washington. Evidently Massey thought I could do something about it.''

The Irishman perused the note. ''The message is cut off here,'' he observed. ''Just who are we to think is supposed to be assassinated, Captain? Is it this *Sew*—? Does that mean Seward, the Secretary of State?''

''I don't know,'' Stephen answered. ''And I only have three days to find out.''

O'Connor raised his eyebrows. ''You wouldn't be thinking of going in there yourself, would you, sir?'' he asked.

Bedford took the playbill out of the other man's hand. ''I would,'' he said.

''Well, I don't know. Washington City's a mighty rotten place, Captain. Last time I was there, they had muddy streets and clogged-up sewers, and hogs was wallowing around in the gutter and dead cats floating in the canal running up to the Capitol—''

''I don't care about what's in the canal, Paddy.''

''Well, it ain't just the canal, Captain Bedford. It's a dangerous place, too. If the pickpockets and cutthroats and thieves don't get you, then the Sisters of Mercy and Charity will. If the town ain't overrun with criminals and politicians, it's festering with lady do-gooders from Massachusetts, like this Miss Dix and Miss Alcott. Either way, a man can't breathe in there.''

"How is it a sergeant in the Confederate Army knows all this?'' Bedford asked. "A sergeant who hasn't been out of my sight in two years.''

The Irishman's face flushed red. "Yes, sir, I guess that's true,'' he acknowledged. "I have been pretty close by. But even so, I've got a few friends over in Washington City. You know—countrymen. They tell me things.''

Stephen looked at him with interest. "Do they?'' he said. "What do these countrymen of yours say is happening in Washington right now?''

"Right now the Unionists are celebrating their victory, Captain. I would say it's no place for a Confederate officer such as yourself to be.''

Bedford clenched his fist. "Then why don't you tell me what a Confederate officer like me should do,'' he said. "Should I stay here in this cold, empty old house, with no family or servants? Should I polish my buttons and go parade around in the streets of Arlington? Should I sit in front of the fire and tell children about the late war? No, Sergeant. As long as I can still serve my country, I will not just . . . sit. I can't.''

"No, sir,'' O'Connor said flatly.

Bedford stuffed the playbill into the pocket of his dressing gown. After a minute, he looked straight at the Irishman. "Don't fight me, Paddy,'' he warned. "Not after all we've been through together. You saw that boy die out there on the lawn a while ago. You even took a bullet in your arm, trying to help him. Don't you think we should at least try to honor his last request?''

O'Connor considered the question a moment. "Yes, sir," he finally answered, "I guess we should."

"Then stand back and let me try to stop these assassins, whoever they are."

"Yes, sir." O'Connor rubbed the bandage on his arm. "Only I think before you go off to Washington City, you ought to consider it's possible these assassins Massey was writing about are planning to kill President Lincoln."

At the sound of the President's name Bedford paused and swallowed hard. After a moment of staring at O'Connor, he walked over to the window and gazed out through the glass. He watched Madison and an elderly black man struggle to heave Massey's body into a wagon. As old Samuel guided the wagon horse off the lawn to the driveway, images of the days of slaves and parties and wagons loaded down with cotton flashed in his mind. All of that had been whisked away, somehow, by the long and violent winds of war—a war started, according to Southern thinking, by the election of one man: Abraham Lincoln.

"Is that something your friends in Washington told you, Paddy?" he asked, still looking out the window.

"That's what they say," he acknowledged. "I hear there's been a rumor of an assassination ever since Sherman set fire to Columbia back in February."

The captain turned around. "All right, Sergeant," he said sternly. "If Lincoln is the target, so be it. I may hate the man for what he's done to the South, but whatever his politics, he is still the President. No handful of rabble-rousers has the right to strike down the leader of this country, and I don't have the right to stand by and let it happen, not when I might be able to do something about it."

"I was hoping to hear you say that, Captain," O'Connor said.

"What?"

"Yes, sir, it pleases me down to the toes. Now, if you don't mind," he said as he picked up his rifle, "I'll be going out to the tack room to gather up my gear, so we can get a good start in the morning. Would you say we'd be leaving about dawn, Captain?"

"Whoa, now. Hold on there, friend. You're not going with me."

"Sir?" He frowned.

"I don't see any reason for you to go. You don't owe any allegiance to the Confederacy anymore, Paddy. Or to my rank, either."

"No, sir, I know I don't." He headed for the door. "But I still owe allegiance to you."

Bedford stopped him. "Now, damn it, O'Connor," he said, exasperated. "You just told me, Washington is a dangerous place—"

"So it is, Captain. Which is why I wouldn't think of letting you go there alone."

"Sergeant, I'm a grown man and a former officer in the Confederate Army. I certainly don't need a protector. Besides, didn't I tell you in the Shenandoah that you don't owe me anymore?"

"Well, yes, sir, I do remember you saying that. But, I don't know, while it's true you have a helping of good sense in that head of yours, I'm thinking you still might be a wee bit impulsive at times. So if you don't mind, I'll just go along and see to it you don't get all that sense knocked out in the streets of Washington City."

"Paddy?" he called out as the Irishman reached the door.

"Sir."

"I appreciate your loyalty, but I don't want you along unless you understand why I want to do this."

"I understand why, Captain Bedford. As you say, I've been with you for two years."

"It's just that after all this futile slaughter, we may finally have a chance to make a man's death mean something."

"Yes, sir."

Stephen was puzzled by his easy acquiescence. "If you understand that," he asked, "why have you been standing there opposing me all this time?"

"I wasn't opposing you, Captain," he denied. "I would never do that. I was merely pointing out the dangers to us both."

Stephen let out a long sigh. "Sometimes, Paddy O'Connor," he said, shaking his head, "for some reason, you look to me very much like a mother hen."

"I do not see the resemblance, Captain," the Irishman replied.

"Well, anyway, Sergeant, when we reach Washington, the first thing we'll do is trace the playbill. Which shouldn't take too long, since there are only a couple of theaters in the city."

"Three that I know of: Washington, Grover's, and Ford's."

"All right, three. I stand corrected."

"And where will we be staying while we're there, sir?"

"I don't know. You know the city better than I do. Pick a hotel."

O'Connor rubbed his whiskers. "Off the top of my head, I would recommend the National Hotel at Sixth Street and Pennsylvania Avenue."

"Don't tell me—you know somebody who works there."

"I believe the main clerk is named O'Leary, sir."

"Is it, really. Imagine that. Well, go on, O'Connor, pack your gear. We'll leave at dawn. And if that's what you recommend, then our first stop will be the National Hotel."

# Chapter 2

Early the next morning, as Stephen and Paddy meandered through the crowded lobby of the National Hotel toward the desk of Dennis O'Leary, two attractive young women arrived in an open carriage outside the building, on Sixth Street. The driver of the buggy, dressed in a lustrous green taffeta dress and matching hat, stepped sharply down to the street, oblivious to the squishing of the mud beneath her stylish black kid-and-satin boots.

"Are you coming, Fanny?" she asked the other woman. She spoke with a crisp New England accent, softened by a warm manner and a natural roundness of tone. Rebecca Windfield was at once the pride and the terror of the Windfield family of Beacon Hill in Boston. Her mother, a rich and very vain woman, was extremely proud of her daughter's rare beauty and charm. The girl was tall and slender, and quite shapely enough to turn any man's head, after all. And, Clara Windfield boasted, daughter Becky was blessed with the same beautiful and haunting face as that Helen of Troy you saw in all the old paintings: the silky blonde hair, the lively and deep blue eyes, and the flawless complexion, as smooth and white as heavy cream.

The Reverend Damion Windfield, on the other hand, while he loved his daughter dearly, sometimes considered her to be, next to the devil, the greatest single threat to his ultimate salvation. At the age of twenty, with a saucy tongue and a flagrant disregard for the proper rules of conduct, she had already frightened away half the suitable young men in Boston. Becky, he believed, was too bold, too adventurous, too blunt, and above all, far too independent to suit any good man of sense. "You'll never catch a man, acting like one," he had told her more than once, adding mysteriously, "You'll surely end up an old maid, and then who will have the last laugh?"

The dark-haired woman in the carriage was quite the opposite. The daughter of the Secretary of State, Frances Seward was small, delicate, and demure. While she was attractive enough, with regular features and a quick smile, she generally preferred to linger in the background on social occasions. Resisting any attention paid to her by any man, she was content to dress 'properly' so as to blend in with the pervading fashion of the day, whether it was as visible as a Madonna hairstyle or as private as a horsehair petticoat.

"I simply can't go up there with you," she said from her seat in the carriage. "A girl simply does not do such things. Not in Washington City."

"Then here, hold the horse." Rebecca promptly handed her the leather reins. "I'll do it myself."

Fanny received the reins unconsciously. "A lady should never go up to a gentleman's hotel room——not even in the daytime," she admonished. "It simply isn't done."

Having heard those particular words a thousand times before, Becky was quite unruffled by them. "Why isn't it done?" she countered. "Ten minutes ago, when I dismissed our driver, you told me a lady 'cannot control a horse.' Now look at you. Aren't you controlling him?"

Fanny stirred nervously when she realized the reins were in her hands. "Well, I guess the truth of the matter is," she admitted, "I just don't understand you, Becky. And neither does anyone else in the family. Oh, they all love you, but for the two weeks you've been staying with us, life has been absolutely chaotic in the Seward household."

"Oh, it has not," said Becky, dismissing the idea, though she found it very flattering.

Frances, however, was deadly serious. "It really has, Becky," she declared. "All of us are shaking our heads, wondering what to do with you. You've got Poppa so confused. Imagine——a man who single-handedly kept France and England out of the War Between the States turns as silly as an old loon in your presence. Did you know that?"

"Does he? I thought he was always that way," she teased.

"Becky," Frances begged, keeping her tone sober, "please don't go in there. Your father let you come to Washington to work for the War Relief Charity, not to go calling on a man in the National Hotel."

Rebecca flicked a lock of her blonde hair away from her forehead. She wore it loose, so that it tumbled down around her shoulders——a style radically different from the current custom of nets in the daytime and flowers and ribbons at night. "That happens to be just what I'm doing, Fanny," she explained. "I'm here to talk Mr. Booth into doing a benefit performance of the Shakespeare play of his choice for the War Relief Charity. Now for goodness' sake, how 'bad' can that be?"

"You could ask someone else," she persisted.

"Well, as it happens, I am planning to ask Laura Keene, too. But if you will pardon my bluntness, Fanny, sometimes only a man will do."

Frances blushed. "If you must have a man, there is John Dyott," she suggested. "He's at Ford's Theater this week. He's acting with Miss Keene in that play, *Our American Cousin.*"

"I don't want John Dyer, or Dyott, or whatever his name is. I've never heard of the man. I want John Wilkes Booth. He is one of the greatest actors in America, isn't he?"

"I don't know if he is or not," Frances evaded.

"Well, I know. Mother and I went all the way to New York to see him last year, when he and his brothers did that performance of *Julius Caesar* in the Winter Garden. They had the audience screaming for more. There must have been over two thousand people jammed in there to see them."

"Becky," Frances said in a lower voice, "I may as well say it: I'm not talking about Mr. Booth's acting."

Rebecca tried to be patient with her. "Then what in heaven's name are you talking about?" she asked. "For once, Fanny, why don't you just say what you mean?"

"All right, then," she replied, drawing closer. "For once, I will say what I mean. What I mean is, his *social* life, his . . . women."

"His women?" Becky echoed, a bit too loudly to suit her friend. "Are you telling me the man's a cad or something?"

"I am telling you, Becky," she said, almost in a whisper, "that John Wilkes Booth has mistresses. He has one right here in Washington, in fact. I shouldn't name names—"

"Oh, go ahead, it's no fun if you don't," Rebecca urged. She was finding the subject quite intriguing.

"Her name is Ella Turner," Fanny blurted. "She lives in the south part of town." The ice broken, the rest of the revelation came more easily. "And there is a woman named Jennie up in Canada," she added, "one called 'Effa' in New York, and worst of all, they say he's secretly engaged to Senator John Hale's daughter Lucy. That's how he got invited to the Inauguration Ball."

"Gracious. I wonder, with all those diversions, how he's ever had time to memorize *Richard III?*"

"Oh, Becky, I don't believe you. Aren't you absolutely terrified to go up there, after what I've told you?"

"Of course I'm not terrified. Why should I be? I'm not one of his mistresses."

"Haven't you been listening to me? John Wilkes Booth has a . . . power over women."

"Well, if he does, it would certainly be worth a trip up a flight of stairs to see it, wouldn't it?"

Frances flung up her hands in frustration, and promptly startled the horse. When he reared, she automatically jerked back on the reins and held him down. After a moment, she sighed deeply and pressed a palm against her bosom. "What on earth am I doing here?" She looked around suspiciously at the people milling about on Pennsylvania Avenue. "Poppa would be absolutely mortified if someone told him his daughter had been seen sitting alone in a carriage outside the National Hotel. He's been so sick since his accident, it could kill him.''

"Oh, Mr. Seward's as strong as a horse, Fanny. And I doubt if a man of his business affairs is anywhere near as naive as you think he is. Surely the Secretary of State of the Union realizes the world is about to change, now that the war is over. He has to know women will demand more freedom now than ever before.''

"If he knows that, Becky, he certainly hasn't told me about it.''

"Well, anyway, all of this is for a good cause, isn't it? And if Mr. Booth does possess this strange, bizarre influence over us poor, defenseless women, imagine what a crowd a charity benefit performance would attract. And crowds, Fanny, mean money—for the widows and mothers of the men who died in the war. Now that's worthwhile, isn't it?''

"Yes," she admitted, "it is. I guess I'm just always horrified of doing the wrong thing. I'm afraid I will compromise Poppa's position, somehow. This town is really very particular about people's reputations, Becky.''

"All towns seem to be, don't they? That's why I've rather given up on the whole idea. It may be a horrid thing to say, but I've stopped thinking about it altogether. If those ladies in the hair nets and lisle stockings want to gossip, then they will gossip. There is nothing I can do about it, one way or the other.''

"Becky, please—''

"I'll be back in a half-hour or so," Rebecca said, patting her friend's arm good-naturedly. "Meanwhile, if you slump down real low in the buggy, maybe nobody will see you.''

Frances gave her a solemn look. "Will you at least promise me you'll be careful?" she begged.

"Oh, don't worry, I'll be careful," she assured her. "But listen—if John Wilkes Booth does start using that power on me—"

"Rebecca!"

"I'll just close my eyes, Fanny, and he'll go away."

Rebecca left the other woman shaking her head and passed beneath the Union flag, through the columns of the portico of the hotel, and into the lobby of the white rectangular five-story building. Even though it was early in the morning, the room was buzzing with men of all descriptions, most of them left over from the Civil War victory celebration the night before.

She had found the demonstration very exciting. With Fanny and her brothers, Augustus and Frederick William, Becky had stared for almost an hour at the dazzling explosions of fireworks over Lafayette Square. Then the three were swept up in the flood of people moving toward the executive mansion. After five minutes of clamoring applause outside the White House, Abraham Lincoln had stepped out on the balcony in a formal black suit and top hat.

When Rebecca saw him raise his hands to the people, she was gripped by the feeling that she was in the presence of a great man. It was strange, at first, how the mere appearance of his gangly, clumsy body brought a hush over the crowd, how his tired, weary face instantly grabbed their attention, how his slow, halting speech riveted them all to the stones they stood on.

But then, as he spoke, she began to see a strength and wisdom flowing out of this man that she had never detected in his photographs. Even at a distance of thirty yards, from a high balcony, he somehow managed to exude at the same time the force of powerful, raw energy and the comfort of solid authority. In the midst of a world blown apart at the seams by Confederate and Union gunpowder, Abraham Lincoln stood head and shoulders above all the others as the only man strong and wise enough to bind the bleeding wounds of a mangled, crippled nation.

"Reconstruction," he had pronounced to the crowd in an oratorical voice, "is fraught with great difficulty," but it is still a task which can be accomplished. "We simply must begin with and mould from disorganized and discordant elements."

If the gathering of the diverse men and women in Washington City and in the National Hotel were any example of those "discordant elements," Rebecca reflected as she proceeded through the lobby, the President was correct: a return to order was going to be very hard, indeed. Ignoring an admiring but rude stare here and there, and paying no attention to the advances of a young man who pretended to know her, she marched straight up to the clerk's desk.

"Sir?" she addressed the pudgy, round-faced little clerk in the long black coat.

"Yes, ma'am?" He turned away from two men at the other end of the desk and raised a thick eyebrow at her.

Rebecca gave the men a quick glance. While the older, bearded one was dully dressed in a brown coat over wrinkled gray trousers, she thought the younger, darker gentleman cut a striking figure in his well-fitting dark gray broadcloth suit and silk top hat.

"Are you Mr. O'Leary?" she asked the clerk.

"Aye, ma'am, that's what they call me."

"Good. Then you're the one my messenger left a note with."

"Well now, what note would that be, ma'am?" He wrinkled his brow.

"The message I sent to Mr. Booth yesterday afternoon," she answered.

"I can't say as I know about that one, ma'am. Could be it got lost in the shuffle of the celebration last night."

"Well, never mind—just tell me what room he's in." Her request drew an intense look from the young man in the gray suit. His stare annoyed her. "Mr. O'Leary—" She waited impatiently.

"Mr. Booth is in Room 20, ma'am," he told her. "Next floor, first door at the top of the stairs."

"Thank you; I'm sorry to bother you," she said and brushed past the two men on her way to the stairs.

At the head of the steps, on the second floor landing, she located the room and promptly rapped on the door. After a minute, she called out his name, then waited again. There was no answer. "Mr. Booth!" She knocked once more.

After a fourth time, she drew a response. "What do you want?" someone asked from behind the door. Low and muffled as it was, she recognized the firm, modulated voice of Mark Antony in *Julius Caesar*.

"Mr. Booth, it's Rebecca Windfield," she announced. "I sent you a note yesterday, about the War Relief Charity. Could I see you a minute, please?"

"I'm sorry," he apologized. "I'm busy."

Rebecca detected, from the corner of her eye, the notice of three or four men who were loitering in the hall, but they didn't bother her. She had come too far to let a few long and prying noses shoo her away now. "Mr. Booth," she said firmly, knocking again, "will you please open the door? I have something for you."

After a long moment of silence, she heard the latch click faintly and the doorknob turn. Then the door cracked open to reveal the actor in a black satin-and-silk dressing gown. She stood in the hall, staring at him. For the first time in her life, Rebecca found herself so profoundly affected by the appearance of a man that she could barely move. Although he was much smaller than he'd seemed on stage, she found John Wilkes Booth instantly appealing—in a very disturbing way. His wavy black hair, thick moustache, and dark, brooding eyes might have been those of any other handsome man but, upon close inspection, she could see a deeply forlorn, longing look about him. She fancied for a moment that his soul had been severely injured and shamed, somehow, and was crying out for help, like a confused and frightened child lost in the darkness of a forbidding wood.

"What is it you have?" Booth asked her indifferently.

Rebecca recovered herself enough to step inside. "What I have is a proposition, Mr. Booth," she asserted, letting the door shut behind her. The sound of the closing door made her uneasy.

He ran his black eyes salaciously over her body. Then he pursed his lips and shook his head. "I'm sorry," he said, turning away. "Not this morning. You look well enough, but I have other things on my mind."

Becky stared at his back in disbelief. While she was shocked at his assumption that she was a prostitute, she was angered even more by the fact that he had rejected her. What other man would have done that? "Sir," she said, bravely moving closer, "what I mean is, my name is Rebecca Windfield and I represent the War Relief Charity.

I would like to offer you the chance of helping your Country repair its wounds by doing a benefit performance, with all proceeds going to the widows and mothers of the dead soldiers on both sides.''

"That's a pretty sentiment," he sighed, easing down into a plain wooden chair in front of a writing desk. His voice sounded sad and distant now. "Sounds like a speech in a play I did once in Baltimore."

Rebecca watched him rudely return to a letter he had been reading. There were twenty or thirty of them scattered about on the desk, among newspaper clippings from the New York *Herald*, the *Times*, the *Tribune*, as well as the Boston *Transcript* and the Washington *Evening Star*. Some of the messages were unopened—including, she surmised, her own.

"Mr. Booth?" She waited. "What do you think of the idea?"

He heard her words, but he was lost in thought, as his eyes were gliding over the page of the letter. "Listen to this." He began reading: *"Please, by all that is sacred, Mr. Booth, come for me soon. My poor, wretched Mother continues to keep me here against my will. She is sitting in her chair in the parlor with me now. She is watching me write these words to you. Oh, Dear Soul, will you save me, Mr. Booth? I will do anything to be free of her. Anything at all. She should have died hereafter, when there was time for such a word."* He folded the letter, stuffed it back into its envelope, and leaned back in his chair. "Have you ever heard anything like that, Miss Windfield?" He looked up at her.

"She sounds very pitiful," Rebecca observed. "Who is she?" She refrained from adding tastelessly, "One of your mistresses?"

But he surprised her. "She's nobody," he answered sadly. "One of thousands. Another lost spirit begging for her freedom. I don't know why, but it's always the same pattern: they call out to me, and then misquote Shakespeare."

"And are you always so cavalier about it?" she challenged. "Surely you're not going to ignore such a desperate plea as that?"

"All I can do is ignore it, Miss Windfield," he replied. "I discovered a long time ago that it isn't really me they want. It isn't even freedom from their mothers or husbands or lovers or fathers they want. They're no different from the rest of this country. They're looking for something or somebody to believe in. They see a man of confidence and bearing and strength on the stage, and they think it's me, instead of a character I'm playing. If they sink low enough, they convince themselves I am their deliverer."

Becky felt an impulse to reach out and touch him—comfort him—but she resisted. "I guess everyone's been hurt by the war, Mr. Booth," she offered limply.

He stood up. "And I have been acting on well-lighted stages all the way through it. Instead of hearing the explosions of cannon and rifles at Bull Run, I've been hearing the cheers of audiences in New York and Boston—the cheers of a wandering people, vainly looking for someone to bring them back together. It's all a ridiculous illusion."

"No, it isn't—"

"Oh, but it is. It's nothing but a lie. Acting on the stage at this moment in history is no better than dancing the Virginia reel on the broken and bleeding back of a dear friend. Which is why I've decided not to do it anymore."

"You don't mean that."

"I mean it," he assured her. "Now, would you please leave me, Miss Windfield? I haven't had breakfast yet."

Rebecca made a move toward the door, then stopped. For a moment she felt offended, but the feeling passed. "I guess I'm spoiled, Mr. Booth," she pressed, "but I'm not very used to being turned away so abruptly. And I've never once failed on a charity mission."

"Well, everybody fails sometime, Miss Windfield. I'm sorry. Please—go. I have other things to think about this morning."

"I won't go until I change your mind about the benefit performance."

He rubbed his high forehead with his thin, white fingers. "Tell your sisters I've retired from the stage," he said, exasperated. "Tell them I am leaving the kingdom to my brother and Edwin Forrest. Maybe they can keep up the illusion; I can't. There's no truth in it for me anymore."

"You're a strange man," she said, without thinking.

Shaking his head, he smiled weakly. "I'm not strange," he denied. "I'm just tired, and hurt, and angry. Like the women in that endless succession of letters. The country I love has been torn apart by the bone and muscle, and I haven't lifted a finger to save it."

"But the war's over, Mr. Booth."

"Yes, but the dear friend's back is still broken, isn't it? And those few men who are responsible for breaking it are still free to keep on pounding away at the arms and legs and head, until finally, someday, even the spirit will be crushed."

Rebecca looked at him curiously. What odd emotions she was feeling at this moment: pity, anger, annoyance, desire—all mixed with fear. It was exciting to talk to Booth, and she was thrilled to hear his magnificent, magnetic voice at close range, but the notion of an injured, crying soul frightened her—especially when it seemed to be reaching out to her.

"I . . . think I had better go, after all." She extended her hand. "Thank you for seeing me."

Instinctively, he took her hand and kissed it gallantly. "It has been a very great pleasure, Miss Windfield," he complimented. "And I apologize for taking you for another kind of woman."

"Well, I suppose Fanny was right, after all." She brought back her hand.

"Fanny?"

"Frances Seward. The friend I'm staying with in Washington. She would die if she knew I told you, but she claims you have a power over women."

"Would that be William Seward's daughter you're referring to?" he asked. "Secretary of State Seward?"

"Yes. She's waiting for me now, downstairs. If she hasn't run off in a blush. Do you know her?"

"No, I don't," he answered on the way to the window. Drawing the curtains back, he asked, "Is that Miss Seward in the carriage with the bay mare?"

"Well, she hasn't bolted after all, has she?"

"She looks quite alone," He turned back to Rebecca. "I have an idea," he offered. "Why don't you and Miss Seward join me for breakfast?"

"Now?"

"Why not?" he said brightly. "We can all three discuss the benefit performance. When I'm in town, I usually eat at Grotier's, down the street. I think you'll find their coffee is especially good."

Becky was rattled by Booth's quick change of attitude and tone. Why, she wondered, was he so interested in the benefit all of a sudden, when not five minutes before he had announced his retirement from the stage? She watched him curiously as he ripped his dressing gown away from his crisp white shirt and quickly slipped into a black suit coat.

"Shall we go?" He stepped up and opened the door for her.

"I'm not sure Fanny is going to be interested in this," she warned. "She's not very adventurous."

"Ah, well, if it's for charity, how could the daughter of the Secretary of State refuse?"

Rebecca smiled uncomfortably and walked out the door, utterly puzzled by this mysterious man. It had been the most peculiar encounter she had ever had. It left her practically speechless.

Downstairs in the lobby, John Wilkes Booth asked Rebecca to go on outside while he had a word with the desk attendant.

"O'Leary," he said, "I need a page and an envelope."

"Yes, sir." The clerk pulled some stationery out of a drawer. While Booth wrote on it, he noted casually, "Fine-looking lass, that one."

Booth didn't seem to hear. He was finishing the message:

> B—Come to Surratt's Boarding House. 7 tonight. Tell others may have new information. —JWB.

"I would like this delivered personally," he instructed as he sealed the envelope.

"I'll get Tommy Burnside to take it over right away, sir."

"I said *personally*, O'Leary. There's five dollars in it for you."

"Oh—well, damned if I wouldn't sing to the gent in his tub for that kind of money, Mr. Booth."

"No need to go that far." He handed him the envelope. "Just make sure he gets it."

"Yes sir." O'Leary nodded and squinted at the two words written on the front of the envelope. In black ink, in an ornate, swirling hand, was the name of the recipient of the letter: Mason Butler.

# Chapter 3

Later, in a stark, gray office on Seventeenth Street, N.W., a large, pear-shaped man in a rumpled black three-piece suit scraped his chair across the oak floor, closer to the fireplace. He eased down into the chair and propped his shiny boots against the brass rail in front of the coal fire. Then he read the note he had just received from the Secretary of War. It was written in a strong, bold hand, in heavy ink:

*Mr. Butler. Please prepare a file on Mr. Donald Massey of your section in advance of a meeting concerning same at 10 a.m., 12 April, 1865. Since the arrival of Gen. Grant tomorrow currently has my entire office in disarray, I will attend you. There is no need for advice or reply in this matter.*

*Edwin McMasters Stanton.*

Pressing his thin, bloodless lips together, Butler wadded the message into a ball and flung it angrily into the fire. While the paper smoldered and darkened on a pile of coals, Butler fumed. He bitterly resented the Secretary's abrupt and disrespectful treatment of him, as if he were nothing more than a forty-year-old junior clerk. Mason Butler believed he deserved a better fate than that. He had been unfairly saddled with menial clerical work in the War Department for over four years. And never once had Stanton or Lincoln noticed his devotion to duty.

His work had not always seemed so bleak. Once he had had a promising political career in the works. When Simon Cameron was appointed Secretary of War under James Buchanan, the great man immediately chose Butler as his unofficial aide and promised him that, within a few years, Mason would land a place in the President's Cabinet. But then, as Butler's luck would have it, the Secretary of State stepped in and obliterated all of his chances in one fell swipe. William Seward had advised the President to replace the great Cameron with an Ohio lawyer named Stanton. After that little shakeup, the triumvirate of Lincoln, Seward, and Stanton fairly ran the country, while the totally ignored Mason Butler languished away in a bog of military personnel paperwork.

But now, after bearing their negligence for all these years, he had begun to take bold steps to move himself up in the organization. And none too soon: his accounts were being cancelled all over town; he was close to losing the big three-story house on K Street, near Stanton's own residence; and collectors were hounding him, showing up at his home frequently, embarrassing him in front of his family and his neighbors. Soon, he comforted himself, all that would come to an end and he would finally get what he deserved.

Just as the paper on the hot coals burst into flames, his young assistant Charles Kirby slid through the door into the room, clutching a stack of papers against his chest. "Mr. Butler?" he chirped in an eager, high-pitched voice.

Butler kept his eyes focused on the burning letter. "Don't stand there with the door open, boy," he growled. "There's a draft in here." Butler cringed every time he heard Kirby's shrill voice. He resented the boy's slender, handsome looks and the ease with which he flew through work in minutes that would take Butler hours to finish. And he resented the fact that Charles came from a wealthy family in Connecticut. Butler had always suspected that Kirby's job had been a present from Stanton himself, though he hadn't yet found any proof of it.

After closing the door, Kirby took a few steps in and stopped in the middle of the room. "There are two applicants for reinstatement outside in the hall," he reported.

"Two deserters, you mean," Butler said, turning to face him. "Call them what they are: traitors to the Union Army."

The boy hesitated, then said, "Their names are Wheeler and Davison."

Butler clenched his teeth. "I know what their names are, Mr. Kirby," he snapped. "You just gave me the papers twenty minutes ago, didn't you? I may look old and useless to you, but believe me, boy, I can still read. Without spectacles, I might add."

"Yes, sir. I just wasn't thinking."

"You never think, do you? Now, what else do you want? You're taking up my heat."

"Sir," he said, advancing, "before you see Privates

Wheeler and Davison, you need to sign these relocation papers for a Corporal Edward Hedgely.'' He handed him the top set of pages from his stack. ''Captain Knight has already signed the release, so it's nothing but a formality.''

Butler took the papers and squinted at them. ''Do I have to remind you, Mr. Kirby,'' he sighed, ''that you do not have the authority to say whether anything is a formality or not?''

''No, sir. I know that. I'm sorry.''

''What's Hedgely's situation?'' Butler asked.

Kirby swallowed. ''It's just that Corporal Hedgely was sent back home to New York yesterday, a week before his release date.''

Butler's eyes skimmed over the paper. ''This says *sickness*,'' he muttered. ''What kind of sickness? I haven't heard about a plague or a fever lately.''

''Uh, no, sir, it was nothing like that. It was a stomach ailment.''

Mason rubbed his thin beard with stiff, cold fingers. ''A stomachache,'' he moaned derisively. ''And yet these papers indicate that Corporal Hedgely is to be in the detachment of troops assigned to General Grant when he arrives in the city tomorrow.''

''Yes, sir, I believe he was.''

''Not *was*, Kirby—*is*. It looks to me as though you're going to have to bring the loafer back, doesn't it?''

''Sir?'' The young man frowned.

''You heard me. I don't care if the war is over, this Captain Knight does not have the authority to release a soldier from the United States Army because of a belly-ache.''

''It's not a bellyache, Mr. Butler,'' Kirby insisted. ''The man is very ill. They're taking him to a hospital in New

York. Besides, it has already been approved; all it needs is a signature from the War Department.''

"I don't see a physician's statement here," Butler said.

"There should be one," Kirby replied, concerned. "Dr. Sykes examined him and—''

"Well, there isn't," Butler interrupted. "So I can't very well sign it, can I? And since Mr. Stanton wants a full show of Army force for the arrival of General Grant, I would suggest we give it to him. Go get this momma's boy and bring him back to his troops.''

"But he's probably in Pennsylvania by now.''

"I don't care where he is, boy. Bring the deserter back.''

"Yes, sir," the young man said, deflated.

"Anything wrong, Kirby?" Butler challenged. "Any complaints with the way I handle my job?''

"No, sir, I'm not complaining. I just don't see why . . .''

"Go on, boy, say it. Why what?''

"Nothing, Mr. Butler.''

"Well, if it's nothing, get out of here and stop wasting my time. Send in those two deserters, and go find your corporal with the bellyache.''

"What if he's dying—''

"Then let the son-of-a-bitch die, Kirby. Then he'll have a legitimate reason for deserting the Army.''

Kirby glared at Butler for a moment, wheeled around, and dashed out of the room.

A few moments later, two men in dirty, ragged blue Union uniforms marched into Butler's office apprehensively. They were wearing heavily soiled shirts, trousers ripped at the knees, and boots that were cracked and covered with gray mud. One of them was a big black man, about thirty, with a grizzly beard and downcast, humble eyes. The other was white, a stocky twenty-year-old with a thick shock of brown hair hanging limply over his forehead and resting just on top of his heavy eyebrows. Tall and erect, he looked Butler straight in the eyes.

"Sir," he announced himself crisply. "My name is Private Wheeler. Private Davison and I were supposed to pick up some papers here."

Butler took a while to examine the two men closely and disapprovingly. Then, without saying a word, he slid a stack of papers off the desk and spent several minutes leisurely thumbing through them. When at last Wheeler began to shift his weight nervously, Mason raised himself up and ambled over to the window, tapping the pages of two particular documents carelessly against his thigh. Finally, after a time at the window, he turned around.

"Mr. Wheeler," he began, "I read here that you and this colored man deserted the Army in October of last year. Is that correct?"

Wheeler glanced at the black man, caught his eye, then nodded to Butler. "It was the second of October," he specified sadly. "The day my son was born."

Butler gave the papers another quick look. "You were in General Curtis's Army of the Border, I see," he went on, "out of Missouri?"

Wheeler cleared his throat. "Yes, sir," he replied. "That's right. It wasn't too long after we licked General Price at Westport that an Indian boy I knew came into camp to see me. He told Ned and me that some of Quantrill's men were raiding my farm, about five miles away. My wife and her two sisters were staying there, and Martha was supposed to be having a baby soon—"

"So you deserted your post and ran to her," Butler anticipated.

"We didn't desert, Sir," Wheeler corrected. "We thought we'd be back by morning. Only when we got there, we found the raid over and the house still burning. Sally and Edna were lying out in the front yard, barely breathing. But my wife was dead, Mr. Butler. Ned found her curled up in the outhouse behind the barn . . . Only I guess God was looking out for us, because the baby inside her was still alive. Ned and I pulled him out—"

"Spare me the details, Wheeler." Butler curled his thin lips. "You're making me sick."

"But it wasn't sickening, sir," he insisted. "Martha was dead and all, but it was still beautiful, wasn't it, Ned? He wasn't nothing but a tiny little baby coming out of a dead body, but he made it just fine. Ned found us a colored woman with milk—"

"Christ, man, I said I didn't want to hear that drivel! It doesn't have anything to do with your desertion."

"Yes, sir." Wheeler bit his lip. "I just thought you'd want to know why we left."

"Well, I don't want to know, so why don't we get on with this? May I have five dollars, please?"

"May you have what, sir?"

Butler sighed condescendingly. "There is a five dollar processing fee," he explained. "Or isn't a pardon from the President of the United States worth that to you?"

Wheeler shook his head. "That isn't in the President's proclamation," he protested. "I know it isn't. I saw it in the paper, and I read very well. Mr. Lincoln said he would issue a pardon to all deserters, if we returned within sixty days of March the eleventh. He said nothing about any money."

"Maybe he didn't. But then Mr. Lincoln doesn't have to handle the paperwork, does he? He can be as soft-hearted and liberal as he wants to be, but it's people like me who must do the real work.''

"I think I understand!'' Wheeler exclaimed. "There is no processing fee, is there? That money's for you! You're taking it!''

Butler wrinkled his long, thin nose. "I wouldn't bother trying to figure it out, boy,'' he said. 'A Missouri rube like you could never understand the complicated procedures of the federal government.''

"Well, I understand enough to know you're stealing money.''

Butler stared at him, unmoved. It didn't bother him in the slightest that he was taking the money for himself. He was only balancing the scales, after all. A few extra dollars here and there was precious little payment for the long, hard years he had been ignored and wasted by Stanton in the War Department.

"Do you have the five dollars or don't you?'' he asked, sounding bored. "I don't have all day.''

"We can't pay it,'' Wheeler confessed. "We don't have a cent. It took everything we had to get us here.''

"That was bad planning, Wheeler,'' Butler said angrily. "But then, what can I expect from a man who would waltz out of an Army camp to visit his wife?'' Butler returned to the desk, drew out a pen, and scratched his signature on the second document. "But I'm more generous than I ought to be,'' he admitted. "Here.'' He stepped across the room and handed the paper to the black man. "As far as the War Department is concerned, Mr. Davison, you are hereby pardoned. Good luck to you.''

The big black man received the paper in his huge, trembling hands. "Is it just me?'' he said, puzzled.

"That is correct,'' Butler confirmed. "You people are

what we fought the war over, aren't you? The government wants you to be free. I'm sure you would never have deserted the Army if he hadn't made you.''

The black man's eyes raised up. ''But if he don't get one, I can't get one neither,'' he stated. ''It wouldn't be right.''

''If you don't leave now, boy, right this minute,'' he warned, ''I'll take it back.''

''I can't leave without him, too,'' he glanced at Wheeler.

''Go on, Ned,'' the other man urged. ''Take it. Leave while you can.''

''No—''

''Ah!'' Butler grunted as he snatched the pardon out of Davison's hands. ''Why must I always be forced to deal with morons? Traitors, deserters—look here, boy . . .'' He brought the paper in front of his vest. ''Is this what you wanted?'' He held it out, ready to rip it apart. ''Is this what you're asking for?''

''No, don't—''

''Do you want it or not? Speak up!''

''Not if he don't get his—''

''Stupid darkie,'' Butler muttered as he jerked his hands apart. With a loud tearing sound, the paper instantly split into two pieces.

''Oh, no.'' The black man stared unbelievingly at the torn paper. ''Sweet Jesus, you shouldn't have done that—''

''You liar!'' Wheeler accused. ''You never had any intention of giving it to him.''

Butler ignored him as he rent the document again. Then, flinging the bits of paper into the fire, he said to him, ''You have less than a month to go, Wheeler. The proclamation states that all deserters who are not pardoned by May 11 will forfeit their right to live in the United States.''

Wheeler clenched his fists until his knuckles turned white. "I can't pay what I don't have!" he cried.

Butler shook his head dejectedly. "Well, I'm sympathetic, of course," he said, "but I've got to do my job. That's the difference between us, boy. If you had done yours, you wouldn't be here now."

"For the love of God, man! What did you expect me to do? They were raiding my home!" Wheeler paused, shaking his head. "All right, look," he said finally, "I'm sorry. I did wrong. But it's done now. The war is over. Can't we forget it?"

"This is your pardon, Wheeler," Butler held up the document. "Do you want me to forget it, too?"

"You bastard," the black man tightened his fists and lumbered toward Butler. "If you tear his papers—"

Mason retreated quickly. "Now, don't you touch me, boy," he threatened. "Or so help me, I'll have you hanged from the gallows."

"I don't care," he mumbled, advancing slowly.

"Hey, I mean what I say now. Don't touch me. Wheeler! Tell him! Get him away from me!"

"I'm going to bust your fat head open, man—"

"Wheeler! If you don't stop him, I swear to God, you'll never see a pardon as long as you live!" Butler backed up until he felt his shoulder blade pressed against the wall. "Wheeler!" he yelled. "If you ever want to live in this country again—"

Just as Davison raised one of his fists high, Wheeler called out to him, "All right, Ned; let him be."

Ned froze. "He tore up my pardon," he said simply.

"I know. But he's going to make you out a new one. Aren't you, Mr. Butler?"

Mason drew in a breath. "It's possible, yes. I can do that. But it's more work. I'll have to add another two dollars to the fee."

"No, you don't—" the black man lunged for him.

"Ned!" Wheeler reached out and grabbed his massive arms. "Let him alone, now. It'll be all right. We'll get the money. Somehow or other, we'll get it." He waited for Davison to relax his muscles and nod; then he guided him toward the door. As Wheeler reached for the knob, he turned his head. "We'll be back," he promised. "If we have to clean spittoons for a month, we're going to earn that seven dollars."

"Why don't you make it eight dollars, Mr. Wheeler." Butler straightened his lapels. "You and your colored man have been very trying."

"Eight dollars! How do you think you can do this? You're nothing but a clerk!"

"Then go complain to somebody, boy," he challenged. "See whose word they take—a clerk's or a deserter's!"

Wheeler hesitated, gritted his teeth, then yanked open the door and let Davison out. But as he was crossing the threshold, he couldn't resist a final word. "Someday, somebody will make you pay, too, Mr. Butler," he predicted. "Because you're a lot worse than any deserter."

"Your fee is now nine dollars, Mr. Wheeler."

"Damn you!"

"One more word, and I'll raise it to ten."

Wheeler's face flushed with his pent-up anger as he stood in the doorway, considering what to do. Deciding finally, he spun around and stormed out of the room toward the stairs.

\* \* \*

The thick, fervid-looking man in a brown suit cast a suspicious glance at the two disgruntled soldiers brushing past him as he ascended the stairs to the second floor of the War Department building. The fifty-year-old Secretary of War lingered a moment at the top of the steps, leaned over the railing, and watched them until they had disappeared. Then he squeezed his heavy, gray-streaked black whiskers in his fingers, tweaked his large nose, and shoved open the door to Butler's office.

He was immediately irritated by what he saw inside. While the clerk's office was quite neat, clean, and orderly, it was also cold, bare, and lifeless. It always struck Edwin Stanton as a kind of tumor on the highly efficient administrative organism he had created and nurtured in the three years he had been head of the Department. But since he had never had any real reason to disapprove of the work carried out in it, he had let it remain as it was.

The occupant of the office rankled him, too. Stanton disliked everything about Mason Butler, from his wrinkled suits and frazzled shirts down to his absurd patent leather boots. But the Secretary was a man with a practical mind and a comprehensive view of things; he would never allow his personal prejudices to affect his professional judgment. As long as the clerk performed his job adequately, he could keep it.

"Mr. Butler?" he said as he entered the room, "I assume you got my message?"

"Oh, yes, sir." Butler instantly rose from his desk, jumped over to the counter under the window, and retrieved a large envelope. "This is it—the Donald Massey file." As he held it out, the paper shook in his fingers.

Stanton calmly took the envelope, slipped out the four

pages of notes, and scanned them quickly. "There's nothing here!" he bellowed, pitching the notes down on Butler's desk. Turning his large eyes toward the other man, Stanton furrowed his brow. "Tell me what you know about this, Butler," he ordered in a sharp voice. "I want every detail."

"Know about what, sir?"

"About Massey's death, what else? Don't tell me you haven't heard about it."

Butler's face suddenly lost its color. "No, sir, I hadn't," he fumbled. "I mean, I haven't."

Stanton considered Mason's reply for a moment, then stuffed his thick hands into his pockets and paced across the floor deliberately. "They brought Massey's body in from Arlington two hours ago," he revealed. "Since he worked here in the Department, they carted him right up to my house. Scared my wife half to death. The poor bastard had been shot in the back."

"Do they have any idea who did it?" Butler asked.

"No idea whatsoever," Stanton said. "Nobody even knows why the man was over there." He stopped in the middle of the room and looked at Butler. "Which brings me to you, Mason."

"Me?" Butler swallowed and wiped his thin lips with his fingers. "I didn't work with Massey, Mr. Stanton," he protested. "I never even saw him."

"Well, you saw him last night. You were seen at the Ferry Inn, drinking together."

"Well, yes, it's true we were there—but we weren't there together. Everybody was celebrating the end of the war. We just happened to cross paths, that's all."

"All right, fine. Then tell me what you talked about when you crossed paths."

"What I meant was, we didn't really talk, Mr. Stanton," Butler's voice wavered. "We just said hello to each other."

"Then Massey never told you anything about his current investigation for the Department?"

"Oh, no, sir. Never. I swear he didn't."

"Nothing about an assassination plot, either?"

"No, sir. Is that what he was investigating?"

Stanton gnashed his teeth, squeezed his beard, and began pacing again. "Don Massey was on a hot trail, Mr. Butler. I know he was. I can feel it in my bones. He knew something was going to happen. Something terrible. The problem is, he never reported it to me. I was hoping he had left a coded message for me in his file, but there was nothing there."

"Too bad," Butler offered.

"I must know what he uncovered, Butler," Stanton growled. "These constant threats of an assassination are starting to wear us down. Mr. Lincoln is thinking more and more about them these days. He even keeps an envelope of them in his desk, marked *Assassination*. If Massey discovered that one of these threats was for real, then the assassin himself may have killed him."

"Oh, I doubt that, sir."

"What?" Stanton responded, interested. "Why would you doubt it?"

"I don't know," Butler answered quickly. "I don't have any reason. I just do."

"I wish I was that confident about it. Well, I've got to go see the President," the Secretary announced abruptly. "And I've got to decide whether or not to tell him about the Massey murder, and my suspicions."

"I hope Mr. Lincoln's all right," Butler remarked limply.

"He's all right," Stanton assured. "I'm just being

cautious. Which reminds me," he added. "With Massey dead and Peterson and Welles out with the flu, we're running short of men. I may have to use you for some extra work later. Will you be available?"

"Yes, sir," Butler replied sharply. "I'll do anything for the Department, Mr. Stanton. You know that."

"I'll be in touch, then," Stanton said as he headed for the door. "Oh!" he exclaimed as he reached it. "I almost forgot. I have a message for you." He crammed his fist into his coat pocket and jerked out a small envelope. "A hotel clerk brought it by downstairs." He held it out. "I told him I'd bring it up."

"Thank you, sir." Butler took the envelope.

"No trouble," Stanton said and left the room.

The Secretary hurried on foot across Seventeenth Street, in the direction of the White House. Ordinarily a man in complete control of his mind, Edwin Stanton now found himself strangely excited and apprehensive about something that had nothing to do with logic or reason. A powerful feeling was urging him on, pushing him through the wooded park toward the executive mansion—a feeling of dread. With no factual evidence to support the idea, he felt almost certain that something ghastly was going to happen.

Soon.

To his surprise, he located the tall and gaunt Abraham Lincoln standing alone in the East Room of the White House. He was staring up at a Roman bust in the archway above the double doors, with his long arms flat against his sides. The great and tireless leader looked exhausted. His sunken cheeks were pale and even more hollow than usual, his dark hair and scraggly beard slightly mussed from lying in bed.

"Good morning, sir." The Secretary tried to sound cheerful.

Lincoln turned, smiled, and nodded congenially. "I hope it's a good morning, Edwin." He rubbed his red, swollen eyes. "It might cancel a bad night."

"I'm sorry if you didn't sleep, Mr. President."

His eyes panned the room. "I slept," he said vaguely. "But not very well. I dreamed it again, Edwin," he confessed in a low, sad voice. "That same haunting dream. I was wandering alone through all the rooms in the White House, searching for these pale, ghostly mourners who kept crying out to me, as if their hearts were broken. I couldn't see them, but their pitiful wailings sent chills up and down my spine. Finally, I wound up here, in the East Room. Over there, under the main chandelier, was a catafalque, with a body in it. I remember, I felt very cold when I saw the tall, hard corpse, covered in a flag. I felt almost frozen. But it wasn't a painful cold, somehow."

"Mr. President, it was only a dream."

He nodded agreeably. "Yes, I know it was. But this was more real than other dreams, Edwin. I remember it all so clearly—like the face of one of the soldiers stationed around the coffin. It was small and round, with a scar the size of a thread running across a dimple in his chin, and tiny black eyes the size of an acorn. I asked this soldier who the dead man was, and he answered with tears in his eyes, 'It's the President.' Then hundreds of mourners suddenly appeared in the room, and they all together burst forth in such a horror-stricken, tormented cry, that it woke me up, and I found myself in my bed, soaked with sweat."

Stanton felt a chill grip his whole body as he watched Lincoln gaze absently around the room, reliving the experience. He collected himself and decided that it was not the time to tell him about Donald Massey. "Mr. President," he said, "considering this fear you have, don't you think it would be a good idea to increase the personal guard?"

"No," he said, slowly shaking his head, "it wouldn't."

"But if you're so concerned about your safety—"

"I'm not concerned about my safety, Edwin." He smiled weakly. "There is no need to be. I've known for years I was to meet a hard and violent death at the hands of some poor Brutus like the one in that bust over the door. There is nothing you, or I, or a hundred extra guards can do about that. When it comes time for a tree or a horse or a . . . President to cease to exist, then he will die, by the will of God."

"But a few guards—"

"No, Edwin," he insisted. "No more guards. Let's not alarm the public when it would do no good. Instead, why don't we think about the matters at hand? I want to assure the Cabinet in that meeting Friday that the Union will be re-established by the time Congress convenes in December. Can I do that? What is happening in Alabama now? Has Mobile surrendered yet?"

"Not yet. But a dispatch from General Canby says he is certain he will take it today. That will end the hostilities altogether."

"Good. That would be right."

"Sir?"

Lincoln placed his hand on Stanton's shoulder. "It would be good timing, Edwin," he said. "It looks to me as though two long and trying chapters in our nation's history may be about to come to an end at the same time. When that finally happens, perhaps our people will at last be able to turn them down and start a new book."

"Two chapters, Mr. President?" he said, puzzled.

"Two." He nodded. "One of them concerns this bloody war that is drawing to a close, Edwin," he answered. "As for the other—unless my brain is in my head merely to torment me with idle dreams—I believe the other concluding chapter belongs entirely to me."

# Chapter 4

A few minutes after twelve noon, Stephen Bedford stopped in front of the entrance to Ford's Theatre on Tenth Street, N.W., unfolded the torn playbill Paddy had found on Donald Massey's body, and compared it to the notice posted on the front door. The two advertisements matched. The top half of the theatre announcement filled in the missing portion of Massey's playbill:

Tom Taylor's Eccentric Comedy,
As originally produced in America by Miss Keene, and
performed by her upwards of
One Thousand Nights,
Entitled

Our American
*COUSIN*

Florence Trenchard . . . . . . Miss Laura Keene

"This is it, Paddy," he said to the Irishman.

"Yes, sir," he agreed, "same thing, exactly. Now if we can fill in the lad's coded message as easy—"

Paddy was interrupted by a sharp, thin voice suddenly shrieking wildly behind them. Bedford wheeled around to see a dark-haired woman struggling frantically with a carriage horse pawing the ground and rearing out of control in the muddy street. But before he could react, the Irishman was already leaping off the wooden planks down to the street and snatching hold of the horse's bridle.

"Don't pull on her!" he yelled at the woman jostling around in the open carriage. "Loosen up, ma'am! Let go of the reins—I'll take them!"

"I can't stop her—"

"Stop pulling on her!" Paddy commanded. "Let me have the reins. Come on, let them drop!" When the leather straps finally went slack, O'Connor locked his massive arms around the horse's head and bore it down against his chest. "Easy now." He held the mare close and rubbed his big palm over her white blaze. "It's going to be all right. Nobody's going to hurt you."

Fanny Seward flipped her tiny black felt hat back off her forehead. "I wasn't *trying* to hurt her," she protested. "I couldn't help it."

Her denial popped a blush of color into O'Connor's cheek. "Oh, no ma'am," he said as he shook his head emphatically, "I didn't mean to say that. You just ain't handling her right, that's all."

"Well, no matter what I want her to do, she does the opposite."

"All you have to do is be gentle with her, ma'am." He stroked the horse's nose, calming her. "Just treat her like a lady, that's all."

"Really?" she said ingenuously. "I had no idea." She settled back in the carriage seat. "I told Becky I couldn't do this," she said, "but she wouldn't listen. She thinks a woman can do anything a man can do."

"Well, if you talk real soft to her and keep her reins loose," Paddy advised, "you'll find she handles like a paddle boat."

Fanny took a deep breath and bravely took over the reins again. "Thank you for the advice," she said shakily. "I think I may be able to handle her now."

"Yes, ma'am." Paddy backed off. "Just remember what I said, and she'll be fine."

Even though she was still flustered, Fanny managed a warm smile. "I'll remember," she said. "You've been very thoughtful."

Stephen snapped open the door to the theatre and waited for Paddy to join him. "You could have asked the lady's name, Sergeant," he scolded him. "It was obvious she liked you."

"Ah, the lass was just grateful, that's all." He colored. "Nothing more to it than that," he muttered as he swept obliviously through the door, in front of his captain.

Inside the dim theatre, the two men were immediately confronted by a slight but shapely woman in an elaborate satin evening gown. She had dark eyes and matted chestnut hair piled high over a pretty face coated with a thick layer of grayish-white theatrical cosmetics.

"What do you want, gentlemen?" she asked abruptly in

a clear, modulated voice. "The theatre is closed during the day."

Stephen politely removed his hat. "Are you Miss Keene?" he asked, undaunted. He recognized the actress from her advertisement pictures. An older woman than the one in the photographs, Laura Keene was still quite attractive, he decided, even if the strata of rouge and carbon black did make her look rather cold and forbidding.

"I'm very busy this afternoon," she began.

But Stephen interrupted her. "Miss Keene," he said, "My name is Stephen Bedford, and this is Patrick O'Connor. We would like to know," he said as he produced Massey's playbill, "if you have ever seen this before."

She barely glanced at the advertisement. "Well, yes, I've probably seen it." She shrugged. "I've probably seen a hundred thousand of them."

"This one in particular," he pressed, "belonged to a man named Donald Massey."

"Mr. Bedford," she contended, "I don't think I know anyone by that name. So, if you don't mind, I have to set up a rehearsal."

"Miss Keene—" He boldly grabbed her arm. "This is important."

She shot a hard look at the fist clutching at her elbow, then glared up at his face. "It just so happens that what I'm doing is important, too, sir," she challenged him coldly. "In fact, 'sir,' " she grunted as she pulled loose from his grip, "my whole career depends on how this play does this Friday night. A word of praise from President Lincoln quoted in the *Evening Star* and I can take my company back to New York, where we belong. Maybe even to Wallack's theatre. But if this play falls on its pointed little head, then I am done for. I'm nothing but a forty-year-old star in a fading constellation.''

"I'm sorry," Stephen apologized. "I don't want to keep you from your work, but if you don't mind, would you answer one question? Have you seen a man with blond hair, about twenty, hanging around the theatre in the past few days?"

Laura Keene rubbed the red marks of his fingers on her bare arm. "He must have been the one here last night," she surmised.

"What was he doing, ma'am?" O'Connor blurted.

She shrugged again. "How would I know what he was doing?" she retorted. "The same as you, I suppose: asking questions. He claimed he worked for the War Department, but he never told me what he wanted.''

Stephen stuffed the playbill back into the pocket of his gray suit. "Are you sure he said he worked for the War Department?" he asked her.

"That's what the man said," she answered. "Now maybe you'll tell me who you're working for.''

"We're looking for Massey," Bedford evaded quickly. "He's a friend.''

She scrutinized them for a moment, then decided, "Well, all right, go ahead and look for him. Ask the actors; maybe they know him. But be quiet about it, will you? We start rehearsal in fifteen minutes.''

"Miss Keene—" he called out to her as she started off.

"Now what, Mr. Bedford?" She looked back wearily.

"Was Donald Massey asking about anybody in particular?"

She sighed. "No," she replied. "Nobody in particular." Then she added, "Except John Wilkes Booth. But that's just natural curiosity. Everybody asks about him.''

Bedford turned the name of the famous actor over in his mind as he replaced his hat and watched Laura Keene hurry past the orchestra seats on the way to the stage apron. "Paddy," he said, turning to O'Connor, "Why don't you go down to the south side of town and start talking to those countrymen of yours? I want to know as much as I can about Private Massey being in the War Department."

"If it's known, Captain, I'll know it by tonight," O'Connor pronounced confidently. "I'll also be asking around for those 'glassy boots' the lad told me about before he died."

Stephen gazed absently at the stage. "Good," he said. "And while you're at it, find out about John Wilkes Booth."

"Booth?" Paddy wrinkled his brow. "Now, Captain, you don't think a man like that could be mixed up in something as bad as this, do you?"

"I don't know what to think yet, Paddy. Just go do it. I'll try to talk to some of the other actors before the rehearsal starts."

"I'm on my way, Captain."

"When you get back, we'll go to see Mr. Seward. He may not be able to tell us anything about an assassination plot, but we're obliged to show him that his name is on Massey's note. At least he'll be warned."

"Yes, sir, I'll be seeing you back at the hotel then," Paddy said and turned around toward the front. "You be careful, now, Captain," he advised as he shoved open the door. On the way out, he waved good-bye.

Stephen walked down to the front of the stage, climbed up on the apron, and crossed under the proscenium into the right wing of the wooden platform. He found no actors loitering backstage, as he'd expected, and the arena was bare and deserted.

As he gazed about the cool, open space, his heart suddenly leaped up into his throat as a loud, cracking sound crashed over his head and reverberated in the rafters and walls. His chest pounded wildly as he strained to hear more. The sound had been almost like a gunshot. But he couldn't be certain he had actually heard it. For the first time in his life, he didn't trust his own senses.

Shaking off a gripping chill, he left the stage wing and walked slowly down a long adjoining tunnel-like corridor, dimly illuminated by one small globed gaslight on the wall. All of a sudden, a low rumbling of groaning voices began to well up around him. He let out a long, halting breath and shuddered as the sound seemed to drift in toward him from the outside, through the cracks and seams of the woodwork. The melange of voices was meaningless and noisy at first, but then he thought he could discern the moans and sobs of a throng of injured people, crying out to . . . him. He tried to swallow with a dry, constricted throat. If he would let his mind go, he could believe there was something or someone supernatural there, lingering within the walls of the theatre, trying desperately to tell him something.

The eerie, disoriented feeling snapped out of his mind when he turned a corner into a well-lit anteroom and discovered a very pretty young woman pacing back and forth in front of an office door. Relieved to see a real presence in the place, he hung back in the doorway for a while, to watch her unobserved. Then she caught him looking.

"Are you Mr. Ford?" she asked immediately.

Stephen was warmed by the husky, sensual sound of her

voice. He decided instantly that this bright and lovely woman, the same who had been at the National Hotel earlier in the day, looking for John Wilkes Booth, was one of the most beautiful women he had ever seen. It was a pity, he decided further, that she was an actress, and one of Booth's mistresses, instead of a lady. This blonde beauty would have graced any Southern plantation.

"Mr. Ford isn't here," he answered her truthfully. "I'm Stephen Bedford. If you don't mind, I would like to ask you a few questions."

"Would you really," she said indignantly, but with interest. "What makes you think I wouldn't mind?"

"Miss Keene said it would be all right," he told her. "The first question is simple: do you know Donald Massey?"

She looked straight at him. "I don't see how it could possibly be any of your business who I know, Mr. Bedford."

Stephen persisted. "Did you know that a man by that name was here in the theatre last night, asking about your . . . friend?"

"My *friend?*" Her face revealed her confusion. "Are you talking about Frances?"

"I'm talking about Mr. Booth."

"Mr. Booth!" she exclaimed, her eyes widening. "Mr. Bedford," she charged, "you are absolutely the rudest man I have ever met. We've known each other a total of three minutes, and already you're insulting me. Whatever you mean by 'friends,' let me tell you, Mr. Booth and I are not it."

"That's not what I wanted to ask you about, ma'am." He moved closer. "You and Mr. Booth can be whatever you want to be. But I must find out all I can about Donald Massey, as soon as possible."

"Well, allow me to give you a piece of advice, sir. You will never find out anything going about it this way." After hesitating, she started for the door.

But Stephen stepped across and blocked the way. "Wait a minute, now." He held up a palm. "Don't go yet, please. You've evaded every question I've asked."

She stood a few feet from him, firm and resolute. "Would you mind removing your hat in my presence?" she snapped.

He yanked it off his head. "I'm sorry," he apologized. "I wasn't thinking."

"I've noticed that."

"I don't know, this investigation seems to be taking me over, somehow," he confessed. "It's almost as if I'm being drawn into something . . ."

She stared at him for a moment, then blew through her teeth. "Well," she announced, "I'm not going to ask what this investigation is, because I don't really care. Now, would you mind moving out of my way?"

"Are you going back to Mr. Booth?" Stephen dug at her. He was shocked at his own rudeness, but for some reason this beautiful and fiery woman seemed to reach down into him and pull it out. She was unsettling—at once irritating and stimulating.

"Why can't you understand," she answered him, "that what I'm going to do is not your concern, Mr. Bedford."

He nodded resignedly and stepped aside. "You're right," he conceded. "It's not my concern. But I could ask your name, couldn't I?"

She stopped; she stood close enough for him to touch. "My name is Rebecca Windfield, sir," she replied.

"I don't remember seeing that name on the advertisement outside," he said.

"And you're not likely to see it there either," she said, looking at him curiously. "If you see Miss Keene, would you please tell her I will be back later this afternoon?"

"This afternoon would be late for the play rehearsal, wouldn't it?" Stephen said. "I doubt if Miss Keene would like that."

She paused at the door, bristling. "Mr. Bedford," she sighed, "I thought, for a minute, when you first crept in here unannounced, that you were nothing but a rude boor. But I was wrong about that. You're also a raving lunatic."

"If we're going to be blunt with each other, Miss Windfield," he countered, "I may as well admit that I have a few doubts about you, too."

"Really. Well, you couldn't even begin to imagine how insignificant your little doubts are to me, Mr. Bedford. Now, good afternoon to you, sir."

"Ma'am." He nodded as she swept past him, brushing the green fabric of her dress against his leg as she went.

Stephen lingered in the anteroom a few minutes, to allow the disturbing effect of Rebecca Windfield wear off. Later, on his way out, his eye snagged on another playbill, lying face-up on a table near the office door. He reached over the table, turned up the gaslight, and read the advertisement, almost in a daze. It was from Grover's Theatre, dated over two years ago:

*J. Wilkes Booth*
*The Pride of the American People*
*The Youngest Tragedian in The World,*
*Who is Entitled*
*To Be Denominated*
*A STAR OF THE FIRST MAGNITUDE*

After a second reading, he dully dimmed the light and looked away from the flame in an effort to sort out the confusion of ideas swirling in his brain. Why, he wondered, was he running into John Wilkes Booth at every turn? Even though he hadn't uncovered the slightest bit of evidence to indicate that the famous actor might be an assassin, still the idea kept stubbornly presenting itself to his mind.

And if Booth were an assassin, was Rebecca Windfield one, too? He shook his head at that notion. He wouldn't allow himself to consider the idea. The woman was too attractive, too stimulating, too . . . exasperating for him to believe that of her.

To kill the thought, he stepped out into the hall again. Once more, he was seized by a cold, deadening feeling in the pit of his stomach. As he strode rapidly down the dim corridor, that feeling turned into a vague, unexplainable sense of dread.

Seeing the actors gathering in the wings for the rehearsal didn't help. He paused long enough to imagine in the faces of each member of the cast a terrible, black gloom. Then he jumped down from the stage and hurried as fast as he could toward the exit.

Only when he reached the light outside did the cold, dismal feeling leave his body.

# Chapter 5

"Hey, watch out for the freedmen!" a shoeshine boy yelled at Paddy as a crowd of black people turned around a corner and headed toward him.

The Irishman leaped out of the muddy street as the pious-looking congregation of a hundred former slaves marched obliviously through, singing "My Country 'Tis of Thee." Tailing twenty feet behind was another troop of a hundred men, this one a rabble made up of Confederate deserters, parading with Hackeston's Rebel Brigade Band and moaning in sombre and morose tones all the verses of "My Old Kentucky Home."

After the last of the drunken deserters straggled by, O'Connor tramped across the street to the Ferry Inn. In front of the entrance steps, a young Union soldier waved a tankard of ale at him. "You heard the latest, Pops?" he saluted him. "Old Canby did it, by God. Mobile's given up without a fight. It's over! Can you believe that? No more hardtack, and no more pork and beans!"

In no mood to converse with anybody on the subject of the war, Paddy nodded his head and kept on walking. He was tired and weary. He had searched two dozen taverns and saloons in Washington City for his Irish friends, and had found no one. They had all left town. Tom McDermott, Mrs. Greenhow's spy, had been hustled out of Washington as a pickpocket; Clarence Day, one of Captain Thomas Nelson's men, had been "sent away" by the police; even Ellie O'Neal, whose house in Swampoodle was an institution, had been "run out of the area," according to a local innkeeper.

Anxious for another drink, he pushed past a couple of policemen escorting a staggering black man dressed in rags, and stepped under the doorway of the inn, which was decorated with boughs of cedar and the blue banner of the 69th New York Regiment. Inside the tavern, he shoved his way through a tangled mass of arms and legs, into a haze of blue smoke, and squeezed out a place for himself at the end of the long pine table in the middle of the room.

"Whatt'll it be, sport?" asked a fat man in a soiled white apron who appeared at his right arm a few minutes later. He was vigorously chewing tobacco and hugging a tray of empty tankards against his belly.

"Irish whisky," Paddy answered.

"Sorry," He shrugged and swallowed some of the tobacco juice. "We got everything from Sneaky Pete to blackberry wine, but one thing we ain't got is Irish whisky."

"Beer then."

"Beer it is."

While Paddy waited for the drink, he listened to a few rounds of "We are Coming, Father Abraham," from a band of Irish-looking soldiers huddled together around a fireplace, then to a rowdy, irritating rendition of "When Johnny Comes Marching Home Again" from a darker group across the room.

. The racket didn't keep him from thinking, though. Paddy O'Connor could not forget for a moment that his captain had sent him on a mission, and that he had failed to accomplish it. He had promised Bedford he would deliver the information he needed, but in five hours of ferreting around the seamiest quarters of the city, he had turned up nothing. For the first time since Antietam, Paddy had let Stephen Bedford down.

Just as the waiter carelessly slammed his pint of beer down on the table, a wide, pink hand suddenly came out of nowhere and curled itself over the top of the tankard. Paddy raised his eyes to see through a veil of smoke a tall, pot-bellied man in plaid trousers, gray vest, and a black wool coat. The man yanked a soggy cigar from between his yellowed teeth, thumped the ashes on the floor, and flashed a wide grin. "You're a Johnny Reb, aren't you, bud?" he said.

"Would you mind moving your hand?" O'Connor asked him calmly.

"Did you see this, boys?" he called to the others in the inn. "A Johnny Reb waltzes in here wearing gray pants and nobody pays him any mind at all. And look at this— look at his face; it's as red as a beet!"

"I can't drink my beer with your hand there," Paddy said firmly.

After hesitating a second, the other man raised his hand off the tankard and smoothed his vest over his protruding stomach. "This is some celebration we have going here, isn't it, Reb?"

"It's mostly noise, if you ask me," O'Connor observed.

"Ha! Sour grapes from a sour loser, is that it? You just can't stand it 'cause we whipped you traitors in the war, can you?" he gloated. "Can he, boys?" He searched the room for moral support. "Poorest excuse for fighting men I've ever seen."

Paddy looked up at him. "At least I was in it," he said pointedly. It was obvious this one was no soldier.

"Are you saying I didn't do my part, Reb?" he huffed. "Just because I didn't shoot a gun—"

"I ain't saying anything, one way or another, Mister," he broke in. "I just want to drink my beer." He raised the container to his lips and let some of the warm beer slide down his throat.

The man in the plaid trousers glowered. "You're a damned cocky Irishman, aren't you?" He looked to the others at the table. "I figure maybe a toast to the Union will take that nasty edge off this traitor. What do you say, boys? Do you figure he owes us a toast for all the misery he's cost?"

"Yeah!" someone responded. "Make him give us a toast!"

"Why don't you leave the man alone, Miller," a tall man in black offered over the foam of his beer. "He's not bothering anybody. You've got no reason to badger him."

"He's Irish," the man next to him offered. "That's reason enough for Miller."

"You shut up, Hinson!"

"Seems a fellow by the name of O'Somebody or Other ran off with Miller's wife last week," Hinson informed Paddy. "If you get my drift."

"You shut up, damn it!" Miller's tone suddenly became hard and mean. "I'm asking this traitor to our beloved Union to have a toast with me, and by God, he's going to oblige me, or else. Waiter!" he called out, "give me an ale! Give me two ales!"

The noise in the room softened as everyone turned his attention to Paddy's table. When the fat waiter lugged over the two pints of ale, each man in the room suddenly fell quiet. All eyes locked on O'Connor.

"Well, Reb?" Miller plucked up his pint of ale. "What's it going to be? Are you going to give us loyal Unionists a toast, or are you yellow, too?"

Paddy squeezed the edge of the table with his fists to keep from ramming them into Miller's face. He had to keep calm. What would Captain Bedford do if Paddy O'Connor not only failed his mission, but got himself thrown into jail for fighting, as well? No, he decided, he could never do that to him. As the others watched closely, he slowly lifted his right hand, opened up his fist, and grabbed the handle of his tankard. "To the Union!" he raised it into the air. "Long may she stand!"

As the inn rocked with cheers of relief and joy, Miller shot disgruntled, disappointed glances everywhere. Finally he hollered, "Wait a minute! Hold it! Quiet!" When the clamor at last died down, he slung his wet cigar to the floor and stomped on it with the heel of his boot. "I'm not through with this reb yet," he announced.

"Come on, Miller—" Hinson pleaded. "He did it, now let him be!"

"Back off, Hinson," a faceless voice yelled out of the smoke. "Damned rebel ought to know better than to come in here in the first place."

"Yeah, that's right!" others voiced their agreement.

Miller smirked with satisfaction. "The thing is, we're all celebrating the end of the war here. We need us a song to go with that toast, right, boys?"

"He's right!" the boys agreed. "Miller's right! Let's have a song, Reb!"

"Well now, let's see." Miller scraped his cheek with a long fingernail. "What song do we need for this Irish reb? How about 'Ain't We Glad to Get Out of the Wilderness'? Since you Southern folk hate the colored people so much, let's hear you eat a little Jim Crow!"

As the whole inn guffawed with laughter, Paddy glanced around, embarrassed at all the attention. The other men, now in the swing of the situation, were pounding their fists on the tables and shouting for him to sing. Some looked weak and acquiescent; others had fire in their eyes.

Buoyed by the rousing support, Miller began to push with abandon. "Sing it, damn you, Reb," he ordered Paddy. "And sing it . . . in colored dialect!"

"Yaay!" the gallery yelped its approval. "Do it colored, Johnny Reb!" they urged.

"Climb up on the table here," Miller commanded with authority. "And sing it loud, Reb. Sing it loud enough for God Himself to hear you!"

Paddy looked up at him, straight into his eyes. "I don't sing songs," he stated.

Miller swallowed. "Hell, all Irishmen sing songs," he claimed. "That's how they take our women, right, boys?"

"Right!"

"So either you give us three verses of that song in dialect, or we'll stretch your neck from a rafter till it breaks. And I'll bet there would be plenty of volunteers for that piece of business."

The excited crowd gathered at the table let up a cheer; to a man, they seemed willing and eager to oblige.

After casting an eye at the sea of hard, glaring faces around him, Paddy quaffed the rest of his beer, slowly pulled himself up from the table, and spoke. "I'll say good evening to you gentlemen now," he muttered and turned to go.

But Miller's hand grabbed his shoulder and spun him around. "You're not going anywhere till you sing, Reb," he blustered.

"Don't touch me again," Paddy ordered. His voice was quiet, but insistent.

But Miller wasn't fazed by it. "Now you listen to me, potato-grower," he growled. "I made a promise to these men, and by God, I'm going to keep it."

"Well, I ain't going to—"

"I told you to get up there and sing, damn it!" He shoved O'Connor toward the table with both hands.

The instant Paddy felt himself stumble, he instinctively lashed back with his right hand and slammed the back of his palm straight into the other man's throat. Miller gasped, staggered, and landed on his backside with a loud thud.

"You Irish scum," he croaked. Fumbling frantically with his coat, he pulled a small ivory-handled pistol out of a pocket. "I'll strew your brains all over this floor—" He started to rise up.

But the Irishman was too quick for him. Before Miller could level the Derringer at him, Paddy had pounced on the man's wrist and was jerking him up on his feet. As the other men watched in stunned silence, he spun Miller's body around in a circle and slung him down against the table. The pine boards split, splintered, and crashed to the floor under the impact of his weight.

On top of a mass of broken boards, Miller scrambled grunting to his knees, scooped up the pistol from the floor, raised it, and pulled the trigger. Before the powder exploded, Paddy ducked, and the bullet whizzed past his head and thumped into a cedar rafter. Instantly the Irishman lunged for Miller. Now he heaved him off the floor by the collars and rammed his fist into the soft flesh of his belly. When Miller folded, O'Connor snapped hold of his pistol hand and brought the forearm down with all his might against his own bent knee.

When the two limbs met, the sound of Miller's bone cracking rang out as loud as a gunshot in the smoky room. Shrieking in agony, he dropped to the floor, clutching the broken arm to his breast. For an instant, everyone in the inn stood silent, awed by the display of strength and violence. Then, as someone tugged Miller out of the way, another called out to the assemblage: "Are we going to let the reb get away with this, men?"

"No!" came the reply in unison.

"Well come on then; let's do something about it!"

While two men in Union uniform kicked aside the table debris, two older men in broadcloth pushed aside the chairs. Then the others began to inch slowly toward O'Connor.

Paddy started his retreat slowly and carefully. He knew that no one man was a match for this mob of at least thirty scowling men with a lust for vengeance in their eyes. As they moved toward him, he felt his way with his hand behind his back.

"You don't look so mean now, Reb," one of the men laughed. "Look at him run, like Beauregard out of Columbia!"

"Yellow-bellied reb!"

"Let's give him a taste of Union justice, men!"

Paddy eased backwards, keeping the others in view, groping behind him with his hand. "I don't want no trouble," he told them. "But I'll fight, if I have to."

"Well, get ready to fight, Johnny Reb."

"Somebody get a rope!" Miller bellowed. "String him up!"

"Yeah, let's hang the bloody bastard!"

O'Connor suddenly felt rough, splintery boards against his fingertips. He knew his back was only a foot away from the wall now. Around him angry, blood-thirsty eyes were glaring and boots were clumping down on the pine floor, drawing closer and closer. Paddy knew there was nothing he could say to stall such men as these. He would have to stand and fight them as long as he could.

Then, as he braced his body for the rush, a sharp voice rang out above the noise. "Here you go, lad. Catch!" Paddy looked up just as a short and heavy hickory stick flew softly out of the smoke in his direction. As he plucked the stick out of the air, a tiny red-headed man in an ill-fitting brown suit squeezed out of the mob and planted himself against the wall, next to Paddy.

"Hardie O'Riley's the name, gents!" he shouted. "And that little device there my friend is holding is what we Irish folk like to call a shillelagh. The finest weapon on God's green earth. And as the Lord provides the needy, I happen to have one, too." He whipped out another club from under his big coat.

"Put your stick up and get out of the way, shrimp!" a stocky man in a three-piece suit threatened. "Or we'll hang you, too."

"Then come and hang me, lads," he brandished his cudgel. "I'm ready to swing whenever you are."

"Don't you realize you're siding with a Johnny Reb, man!" the stocky man accused.

"The war is over, gents! The only rebs left now are the ones in the history books."

"Don't listen to him!" Miller cried out from across the room. "Kill him, too! Go on—kill both of them! What's the matter with you? There are only two of them!"

"Make that three," said another man stepping out of the crowd. "Robert J. O'Rourke's the name, of the 24th Massachusetts Regiment."

"Sean O'Hara makes it four." The next man broke through.

"Make it five." Another appeared.

And others came forth:

"Six."

"Seven."

"Eight."

"Good lads!" O'Riley beamed. "Now, if you think you're ready for us, gents," he announced, swashing his shillelagh through the air, "come have a run at these Irish sticks of ours."

With whoops and roars and angry cries, the thirty all at once charged the eight. But the fight that followed lasted only a matter of minutes. The Irish Americans swished their shillelaghs around in a dazzling show of power and finesse and reckless abandon. As they formed a line of swinging clubs, the larger challengers stopped abruptly and dropped to the floor like splattered flies. Right and left, O'Riley and his men banged wildly away at heads and chests and stomachs. Tables crunched, chairs splintered, mirrors and windows shattered; eyebrows and noses and cheeks split apart and poured out blood. And yet no man in the 24th suffered so much as a scratch.

"Come on, lad, time to go." O'Riley pushed the bigger O'Connor past a wall of cudgels out of the inn. "You'd better be moving on, quick as you can," he advised O'Connor on the street.

"What about the others?" Paddy gestured toward the inn. "We can't be leaving them in there—"

"Ah!" Hardie grinned, flashing a gap in his front teeth. "Don't worry about the 24th. They'll be fine. Now what's your name, lad?" he asked.

"Paddy O'Connor," he answered.

"Well, now, that's a fine name, I would say. I'm glad to make your acquaintance. But let's be going now, while we can."

As they walked briskly down the street, Paddy muttered an embarrassed thanks for O'Riley's help.

"The help was nothing." Hardie dismissed it with a wave of the hand. "To tell you the truth, I was hating their raspy singing so much, I was looking for an excuse to spring into action. But let me be giving you a word of advice, Paddy O'Connor. I wouldn't be taking myself into any more drinking halls in Washington City, if I were you. Word travels fast in this old town. Next place you go, they'll be ready for you."

"Even if they are, I've still got to go," Paddy said soberly.

The little man stopped him. "Now wait," he said, "I'm not just whistling a tune here, lad. What I mean is, they'll kill you, sure as heaven. And they'll think nothing of doing it."

"Maybe so, but I've still got to try to get some information for Captain Bedford," O'Connor said stubbornly. "I decided back there, I won't be going back until I do. You

see, the captain is on this important mission which he took
on his own self—''

"Now don't be telling me any more of that," O'Riley
cut him off. "I don't want to know about it. There are too
many people around here looking to hang a spy these
days."

O'Connor looked straight at him. "Hardie," he said,
"Captain Bedford wants me to find out about two people:
John Wilkes Booth and Donald Massey."

"Donald Massey!" he exclaimed. "Oh, no, Paddy—''
He turned to go.

"You know him!" Paddy grabbed his arm.

"I don't know anything, O'Connor," Hardie insisted
firmly.

"You know Massey," Paddy charged. "I can see it in
your eyes."

"You're seeing things, lad."

"Hardie, tell me!"

With difficulty, O'Riley shrugged off Paddy's big hand.
"All right, all right," he relented. "I did know Donald
Massey. He was a countryman, and he worked for the War
Department. Only they tell me the poor lad was killed last
night, over in Washington."

"He was," Paddy confirmed. "I was there."

O'Riley cocked his head. "Well then," he declared,
"you don't need me to tell you anything, do you?"

"We need to know who shot him, Hardie," Paddy
pressed. "We might be able to stop something real bad
from happening, if we know."

"Well now, I'll swear to you, lad, I have no idea who
shot him."

"Massey said it was a man with boots that shined like
glass. Do you have any idea who that would be?"

Hardie hesitated, then shook his head. "I couldn't say," he answered.

Paddy sighed. "You're lying to me, Hardie O'Riley," he said sadly. "I can hear it in your voice."

"I'm sorry, O'Connor. You just ask too much of a man, that's all. I don't mind cracking a few skulls in a saloon now and again. But this kind of thing you're poking around in is something else."

"All right. If you won't tell me about it, I'll just have to try somewhere else. I'll find another saloon."

"Don't do it, lad. Sure as praying, somebody will be there waiting for you. You won't have a chance."

"I've got to do something, Hardie."

"By the saints, you're a hard-headed man, Paddy O'Connor."

"All I know is, whatever it takes to serve Captain Bedford, I'm going to do it."

"Well God preserve you then."

Paddy looked at him a moment, then extended his hand. "Good-bye, Hardie," he said. "I'd be grateful if you thanked the others for saving me."

"Saving you for what? For another clutch of villains as bad as that one?"

"I'll be on my guard," Paddy said.

O'Riley sighed resignedly, took O'Connor's hand and shook it. "All right then," he said, "at least let me go with you. I may not be big, but you see I can shake a cudgel hard. And two shillelaghs are always better than one."

Paddy shook his head. "This is my job, Hardie," he declined. "I'll have to be doing it myself. Unless," he added, "you want to tell me about Donald Massey or John Wilkes Booth."

"Damn it, lad," O'Riley groaned. "I've said all I can say about Donald Massey. I'd as like be cutting my own throat and a few others besides if I said another word."

"Then what about Booth?"

Hardie paused. "The same goes for Booth, Paddy," he answered.

Paddy nodded understandingly. "It's all right," he declared. "I'll find out about him myself." He started plodding south, through the mud, toward the War College.

Before he had gone ten yards, a thin voice shouted behind him. "You're crazy, Paddy O'Connor!" O'Riley hollered. "You know that?"

Paddy kept walking.

"Paddy O'Connor!"

The Irishman stopped, took a deep breath, and turned around. O'Riley was standing in the street, one hand on his hip, the other with his shillelagh resting on his shoulder. "What is it, Hardie?" he yelled back.

"You're going the wrong way, O'Connor!"

"What?"

"I said, you're going the wrong way! If you want to know about Mr. John Wilkes Booth, you'd best be headed for that boarding house he's always hanging around."

"What boarding house?"

"Well, by the saints, O'Connor, if you weren't just standing there in the street, I'd be showing you now, wouldn't I?"

# Chapter 6

Across the broad path in front of Mary Surratt's boarding house on H Street, N.W., Hardie O'Riley stretched out his arm, clasped hold of Paddy's fingers, and shook them vigorously. "I guess I'll be seeing you then, lad," he announced amiably. "Top of the evening to you."

"You're welcome to stay a while," Paddy offered in a low voice.

He let go of O'Connor's hand. "Now I've already told you," he replied, "I'll not be taking any part in this unholy business of spying. On the other hand, I promise you, if you've made up your mind to do it, all you have to do is stand right there and wait. Count on it, Paddy O'Connor, more trouble than you have ever seen will come ambling down that street before I crawl into my bed tonight."

Paddy watched the little man linger a moment, then suddenly burst away down the path and vanish in the misty evening. O'Connor drew in a long breath, walked across H Street, and sidled against a wall in the alley next to the boarding house. While the gray overcast sky above him and the wide streets around him gradually became dark, he waited for something to happen.

Time passed and he grew more and more anxious. He pondered what he should do. He had promised Captain Bedford to meet him back at the hotel. Should he honor that promise or stay there and attempt to salvage the mission Bedford had sent him on?

Before he could make a decision, his eye caught on a couple of spectral figures draped in dark, flowing cloaks, sweeping across the street toward him. Shrinking back into the shadows as they approached the front door of the boarding house, Paddy held his breath and strained to hear as one of them began talking, his clear and distinct words hanging heavy in the damp night air.

"I'm sorry, Wilkes," he was saying in a deep voice as the two paused at the doorway. "You know I hate to oppose you in anything, but I can't help how I feel about this. I just can't believe in those rascals you've hired."

The second man straightened his top hat on his head. "Well, thank God, you don't have to believe in them," he said. "You ought to realize, Michael, that these men are of a different order from most of the men you and I have known. They respond to nothing in life but jobs and money. For one or the other, they will do anything they're told to do."

"But what I'm concerned about is, they can't possibly know what kind of man you are—"

"It doesn't matter what they know, Michael, as long as

they understand the color of my gold——'' His words were
cut off to Paddy's ears by the door slamming shut behind
them.

O'Connor stood still for a breathless moment, then eased
hesitantly out of the darkness, trying to collect his thoughts.
He knew he had just heard something important, but what
did it mean? He hadn't understood enough to report to his
captain yet. He ran the words he had heard through his
memory again, and then finally made a decision: he would
stay here and try to learn more.

Checking to make sure that nobody was watching, he
slipped around to the front of the house, and paused in the
pale light at the door. After breathing in and out three
times to strengthen his resolve, he quickly grabbed the
doorknob, twisted it, and shoved in the door. To his great
relief, the dim foyer was empty and silent. Seconds later,
he heard, though faintly, the commanding voice of the
second man, drifting down the stairs from a room on the
second floor.

Knowing that he had to go where John Wilkes Booth
was talking, Paddy proceeded carefully up the creaking
steps to the second floor landing. With his breath short and
halting and his heart pounding in his chest, he crept silently down the hall, past the cracked door, then ducked
into a dark corner, beyond the rim of light made by the
tiny gas fire on the wall.

Inside the room on the second floor of Mary Surratt's
boarding house, a faultlessly dressed John Wilkes Booth
stood with his back to a coal fire, rocking back and forth
on his heels as he scrutinized the five other men in the
room. His friend Michael O'Laughlin had been right about
one thing: men like George Atzerodt, Lewis Powell, Davie

Herold, and Mason Butler were totally incapable of appreciating the parts they were about to play in the most powerful act of drama in the history of America. No matter how well he explained it to them, they could never understand the importance of the grand and climactic scene that he had written and which they were to perform.

Atzerodt, leaning forward in a chair and wiping the blade of a Bowie knife on his muddy trousers leg, was an unemployed coach-maker. In the early years of the war he had scrounged out a few dollars smuggling Confederate soldiers from Maryland across the Potomac to Virginia, but now that his commerce had dried up completely, he was in desperate need of money. His rough wool overcoat, his wrinkled brown suit, and the once-expensive curled hat which he wore low over his weather-beaten square face, constituted all his worldly possessions. He was destitute and hungry, sworn to commit any crime for payment of gold.

Pacing up and down in front of Atzerodt was Lewis Powell, a tall, robust man of twenty-one, who had a habit of shuffling about a room with his hands crammed into the pockets of his overcoat as he peered at you from under the brim of his hat, and all the while hummed nervously in a tenor voice. While Powell came from a respectable line of doctors and Baptist preachers, he had never amounted to anything his relatives could be proud of. Loaded with a cache of money, he believed he could go home to Virginia, marry his fiancée and, for the first time in his life, stand up and be counted as a worthy member of the Powell family.

Across the room, near the door, Davie Herold drew his arms into his stout little body and shivered, while his dark, round eyes suspiciously followed Powell's every movement, as if he expected him to pounce his way at any second. Unlike Powell and Atzerodt, Davie, a drug clerk at Thompson's Store on Pennsylvania Avenue, was a native of Washington. But like them, he needed money badly. His father had died recently, and he could see no way of supporting his mother and six sisters on his meagre salary alone.

Mason Butler, sitting on a maroon Victorian sofa by himself, was also watching Powell. He disliked the attractive young man and considered him inferior. Butler, after all, was not in this conspiracy merely for money, as Powell and the others were. He also wanted the position in the government that Cameron had promised him years ago—the place Lincoln and Johnson and Stanton had unjustly denied him. He wanted justice.

"Will you stop pacing and light somewhere," he barked at Powell. "You're making me sick, all that going back and forth, back and forth—"

Powell stopped in the middle of the room, turned, and faced him. "Do you think I care what makes you sick, old man?" he challenged. "I couldn't care less if a mole like you lives or dies."

"You think anybody cares about *you,* preacher-boy?" Atzerodt broke in.

"All right, be still, all of you," the fifth man cautioned them. "We're not here to fight. It's natural to be a little shaky, with the fourteenth only two days off, but let's not let it get the best of us."

"Thank you, Michael," Booth said to the intense-looking man with the thick moustache and the penetrating eyes. He could always count on his school chum from Baltimore for support. While the others were there merely to do his bidding, O'Laughlin cared for him and believed in him.

He understood the agony the actor felt at the defeat of a glorious South he had never had a chance to defend.

"Why are we meeting again, anyway, Booth?" Butler demanded. "I'm taking a big chance, coming here."

"We're all taking chances, Mason," the actor said. "Which is why we must make sure the plan is right."

"Oh, no," Powell complained in his high voice. "Not another rehearsal. We all know what we're supposed to do. We've gone over it a hundred times."

"Shut up, Powell," Atzerodt muttered. "Let Mr. Booth do it the way it oughta be done. I reckon for sure, ain't none of us smart enough to figure all this out."

Lewis scowled at him from under his hat. "Do you really think killing the President, the Vice President, the Secretary of State, and the Commander of the Army requires any brains, Atzerodt?" he retorted.

"Maybe it don't," he conceded. "But I reckon killing 'em and getting away with it does."

"He's right, Lewis," Davie Herold put in weakly.

"Who the hell asked you, nitwit?" Powell wheeled around.

"I just think it's a real good plan, that's all," Davie said defensively.

"Oh, good. A knuckle-headed drug clerk has now expressed his approval of the plan, so we can all relax."

"Why don't you sit down, Powell," Booth ordered.

"I don't want to—"

"I said, Sit down!" Booth boomed in a blood-curdling voice. "Thank you," he said politely when Powell took his seat. "Now, gentlemen," he addressed the others, "if you don't mind, why don't we look at the plan? The four assassinations will take place on Friday, March 14, at exactly ten p.m.'' He turned to the coach-maker. ''George, tell us what you're supposed to do.''

Atzerodt sheathed his Bowie knife behind his belt and cleared his throat. ''Well,'' he began, ''I'm supposed to go in this room in the Kirkwood House, right over the Vice President's place, and stay there all day. At ten o'clock at night, I'm to sneak downstairs and kill Mr. Johnson, and his secretary, too, if he's in the way. Then I take off for parts unknown.''

''Not parts unknown, George,'' Booth corrected. ''For Maryland.''

''Yessir; Maryland.''

Powell leaned forward in his chair. ''Tell me something, Atzerodt,'' he challenged. ''Have you ever killed anybody? Do you know what it feels like to take somebody's life? Are you sure you can do it?''

''Why don't you leave people alone, Powell?'' Atzerodt retorted angrily.

''Just answer my question, Atzerodt: have you ever committed a murder?''

''I reckon it's none of your business whether I have or not.''

Powell threw up his hands. ''There you have it, friends—a weak link in the chain. Exactly what every conspiracy needs.''

''Don't worry about George,'' Booth advised. ''He'll do his part. I've picked all of you very carefully. There are no weak links in this chain. Now, Lewis, explain what you and Davie will be doing while George is executing Mr. Johnson.''

The man shrugged. ''All right. My job is simple. First, Davie goes up to the front of William Seward's house and delivers a package of medicine from Thompson's Store.

While he's getting everyone's attention, I crawl inside and sneak up to Seward's bedroom and slit the old bastard's throat. This should be easy pickings for me. I did it a dozen times when I was spying for Mosby.''

"And your escape route?''

"While the dimwit stays behind, I cross Anacostia Creek and head south for Surratt's Tavern.''

Booth nodded his satisfaction. "Good.'' He rubbed his eyes. "That will take care of the Vice President and the Secretary of State. Michael, what about General Grant?''

O'Laughlin glanced at the other men in the room, then looked at Booth. "The General is scheduled to be at Ford's Theatre Friday night, Wilkes,'' he responded, "watching *Our American Cousin*. At exactly ten o'clock, I will step out of a darkened corner, aim a rifle at his heart and, God help me, pull the trigger. In the confusion that follows, I will escape through the back door of the theatre, mount my horse, and head home to Baltimore.''

The actor allowed O'Laughlin's words to sink in for a moment. "And at the precise moment Grant is shot,'' he informed the others, "John Harrison Surratt will fire a single round into the President's head, from his position on the opposite side of the theatre.''

The dim room suddenly became very still as each man lowered his head and considered, as if for the first time, the full impact of the violence of the actor's scheme. After they had held their eyes to the floor for a respectable time, Lewis Powell raised his head and broke the stony silence.

"Where is John Harrison Surratt?'' he asked Booth, regarding the son of the owner of the boarding house. "It seems to me the man should be here now, with the rest of us.''

Booth plucked up the sooty poker and jiggled the coals

in the fireplace. "Surratt is on his way down from Canada," he replied. "John is a careful man; he's in the process of setting up a series of witnesses in New York. If they have to, they will testify that he was there on the fourteenth."

"That's fine for him, but I've heard the man's a bit unpredictable on occasions," Powell said. "What if he doesn't get here on time? What good will it do for us to kill the others if Lincoln is left alive?"

"That's why we have Mr. Butler," Booth gestured toward the clerk. "Not only has he been providing us with inside information on the movements of Lincoln and his cabinet, but he also acts as an understudy to Surratt."

"As *what?*" Atzerodt asked.

"If Surratt fails, it becomes Mason's job to kill the President."

Powell looked dubiously at Butler. "Do you mean to say our lives may depend on this mole here?"

Mason glared at him, but said nothing.

"I assure you, Surratt will be here, Lewis," Booth promised. "But in the event that he doesn't make it, let me remind you it was Mason who silenced that War Department detective Massey—"

"Silenced him with a bullet in the back, you mean," Powell amended. "Any mole can do that."

"Watch what you're saying, Powell," Mason clenched his teeth.

"Uh-uh, I don't think I like this." Lewis popped up from his seat and began pacing again. "I'm not convinced we're going to get away with it. Sure, there will be a lot of confusion with four political assassinations happening at once, but it won't be enough to shield all of us. The police will be searching every house and tavern in the city. They'll block the roads and close the ferries—"

"No, they won't," Booth interrupted.

"Yes, they will. I know how they work."

"Let Wilkes explain, Lewis," O'Laughlin put in. "He's worked everything out."

"Has he? Then convince me, Mr. Booth. Tell me, in all this chaos, why won't the police be clapping handcuffs on anything that moves?"

Booth smiled. "Because they will have already arrested the man they believe assassinated the President," he returned.

"Meaning who?" Powell sneered.

"Meaning me."

"Now just a minute, Booth," Butler grumbled. "I'm not sure I like the sound of that. Nobody told me about that."

"Nobody told me either," Atzerodt offered.

"You'd better explain yourself, sir," Powell threatened. "Or else we'll all of us get up and walk out of here right now."

Booth leaned the poker against the fireplace stones and sauntered over to the windows and back, thinking, choosing his words. He came to a sudden halt in the middle of the room, eyed each man closely, then spoke. "What will happen," he explained, "is this: the police will arrest me and charge me with the assassination of Lincoln and Grant and quickly connect me with the other two killings. This arrest will focus the attention of the world upon me. I will then step forth on the greatest stage, in front of the largest audience in the history of mankind. The ears of fifty million people around the globe will ring with the sound of my voice. I will tell my friends in the South that it is time to rebuild. I will tell them the tyrants who hoped to break our backs no longer live—"

"Wait a minute!" Powell broke in. "You must think we're all idiots, Booth. I don't care what you do to yourself, but I'm not going to let you sacrifice me for some ideal—"

Booth shook his head emphatically. "No one will be sacrificed, Lewis," he assured him. "When the excitement dies down, I will show that I have plenty of witnesses to testify that I was sitting innocently in a balcony box in front of everyone when the fatal shots were fired. By that time all of you will have disappeared into the night. Within a day I will be a free man, having finally performed the leading role in a real-life drama—one that is destined to change the course of human events forever.

"Why should the police arrest you, of all people, when these men are killed?" Powell asked.

"They will arrest me because a policeman is a short-sighted man whose intelligence is limited to a consideration of physical facts and evidence, Mr. Powell. And we will see to it that he has enough evidence to connect me with all four assassinations. Evidence he can't miss."

"What kind of evidence are you talking about?"

Booth clasped his hands behind his back and looked directly at Powell. "On the morning of the fourteenth," he said, "I will leave a signed note at the Kirkwood House, requesting to see Mr. Johnson. When that note is discovered, the room I'm going to rent there will be searched."

"You mean the one I'll be using," Atzerodt guessed.

"Yes. In it the police will find these two items," Booth said, digging into his pockets. "An Ontario bankbook in my name and a handkerchief with my mother's name embroidered on it." He handed the two objects to the coach-maker. "Leave them where they will be easily found,

George," he instructed. "They will lead the police straight to me."

Atzerodt held them out for the others to see.

"As for Mr. Seward," Booth continued, "I now know two ladies in his household. In the next two days I will make it a point to annoy them by continually prying into the Secretary's affairs. When he is murdered, they will instantly accuse me. For added measure, the medicine Davie will deliver at Seward's doorstep will have been ordered by me."

"Well, I'll admit it sounds pretty clever so far," Powell conceded grudgingly. "But the main arm of the police will be looking at the killings at Ford's."

"Yes, they will. Which is why Michael will inform the General tomorrow night that I am requesting him and Mrs. Grant to join me in my box for the evening performance of *Our American Cousin*."

"Ah, I see. You will be sitting next to Mrs. Grant when her husband is shot," Lewis deduced. "Damn! The best witness in the world!"

"But a *delayed* witness," he qualified. "She will be too upset to speak up until the next day, at the soonest. By then I will have had my hour upon the stage."

After a pause, O'Laughlin asked Booth what evidence he was laying for the Lincoln assassination.

"That's what I'll be doing all day Friday," the actor replied. "Every one will know that I am going to the play. I will visit Harry Ford at the theatre; I will discuss the play and politics with John Coyle, the newspaper editor. And finally, gentlemen, I will give a letter to an actor friend of mine to be published on March 15 in *The National Intelligencer*."

"What kind of letter?" Butler wondered.

Booth made a theatrical gesture with his hands. "A signed letter which will seem to convict me," he answered. "But actually it will not. It will end with these words:

> *For a long time, I have devoted my energies, my time and money, to the accomplishment of a certain end. I have been disappointed. The moment has arrived when I must change my plans. Many will blame me for what I'm about to do, but posterity, I am sure, will justify me.*"

"What does all that mean?" Atzerodt asked.

"It will seem to mean the assassination," Booth told him. "But when I am questioned, I will explain that it actually means my retirement from the stage."

After a long stretch of silence, Powell peeled off his hat and put it back on again. "So," he said to Booth, "all the time we're making our getaways, the four arms of the Metropolitan Police are following all this planted evidence to you. By the time they realize you are innocent, we will be gone."

Booth nodded. "And most important," he added, "I will at last have done my duty for my bleeding brothers of the defeated South."

"And nobody's caught," Atzerodt put in.

"Nobody's caught," Booth confirmed.

Powell nodded. "Well, I have to say, it is smart, all right."

"Smart!" O'Laughlin burst out. "Great day in the morning, man! It's inspired! It's an airtight plan. A damned brilliant plot!"

Booth smiled with satisfaction. "I believe it will work perfectly, if everyone—" he began, but before he could finish his sentence, the door to the room swept open, and a middle-aged woman in a long gray dress rushed in.

"Wilkes!" Mrs. Surratt whispered excitedly. "Hurry!"

"What is it? What's wrong?" Booth demanded.

She tried to catch her breath. "I just saw . . . someone in the hall," she breathed. "I think he was listening!"

"Oh, God." The actor instantly brushed past the flushed woman and darted out into the hall. His eyes quickly scanned the corridor. "Where is he?" he asked her. "I don't see him."

"He was over there, by the window." She pointed at the end of the hall. "He was just standing there."

Booth sprang over to the window and peered out the glass, down to the ground below. "I see him." He detected a moving shape. "He's running across the yard. Let's get him."

Quickly, the five men and Mrs. Surratt scrambled down the stairs and poured out the front door. "There he goes," Lewis Powell huffed as a bulky figure split away from the house and began hustling down the dark street.

"I'll get him," Atzerodt whipped out his Bowie knife and scudded after the fleeting man. He stumbled against the carriage block, recovered his balance, and kept going.

After the coach-maker had vanished into the darkness, Booth addressed the woman. "Mary," he asked worriedly, "how much do you think he heard?"

"I don't know," she said shakily. "I've been downstairs for an hour. He could have been listening all that time."

"Damn!" Powell exclaimed. "This just about breaks the chain, doesn't it?"

Booth nervously slid his palm over his high forehead and dug his fingers through his black curls. "All right," he said after a minute, "there's no need for us to panic. When George brings the man back, we will simply find out how much he knows."

"Don't look like George is gonna be bringing him back, Mr. Booth," Davie Herold reported. "Look."

Booth stood still as the coach-maker came forward, panting, stuffing his knife behind his belt. "What happened?" he asked him.

"I lost him," Atzerodt lowered his gaze. "I reckon he ducked into an alley somewhere."

Powell grabbed the actor's elbow. "Booth," he warned, "that ape we just saw loping down the street could get us all hanged."

"I know he could, Lewis," he jerked his arm loose. "George," he ordered the man with the knife, "I want you to go find him. We can't make another move until we do something about this."

"Ain't no way I can find him now, Mr. Booth," he replied. "The man's gone."

As Booth gnashed his teeth and slammed his fist into his palm, Mason Butler stepped forward. "How much is it worth to you to have this problem taken care of, Mr. Booth?" he inquired in a businesslike tone of voice.

Booth shot a suspicious glance at the clerk. "It's worth the whole scheme, Mason," he answered.

"What would that be, translated into dollars?"

"Dollars!" Lewis Powell snatched his collar. "Now you listen here, you bastard—"

"Booth—make these yokels go away," the clerk gulped. "I mean it. I won't say a thing with them here."

"You slimy mole—"

"Booth—"

"All right, go on, all of you," the actor ordered them. "Disappear."

"What about this . . . creature here?" Powell squawked.

"I'll take care of it, Lewis," Booth said. "Now go— before the other boarders come out. Hurry!"

"We'll be in touch, Booth," Powell cautioned as the others broke away into the night. "Watch what you agree to with that mole."

A while later, in the upstairs room of the boarding house, Booth stood next to the dying fire and watched Butler straighten the lapels of his suit and buff his patent leather shoes on the backs of his trousers. Then he posed a question to him. "Are you trying to tell me you know this man, Mason?" he asked.

"I know him very well," he replied calmly. "As a matter of fact, I shot him last night."

"He didn't look shot to me," Booth returned.

"Maybe he didn't, but he was. Anyway, my point is, since I'm the only one who knows who he is, I'm the only one who can move him out of the way of your scheme."

"Move him for an extra fee, you mean."

"Yes, that's right. A fee of one thousand dollars. Half of what I owe on my house. I would ask for more, but you will find I'm not a greedy man, Mr. Booth."

The actor considered the sum. "All right," he agreed, "you've got it. Now get out of here and take care of him."

"That I will gladly do," Butler smiled, nodded, and headed for the door. Then he paused and looked back. "There is one other thing I will need," he added. "It's an insignificant little thing to you, but it would be very important to me."

"Don't push me, Butler," the actor warned. "Instead

of making deals with you, I ought to be throwing you out on your ear.''

But Butler was unruffled by the threat. ''You're not that kind of man, Mr. Booth.'' He grinned. ''Which is why you've hired us to do your dirty work. You may be rich and famous, but down deep, you're no different from any other play-actor, are you? You're nothing but spit and polish and a lot of bluster.''

''Get out of here, Butler.''

''I'm not going anywhere until I'm assured of proper payment for this murder you want me to commit for you.''

Booth felt his flesh crawl at the cold, hard sound of Butler's words. ''My God,'' he said, recoiling, ''I never wanted to have an innocent man murdered. How suddenly things can change. Only a few moments ago we were all agreeing that my plan was perfect.''

''It's still a good enough plan,'' the clerk contended. ''It can work. All you have to do is agree to my little proposition.''

The actor rubbed his forehead. ''I've already agreed to a thousand dollars, man—what else could you want?''

''That was very generous of you, Mr. Booth, and I thank you for it. But you know, sir, sometimes a man needs more than money. You see, for years I have been giving my heart and soul in the service of my government without so much as a complaint on my part. But in return for my faithfulness, I have been treated as nothing more than a second-rate clerk. A nobody. Well, now I think it's time for me to be a somebody. I want what you have, Booth: position and respect. I deserve those things.''

''Well, I certainly can't give them to you—''

''Oh, but you can,'' he differed. ''You can give them to me by using this play-acting bluster you're so proud of.

You see, when you tell the world about these dead tyrants of government, I want you to convince them there are certain men of quality who have been cheated out of their rightful public offices by Seward and Lincoln and Stanton. Men like Mason Butler.''

Booth clenched his teeth. "You're disgusting, Butler," he said. "Do you expect me to cheapen my one great moment with an advertisement for you?"

"Well, do you expect me to murder a man for you, just because you ask me to?" he countered.

Booth sighed deeply, wrinkled his brow, and ambled over to the window. "Why in God's name did this have to happen?" he muttered. "I had everything under control only fifteen minutes ago!"

"What is it going to be, Booth?" the clerk demanded from the door. "I've made my proposition. Now, do you want this done or not?"

The actor stared out the window, silent.

"Booth," Mason pressed. "I'm waiting for an answer."

"Why did he have to be there?" the actor mumbled absently. "Why, of all the times of his life, did he have to place himself there, tonight?"

"Booth!" Butler growled impatiently at the man's back. "I'm asking for your answer."

"He's going to be another human sacrifice to the dead body of a lost cause."

"Are you listening to me? Do I kill him or not?"

"Yes, damn it!" Booth cried out. "Kill him! Kill him!"

# Chapter 7

Stephen Bedford felt very uneasy as he stepped down out of his carriage on the sidewalk in front of the Seward house a few minutes later. Gazing apprehensively around the dark streets of Lafayette Square, he wondered where on earth Paddy O'Connor could be. He had waited for him at the hotel until the last possible moment, but the Irishman hadn't shown up. Bedford's first impulse had been to go find him, but he knew he couldn't. The assassination attempt was only hours away now, and he had learned practically nothing in the one day he had been in the city. He simply had to talk to Secretary of State Seward.

Pausing in front of the three-story house, Stephen sucked in a deep draught of the cool night air, straightened his waistcoat, and clacked the ornate brass door-knocker twice.

Instantly he heard feet shuffling behind the door, then a woman's voice calling out to someone and the soft sound of the oak door swinging open.

The thrill of seeing a beautiful, statuesque blonde woman in a green gown standing in the pale yellow light of the Seward house confounded him into silence. For a moment, all he could do was swallow hard and smile awkwardly at her.

Rebecca Windfield, on the other hand, appeared altogether unmoved. "Yes?" she said to him.

"Uh, excuse me—" he fumbled.

"Is there something I can do for you, Mr. Bedford?" she asked. "Or did you just come here to stand and gape?"

"I'm sorry, Miss Windfield." He quickly removed his hat. "I didn't mean to stare—"

"That's all right—if you'll tell me what you want."

"It's just that I wasn't expecting you to answer the door," Stephen explained.

She looked directly at him. "Bell is traipsing off somewhere on an errand and Fanny isn't feeling well," she replied coolly, "so I'm answering doors this evening." When he didn't respond, she added, "I'm sorry if you find that shocking."

"That wasn't what shocked me," he said quickly. "What I mean is, I didn't expect you to be here."

"Why shouldn't I be here?" she wondered. "I live here."

He hesitated, befuddled by her words. "I was looking for the residence of Mr. Seward—"

"And you found it." She started to close the door. "Now, if you don't mind, Mr. Seward needs a good deal of peace and quiet."

Collecting himself, he reached out and grabbed the edge of the door. "Whoa now," he protested. "Not so fast. I may be acting like an idiot, but I'm not going to be turned aside that easily."

She glared at him. "Mr. Bedford," she said, "did you really think I would be impressed that you followed me here, like a little puppy?"

"Well, I hate to disappoint you, ma'am, but as it happens, I didn't follow you. I had no idea you lived here. As a matter of fact, I've never thought of you as living anywhere. I'm here to see Mr. Seward."

"Now, Mr. Bedford—"

"I sent him a note this morning, Miss Windfield," he said sternly. "I had no idea he had a professional actress as a house guest."

"I am not an actress, sir," she corrected. "Professional or otherwise."

He wrinkled his brow. "But you were at Ford's Theatre this morning," he reminded.

"Not that it's anything to you, Mr. Bedford, but I happened to be there to talk Miss Keene into doing a benefit performance for the War Relief Charity of Boston. Which I represent, by the way."

"Do you really?" He grinned.

"Yes, I do," she replied stiffly. "Is that so funny?"

"Well, no, not exactly. I was just remembering what a friend said once. He warned me that Washington City was overrun with lady do-gooders from Massachusetts, and sure enough, there you are, as big and beautiful as life. Standing right in the way of where I want to go. It's almost like fate, isn't it, Miss Windfield?"

"It's not in the slightest like fate," she disagreed.

He couldn't resist sliding his left hand up the edge of

the door and touching her fingers. Her warm, satiny skin excited him. "I wish you were a little upset that I didn't come to see you," he said.

"Good night, Mr. Bedford." She pushed against the door.

But he held firm. "All right, ma'am," he said, changing his tone of voice. "I may as well tell you, I'm not playing games. I came here to see Mr. Seward, and damn it, I'm going to see him!"

They looked at each other tensely for a moment, neither of them yielding an inch. Then a woman's voice called out weakly from inside the house. "Becky? Who is it?"

"Now look what you've done," Rebecca complained to him. "Frances was going up to bed. Couldn't you just leave, Mr. Bedford? Please?"

"I'll leave, if you give me ten minutes with Mr. Seward," he proposed.

"No."

"Five minutes."

"No!" She shoved hard against the door.

"Becky?"

Rebecca pressed her lips together tightly, hesitated, then relaxed, letting the door open. "Very well, Mr. Bedford," she gave in. She took a few steps into the foyer and introduced him to Frances, who was standing at the foot of the stairs with a supporting hand on the rail. "Mr. Bedford is in town doing some sort of investigation," Rebecca revealed. "He wants to ask some questions."

"You're the gentleman in front of the theatre, aren't you?" Frances recognized him.

"Yes, I am," Stephen said. "I hope you didn't have any more trouble with that mare of yours."

"Oh, no." She smiled. "No trouble at all. Thanks to your friend. He's not . . . with you this evening?"

"No, Miss Seward, he isn't."

"Oh, I didn't mean to say that I was *looking* for him," she assured him.

"No, ma'am."

She touched her reddened cheek with her fingertips. "It's just that he was so kind, I wanted . . . to thank him," she faltered. "Again," she added quickly and clumsily.

Stephen glanced at Rebecca, who was watching him closely, and then back at Frances. "I wish more than you do that Paddy was with me, Miss Seward," he offered, "but he's attending to some business for me right now."

"I seem to remember he was wearing Confederate trousers this morning," she ventured.

"Yes, ma'am, he was," Stephen confessed. "Evidently he likes the cut. He won't take them off for anything."

She dropped her eyes to the floor, embarrassed. "I mean, was he once a Confederate soldier?" she asked.

"We both were," Bedford explained.

"I should think you would have told us that, Mr. Bedford," Becky said, offended.

"I thought it showed."

"Well, I suppose it does, now that you mention it. If all Southerners have your manners, it's no mystery why we won the war."

Her words cut into him. Digging his nails into his palms to stay calm, he said to her, "I wish to God it were that simple, ma'am. But I'm afraid it takes more than a clash of manners to kill 800,000 American men. It takes a little hate and ignorance, and misunderstanding, too."

The room was cold and silent for a while, as all three of

them stood as still as statues in a park. Finally, Stephen stepped closer to Fanny. "Miss Seward," he began, "I came to see your father. I must talk to him."

"I don't understand," she said, surprised. "Surely he doesn't have anything to do with your investigation."

"I can only tell you it's very urgent, Miss Seward."

"Well, even if it is, what you're asking is impossible. He isn't up to it. He's been bedridden since his carriage accident three days ago."

"But hasn't he mentioned the note I sent him? Surely he'll want to see me for a few minutes, anyway—"

"I don't think so, Mr. Bedford." She shook her head. "He's much too ill, really. The only time he even talks is when Becky is around."

He turned to Rebecca. "Then you take me up to see him," he ordered.

"I will not."

"It could mean his life, Miss Windfield," he stated.

"You're exactly right, sir. It could."

Stephen glanced up the stairs and made a decision. "Well, I hate to oppose a couple of lovely ladies," he said, "but I'm going up those stairs, no matter what you say."

"Sir!" a loud male voice called out to him. "You will do nothing of the kind. Don't you move another inch!"

Stephen turned to see a slight, stuffy-looking round-faced man with thin brown hair and curly muttonchop sideburns that looked pasted to his cheeks. He was standing in the doorway to the parlor, wearing a solemn expression and fidgeting nervously with the corner of his vest.

"I would appreciate it if you would leave peaceably, Mr. Bedford," he pronounced in a low, strained voice. "It would save me the trouble of having you thrown out."

"Frederick!" Frances rebuffed him, "what's the matter with you—"

"Go to your room, Frances," the Secretary's son said, pointing to the stairs. "Both of you. The visit is over; this uninvited 'gentleman' is leaving."

Even though Frederick Seward's words grated on him, Bedford tried to be polite. "Sir," he explained, "I realize I wasn't invited, but I did send your father a note."

"I know you did," he acknowledged scornfully. "I read it. Now let me assure you that no one in this house has any interest in what a former Confederate officer has to say on any subject. So if you will please go . . ."

"Frederick, there's no need to be rude," Fanny admonished. "He's not bothering you."

"He is bothering all of us, Frances."

Stephen stepped toward the other man. "Mr. Seward," he advised in a clear, calm voice, "whatever you think I'm doing, let me tell you, I'm not here as a Confederate officer. I'm here because I have reason to believe your father is in great danger, and I think I can help him."

"Help him, indeed." Seward smoothed his cravat against his collar. "Why in heaven's name would you want to help my father?"

"Because he's a decent human being, Mr. Seward," Stephen answered. "I may not agree with the man's politics, but that doesn't mean I can stand by and let him be assassinated."

"Assassinated!" Frances cried out. "Oh, Frederick—"

"Be still, Frances," her brother scolded. "Are you going to believe the word of a Southerner? Can't you tell the man's lying?"

"But what if he isn't lying?"

Frederick rubbed his shaven chin. "Hush girl," he said

stubbornly. "Go to bed. You and Rebecca both go upstairs and attend to your sewing, or gossiping, or whatever it is you do."

"Oh, Becky—" She grabbed Rebecca's arm. "Is it possible? Would they actually *kill* him?"

"Calm down, Fanny," Becky said, and squeezed her hand. "Nothing's happened yet. Your father is still safe in his bed upstairs."

"But what if they do try to murder him? They could do it while he's sleeping—"

"Mr. Bedford," Rebecca applied to the captain, "is your evidence strong enough to warrant all this?"

"You're asking *him?*" Frederick broke in angrily. "A Southerner?" He wheeled around and stormed away into the parlor. At a writing desk near the fireplace, he whisked off a stack of papers and returned to the foyer, waving them in the air. "These are reports we just received on the Southern prison camp at Andersonville, Georgia," he panted excitedly. "Would you like to hear about the place, Mr. Bedford?"

"I already know about it, Mr. Seward," Stephen admitted with shame.

"Well, did you know that the ground of this filthy prison is covered with human excrement, that prisoners are allowed to die of starvation and naked exposure, that your Captain Wirz freely admits he has killed thousands of sick and injured Union soldiers for the pure *fun* of it!"

"I'm aware of the Andersonville prison, sir," Stephen tried to cut him off. "I know it has been a disgrace."

But Seward was brimming with anger and revulsion. "This is your glorious Southern tradition, Mr. Bedford," he contended, "not those sprawling plantation homes and loyal slaves singing 'Old Black Joe' in the moonlight we always hear about. Twelve thousand defenseless men have been brutally and sadistically murdered in that hellhole, and not one single Southerner has lifted a finger to stop it. Not one!''

Bedford felt a knot form in his tight throat. "Maybe now we can," he offered. "Maybe we can finally get rid of this death cloud that's been hanging over all of us for four years. You're right about the Andersonville camp, Mr. Seward. It is deplorable; it violates every shred of human decency in my soul. But can you defend Sherman's bloody march to the sea any better? Thousands of homes blown up or burned, animals mutilated, women raped, households separated forever—a South already broken and down on its knees, slashed and butchered by a godless madman, hungry for headlines?''

"Sherman's march was an act of war, sir," Seward muttered weakly.

"And acts of war sicken me, Mr. Seward. Which is why, when I uncovered a plot to assassinate the Secretary of State, I thought I should do something about it."

"Just say your piece and be gone, man," Seward wavered uncomfortably.

"All right. My piece is that on the fourteenth of April, your father may be assassinated. I don't know any more than that, but it was enough to scare me. Now I'm done with it. I leave the rest up to you."

Seward rolled the reports and squeezed them in his fist. "Fine. Now you can leave, Mr. Bedford." He thumped them against his thigh.

"Yes," Stephen fumed. "Now I can leave."

"Mr. Bedford—" Frances called out as he started for the door.

He paused. "Will you tell your father what I just said, Miss Seward?" he asked her.

"My sister will tell him nothing," Frederick broke in.

"For the love of God, man—"

"He will hear about none of this, sir," he swore loudly. "None of it!"

Boiling with frustration, Stephen glared at Seward, then looked at the two women next to the stairs. Frances was hanging on to Rebecca, sobbing. But his eyes were drawn like a magnet to the blonde woman. For an instant he thought he saw a glint of warm sympathy in her eyes. But then, he decided, he was only imagining things.

"Captain," snarled Seward in a final shot as Stephen jerked open the door, "you can tell your Southern friends that this devil Wirz will be dealt with."

"I'll do that." Stephen crashed through the front door and out of the house. He came to a halt in front of the closed door, slipped on his hat, and listened to Frederick Seward's loud, shaky voice issuing another command inside. Frances, he concluded, would probably obey her brother to the letter. She would keep her silence, and William Seward would never be told of his own destiny.

Disgusted, he pushed a breath of air through his teeth and started for his carriage. Just yesterday he had believed peace had come at last. Today he was alone on a street in the Union capitol, and Paddy was missing, and he was tired and angry and about to explode with frustration. Time was drawing near, and he had accomplished nothing. . . .

As he marched toward the curb, he heard the door of the Seward house crack open and then slam closed behind him. Then a husky woman's voice cried out: "Mr. Bedford!"

Recognizing it as the voice of Rebecca Windfield, he hesitated, but then kept going.

"Mr. Bedford! Wait!"

He drew close to the carriage parked on the curb.

"Mr. Bedford! Stephen!" She hurried after him down the walk. When he turned around, she stopped abruptly and gathered her poise. "Are you hard of hearing or something?" she blurted.

"No." He stepped over to the carriage and picked up the tether weight, "I just think I've probably heard enough tonight."

"Well, I can't very well blame you for thinking that," she granted.

He looked at her. She stood erect and proud on the sidewalk; yet he could see, even in the dim moonlight, a softness in her expression that wasn't there before. It stirred his desire. He longed to reach out and grab her and pull her body next to his. "You almost sound civil," he commented as he flung the weight into the carriage.

"A lot you know about being civil," she returned. "Why didn't you tell me what you were doing?"

"You didn't ask."

"You let me think you were nosing around the city on some silly investigation or other, when all the time you were trying desperately to save Mr. Seward's life."

"Don't make me sound noble, Rebecca," he said, using her given name for the first time. "I'm not. You saw how I handled myself in there."

"Oh, don't mind Frederick." She smiled. "He's not as bad as all that. You just caught him at a bad time, that's all. The poor man has an awful lot to contend with. His mother is an invalid, his father is bedridden, Fanny is ill most of the time, and I'm hanging around to ruffle his feathers—''

''And just as he gets those damned Andersonville reports, I bring him this news about the Secretary.''

''Yes. Can you blame him for acting so . . . pompously?''

He raised his eyebrows. ''You know something, Rebecca, you're a very wise lady,'' he complimented her. ''I believe I'm going to have to be careful around you.''

''That would be a change.''

He winced. ''But Lord—what a tongue you have.''

''A woman's tongue is a woman's sword,'' she responded immediately. ''A weapon issued at birth.''

He smiled at her. ''Well, put up your weapons with the rest of us, ma'am,'' he said. ''The war is over.''

''Mr. Bedford—''

''What happened to 'Stephen'?''

''All right . . . Stephen—I just wanted you to know that as soon as I go back inside, I'm going to tell Mr. Seward that you were here. I will warn him about a possible assassination attempt.''

He ached to reach out and touch her. Instead, he tipped his hat politely. ''I thank you for that,'' he said, ''but be careful not to upset him too much when you tell him.''

''Oh, I won't,'' she promised. ''He likes me.''

''Yes,'' he replied, climbing aboard the carriage, ''that's what I'm talking about.'' Gathering up the reins, he clucked to the horse, and the carriage thrust ahead with a jerk. But then, twenty feet away, a thought suddenly leaping into his mind, he snapped back on the lines and stopped in the middle of the street. Acting on an impulse, he bounded out of the carriage and marched straight for Rebecca.

He caught up to her a few feet from the house. Without a word he clamped his hands on her shoulders and spun her around. Before she could blink an eye, he surrounded her in his arms and pulled her soft body to his chest.

"What are you doing!" she strained against him. "Stop it!"

Undaunted by her words, he tightened his hold on her, eased his face closer, and pressed his lips to hers. In the panting space of a few strong heartbeats, his whole body stiffened as he felt her heavy breasts mashing against him and her warm, moist lips separating under his—responding to the kiss, he thought. But then she wiggled out of his arms.

"You boor!" She whacked his cheek with the flat of her hand. Agitated and flustered, she backed away from him, gasping for breath. "Dear God, sir," she huffed, "what kind of manners do they teach in the South, anyway?"

"I'm sorry, Miss Windfield," Stephen apologized.

"You . . ." she groped for the right word.

" 'Boor' was appropriate," he said as he rubbed his stinging cheek.

"You . . . Reb!" she erupted, then gathered her skirts, wheeled around, and ran. In a rush of green taffeta and swirling blonde hair, she swept off the walk into the yellow light of the foyer and, with the rude slam of the oak door behind her, disappeared into the house.

# Chapter 8

Stephen was still puzzling over Rebecca Winfield and her blistering slap when he unlatched the door to his room at the National Hotel. He could hardly regret kissing the lady, but for the life of him, he couldn't understand her reaction to him. She was unlike any of the Southern ladies he had courted. She was feisty, aggressive, and direct—and the most exciting woman he had ever known.

The image of the beautiful Rebecca clasped in his arms, with the moonlight dancing in her flowing blonde hair, was lingering in his mind as he kicked open the door and stepped inside. Then a voice rang out at him from the darkness.

"All right, lad. Hold it right there!" a man bellowed. "Make another move and so help me, I'll run you through!"

"Paddy?" Stephen squinted his eyes. "Is that you?"

"Captain Bedford—"

Stephen quickly lit the gaslight and gazed around the room. To his surprise, he discovered the big Irishman hanging close to the facing of the closed window, with the pummel of a sword pressed against his chest. "Paddy?" He moved toward him. "What's going on? What's wrong?"

"Sorry, Captain." O'Connor relaxed. "I didn't know it was you. Here, you can have your sword back; I didn't hurt it any."

Stephen grabbed it and flung it on the bed. "I don't care about the damned sword," he said. "What are you doing, hiding here in the dark? This isn't like you."

O'Connor reached over and parted the curtains and peered through the window glass. "I wasn't hiding, Captain," he explained. "I was just standing here looking out the window." He added "Seeing who I could see."

"Well, who are you trying to see? Who's out there?"

"I don't know who it is." He turned away from the window. "Just somebody that's been following me."

"Well, let's go out and get him."

"No, wait." He held up his hands. "That wouldn't do any good, Captain. This ain't a fight, or anything like that. There are so many people in this, it wouldn't even matter if we did get him."

"So many people in what, Paddy?" he asked, trying to be patient. "What are you talking about?"

O'Connor stuffed his hands in his pockets and paced a few steps. After lumbering back and forth over the floor a couple of times, searching his mind, he finally stopped and described for Stephen the scene at Surratt's boarding house. His report was earnest, but confused. He hadn't heard much of what was said. He had forgotten some of what he had heard. And of the two men he had actually seen, he had recognized only one. But of this he was certain: there was to be a quadruple assassination on the fourteenth of April, and the man planning the murder was one of the most famous actors in America.

"John Wilkes Booth," Stephen repeated the actor's name when Paddy had finished. "I had a feeling he was involved in this."

Paddy's eyes grew round and large. "Captain, I've got to tell you, this Booth is a spooky one," he stated resolutely. "And these lads of his are ten times more coldblooded than he is. It was like a pit of snakes in that room. Just hearing them talk made my flesh crawl. But the thing that keeps bothering me is, I didn't know any of them."

"But we do know their leader," Stephen pointed out.

"Well, yes, sir, but what good does that do? Booth's not going to kill anybody. Look, maybe we ought to be going to the police, Captain."

"Do you think the police would listen to a couple of Southerners trying to save President Lincoln's life? Uh-uh. They'd never believe us. What about your countrymen, Paddy?" he suggested eagerly. "Wouldn't they give us a hand?"

The Irishman shrugged. "Aye, they would, Captain," he agreed, "but there ain't enough of them left to help. The government ran them off."

It was Stephen's turn to pace now. "Well, since we don't have enough time to round up the old company," he reasoned, "the only thing we can do is go to the War Department."

"That wouldn't do any good either, would it?" Paddy said.

"Maybe it will. If we claim we know all about the death

of one of their detectives, Donald Massey, then Stanton himself will have to see us.''

''Well, all right,'' Paddy conceded, ''but you might remember the man's a Yank, Captain. He might not believe you any more than the police.''

''No, but it's all we have time to do, Paddy,'' Stephen declared. ''The first thing in the morning, we'll go see him.''

''Yes, sir,'' he said, making another check at the window. ''I sure hope it works. Somebody has to stop this, Captain. We can't let a thing like this just . . . happen.''


A while later, after Stephen had told Paddy about his visit to the Seward house, the Confederate officer picked up the sword off the mattress and laid it against the wall. Leaning back against the headboard, he stared vaguely at the flickering gaslight on the wall above Paddy's bed. Before long a chill began to creep into his body, then he felt that same gnawing, freezing sensation that had gripped him earlier in the day, at Ford's Theatre. It was a shuddering apprehension of dread, a feeling that no matter what he or anyone else would do, some ghastly and horrible event was going to occur.

''Captain?'' Paddy turned toward Stephen and propped himself up on his elbow. ''I was just thinking about what you said. Are you sure this Miss Seward was the same lady we saw fighting her horse in front of the theatre this morning?''

''I'm sure, Paddy,'' he replied, relieved to hear the other man's voice. He had been silent for several minutes.

''Well, fancy that.'' He rolled over on his back.

''Frances Seward seems to be very sweet, Sergeant,'' he

offered. "But now, I won't say how smart she is, the way the lady kept asking about you all evening—"

"Aw, Captain—"

"Just watch your step with her, old friend," he warned. "I'm afraid she's already got her cap set for you."

"Aw, I doubt that, Captain." He dismissed the idea with a wave of the hand.

Stephen looked at him, surprised. "Don't tell me you don't mind, Paddy," he said. "You? The woman-hater?"

"I never hated any woman, Captain," he denied. "I just never seen one I liked particularly, that's all."

"But you do like this one?" he led him.

"Ah!" he grunted and rolled over on his side. "All I know is, a man's got more important things to think about than a young lass who can't even handle her mare, for the love of the saints."

"What about when this is over, Sergeant?" he said to his back. "What then?"

"Well now, I couldn't hardly be saying that, could I?" he mumbled. "We'll just have to see. Now, would you mind turning off the light there, Captain Bedford? We've got a fine lot of things to do tomorrow, and it's sleep we're needing now, not idle talk."

Stephen smiled, pleased by Paddy's interest in Frances Seward. He had always believed the big rough Irishman needed a bit of feminine softness and warmth in his life. But then, he had to admit, so did he.

He reached over Paddy's bed and shut off the flame.


Below the room, on Sixth Street, in almost exactly the spot Rebecca and Frances had parked their carriage early that morning, a large, pear-shaped man in a black overcoat stood propped against a tree, watching the window as the light went out. Lingering a while to make sure the occupants of the room were out for the night, he finally decided it was time to go home. He plucked a linen handkerchief out of his coat pocket, wiped the tops of his boots with the corner of it, and stuffed it into his vest. Then he began sauntering casually down the street.

He had a certain job to do, and it had to be done before Friday night. The man who had eavesdropped on the conspiracy meeting—the man who could identify him as the murderer of Donald Massey—would have to be eliminated immediately. And so would his sporty young friend, Captain Stephen Bedford.

The man crossed Sixth Street and paused on the curb on the other side. He turned around and stole a last look at the National Hotel window. This murder, he decided, like Booth's murders, would take extremely careful planning. It would have to be done very cleverly, under the cover of darkness. And it would have to be done from behind.

That, after all, was Mason Butler's way.

# Chapter 9

At 9:35 the next morning, April 13, 1865, Stephen was poised on the sharp edge of a straight wooden chair near Edwin Stanton's desk, nervously tracing the rim of his hat with his index finger while he waited for the Secretary to finish reading a certain document. Bedford was struggling to hold down his temper. He had just witnessed a severe, almost merciless interrogation of his friend Paddy O'Connor. Stanton had launched such a salvo of questions at Paddy that the Irishman was thrown into hopeless confusion. He had finally had to ask to leave the room, flustered and embarrassed. Stephen was now waiting for the former lawyer to examine his offering—Massey's coded message, the only tangible bit of evidence he had to show him.

After deliberation, Stanton carefully laid the note down

on his desk and swung around to face Stephen. "Well," he said, adjusting his spectacles, "I knew Massey was onto something. I only wish he had been able to report to me what it was."

Stephen felt a surge of relief at his words. "Then you do believe there's a plot to kill the President?" he exacted.

"Oh, yes," he nodded. "There is always a plot to kill the President. Five plots. Ten. Maybe twenty."

Stephen's face was crestfallen. He stirred uncomfortably in the hard chair. "But this one is for real," he pleaded. "You heard what Paddy said about the assassins."

"I heard a very emotional man describe a strange, invisible meeting in a boarding house somewhere in the bowels of Washington city at some undisclosed time last night. You think about that, son. How much of it sounds real to you?"

"However it sounds, what he says is true, Mr. Stanton," Stephen protested. "Paddy never lies."

"Oh, I'm sure he wasn't doing that," the Secretary replied in a concerned voice. He drummed his fingers on the arms of his chair. "All right," he said after a minute, "what if what he says is true? Can you tell me what this coded message has to do with that particular meeting? I'm sorry, but this dull old head of mine fails to see any connection between the two."

"I'm not sure what the connection is, Mr. Stanton." Stephen jumped up from his seat. "At least I can't explain it. But I know there is going to be an attempted assassination. I know it in the bottom of my soul."

Stanton leaned back in his chair. "Then prove it," he muttered.

"Sir?"

"I said, prove it. If you're so cock sure that a prominent

actor is plotting four bizarre political murders, then give me something besides a torn message to go on. Make me believe it, too.''

Stephen took a few steps toward the fireplace and stared obliviously at the mantle. Stanton's challenge set his brain to swarming with the events of the past thirty-six hours. He stretched through the confusion for some clear, factual associations to cast back at Stanton. But he couldn't reach them. After a time, he conceded. ''I suppose I really can't make you believe it,'' he sighed. ''Not with facts, anyway.''

''I didn't think so.''

He looked around at the Secretary. ''But it's not just what Paddy heard last night,'' he offered. ''I know it sounds strange, but I can feel it about to happen.''

Stanton shrugged. ''What do you expect me to do about that, I wonder? I don't even know who is supposed to be committing these murders of yours. Or where, or even if they're actually going to be committing them.''

''You could at least tell somebody about it.''

''For instance?''

''Well, Mr. Lincoln, for one. I should think the President deserves to know about any plot to kill him.''

''Well, naturally, I'll tell Mr. Lincoln,'' he said. ''I always do. And just like every other time, he will file it with the other plots in his desk.''

''This is ridiculous.'' Stephen threw up his hands. ''I don't know why I should be pleading to you. I hate Lincoln, and I'm the only one who gives a damn about saving his life.''

Stanton was silent for a while, then peeled off his glasses and wiped them against his vest. ''Why do you hate him, Captain Bedford?''

Bedford frowned. "How could I feel any other way about a man responsible for so much misery?" he huffed.

The Secretary shook his head condescendingly. "You may be a concerned and moral citizen, young man," he accused, "but your attitude is very stupid. Stupid and ignorant. I'll never understand why you Southerners can't see that at this particular moment in history, Abraham Lincoln is absolutely the best friend you have."

"I don't think so," Stephen scoffed.

"Oh, but he is," Stanton persisted. "Lincoln's a very simple man, Stephen. He doesn't drift from one political position to another like Horace Greeley, and he isn't overcome by his base emotions like General Sherman. And, I've got to admit, he never runs over his own people the way I do. The man knows what he believes in, and he accepts it. And you Southerners should get down on your knees and thank the Lord that the thing he believes in most is the people of this country. He wants a reunion in peace. That's his vision of Reconstruction."

"But it's not yours," Stephen prodded.

"No, it's not mine. I'm afraid Reconstruction is going to be every bit as horrible as the war itself, Stephen. But that is natural."

"Natural?"

"I believe this war was meant to be. It was already written in the pages of history before a single shot was fired at Fort Sumter. It was as inevitable as the passing of time. When our two ways of life clashed like two seasons of the year, the result just had to be a violent storm. And never doubt it, Reconstruction will be a whole winter of storms, each one bigger than the one before it. You will need a friend in high places to weather it. A friend like Lincoln."

Stephen shuddered. "Why just Lincoln?" he asked. "If a man like you can see the whole picture, why can't you see it his way?"

"Lincoln is not just a simple man. He's also naive. He believes what you and I can't. Like an adolescent boy, he assumes he can change not only events, but people, too. Which is why he's a great man, and men like us are not. A great man never loses that naiveté. If he didn't believe in his dreams, he could never put everything he has into making them come true."

Bedford ran his fingers through his black hair. This man made him very uneasy. His calculated manner and bluntness were disturbing.

Stanton picked up the torn playbill. "Here." He handed Stephen the message. "Thank you for letting me see this. And thank you for letting me hear Mr. O'Connor's story." When Stephen had taken it, he rose from his chair. "It's too bad about Massey," he regretted. "He was a good worker. I hired him when he came to me for a job last year, after Chancellorsville."

"You hired him as a spy," Bedford prodded.

"Oh, no, there are no spies in this department," he corrected. "Massey's job was purely clerical. He handled unsolicited mail, and he processed suspicious threats to members of the government. Nothing but paperwork. Lately, though, he had begun to investigate certain political threats on his own time. I encouraged him to follow up on them, since I always want my people to be interested in their work."

"But Massey was murdered, Mr. Stanton. Your clerk was shot in the back."

"I know he was." He glared. "We're looking into the matter."

"You're looking into it, but you won't accept the idea that he was murdered because he knew too much about this assassination plot."

"No, I won't. That idea is merely a supposition, not fact."

"Well, damn the facts!" Stephen barked. "And damn all this talk about the great Mr. Lincoln. If you really believed he was a great man, you would do something to save him!"

Stanton pursed his lips, pulled at his long gray-and-black beard, and regarded Bedford closely. "I'll tell you what I'll do," he proposed. "I don't have time to investigate this myself, but I will assign a department man to the case. Would that satisfy you?"

"If that's all the help I can get," he agreed reluctantly.

The Secretary shot Stephen a stern glance, then walked back to his desk, eased down in the chair, and flicked up a pen. "It's all I can offer." He began scratching out a note. "I'm turning you over to a man who was with Massey the night he died. Since the fourteenth is so close, I'm instructing him to drop all his other duties and concentrate entirely on your case."

Bedford watched his pen scribble across the page. "Mr. Stanton," he said, "I appreciate your help, but considering the nature of Booth's plan, don't you think you should be doing more than this? Don't you think the whole department should be involved?"

"I would like to oblige you with that, Captain Bedford," he replied as he continued writing, "but we have a hundred other jobs to do. You'll just have to be content with this." He finished the message with a sweeping signature, blotted the ink, and folded the paper neatly into quarters.

"Take this note to Mr. Dearing across the hall," he directed. "He'll take care of you."

Stephen couldn't help but feel a sting of resentment at being herded about this way, but he kept his composure long enough to thank Stanton for his time and aid. At least, he tried to console himself, he was finally accomplishing something.

With the message in hand, he marched straight out of the office and across the hall into another smaller room. Inside, near an unlit coal stove, he found a very skinny bald-headed man with sallow cheeks and a long, thin nose. He was curled up with an ink pen in front of a neat stack of papers and packages.

"Good morning." He looked up.

"I'm Stephen Bedford." He handed the skinny man Stanton's message. "I was told I should see this man."

"Yes, sir." He creaked to his feet.

Bedford took a moment to survey the close little office. It was half the size of Stanton's, but so neat and orderly it looked spacious. "There was supposed to be a Mr. O'Connor waiting here for me," he prompted the other man. "Have you seen him?"

"Oh, yes, sir, I saw him," the clerk answered, scanning the note. "He was here, but he lit off about five minutes ago. He said for me to tell you he'd meet you back at the hotel."

"That's strange."

"Well, he was kind of restless, you know?" He nodded his head knowingly. "If you ask me," He offered slyly, "he was in the process of letting a woman crawl up under his skin. I've seen it happen before."

"Could be," Stephen granted, thinking of Frances Seward.

"Will you come this way, please?" He returned the message to Stephen. Without saying another word, the thin man led him down the corridor, up a narrow set of stairs, along a wide landing, and finally to a closed door at the end of a long hall.

"Is this it?" Stephen asked, gazing around. This part of the building felt lonely and isolated; the clammy air seemed to stick to his skin like cold sweat. It made him shiver.

"This is it," he confirmed. "Just knock on the door and go in," he counseled.

"Thank you, Mr. Dearing."

"You're welcome, sir. Good luck," he said ominously, and strolled away down the hall.

Bedford rapped on the thick door a few times, cracked it open, and walked in. Before he could take two steps, a bright, eager-faced young man sprang away from his tiny desk and greeted him.

"Good morning, sir," he chirped in a shrill voice. "My name is Kirby. May I help you?"

"Yes, if you don't mind—" He gave him the message.

"Kirby!" the other man in the room growled from his desk. "How many times have I told you not to shout!" The second clerk was large and doughy, with a homely horseface and thin, white lips. As his eyes met Stephen's, they seemed to draw back into his head for a moment; then his big oblong face became rigid. "What is it?" he snarled. "What does he want?"

"Mr. Stanton sent him," Kirby explained.

"Sent him for what?" he grunted. "I've got enough to do around here as it is."

The young clerk advanced briskly. "The Secretary is giving you an investigative case," he announced excitedly.

"What?"

"It says so in this note."

"Let me see that." He snapped the message out of his hand. Squinting at the words, his face gradually began to soften. Soon his mouth was forming a smile. "Well, I'll be damned." He grinned. "Isn't this something?"

"It's exactly what you've been waiting for, sir." Kirby beamed. "A real case!"

"What are you going on about, boy? It's not your case, is it?"

"No, sir—"

"Well then, shut up and go on about your business," he croaked. "That is, if you have any business."

"Yes, sir," he replied in a lower voice. "I was just being happy for you, that's all," he muttered.

The older clerk watched Charles Kirby settle down in his chair, then scowled his big face at him. "What do you think you're doing, boy?" he challenged. "Did I ask you to go back to your desk?"

"I was just doing what you said, sir," he answered. "I was going about my business."

"Don't you mock me, Kirby. Get out of here. Go on, lose yourself. I've got some work to do with this man."

"I'm sorry, sir."

Stephen watched with irritation as the scolded young man evacuated the room in a flash. He was annoyed further by having to wait a full five minutes for the other clerk to strain his eyes over the Secretary's thickly written note.

Finally, the man peered up from the paper. "An assassination attempt, huh?" he murmured.

"That's right; four of them."

"Four of them," he echoed. "Really."

"Four men will be killed tomorrow night, if we don't do something to stop them."

"I see," he nodded. "Well, that would certainly be a terrible thing to happen, wouldn't it? I guess I'll have to look into it."

"I was hoping we could do more than look into it, sir." He approached the desk. "I was hoping that with the influence of the War Department, we could go out and recruit a number of people to work with us on this. With a proper work force, we could track down every lead we have."

"Could we really? Well that's very clever."

Stephen drew himself up at his scornful tone of voice. "Look," he said, "I don't want to try to tell you how to do your job—"

"Then don't," the man commanded. "I will try to tell you something, though. I'm good at my job, sir. I have as much talent and experience as any two other men in this department. Add to that the fact that I'm more dedicated than any of them, including Edwin Stanton, and I think you can assume I will be able to go about this case without any amateur advice from you or help from people dragged in off the street. Do you understand what I'm saying?"

"Yes, I understand," Bedford said through clenched teeth.

"Good. Then why don't we begin at the beginning? I want you to tell me about this alleged assassination. Facts, rumors, lies, everything. In other words, let me know what you know."

"That's fair enough," Stephen acknowledged. "Let's get to it."

"And I also want to know who else you've been confiding in. I don't want unauthorized people going around with confidential information.''

"Fine. I'll tell you everything. May I sit down?''

"Go ahead, sit, Mr. . .?''

"Bedford.''

The clerk rose to his feet and extended his hand. "I'm very pleased to meet you, Mr. Bedford,'' he said. "I'm sure we're going to work very well together.''

Shaking the clerk's hand, Stephen said, "And your name . . . ?''

"Oh, don't you know my name?'' He slipped his sweating hand out of Stephen's grip. "I'm terribly sorry. I naturally assumed since you walked straight into my office, you would know who I am.''

"I should have asked—''

"Well, it's Butler, sir,'' the clerk told him with satisfaction. "Mason T. Butler.''

# Chapter 10

After leaving the War Department building, Stephen began walking down Pennsylvania Avenue toward the great dome of the Capitol rising out of the trees in the distance. Oblivious to the crisscrossing of coaches, buggies, horses, and carriages in the corrugated, rain-rutted street around him, he thought about what he had just heard from Edwin Stanton and Mason Butler. He was furious with them. One had been too busy and the other interested in nothing but promoting himself. If the assassins were to be stopped tomorrow, he decided, then he and Paddy would have to do it themselves. Somehow.

As he straggled along the thoroughfare, he gradually became aware of the buzzing sound of excited human voices down the street. Drawing closer, he could make out the swelling cheers of a few men, followed by a blast of clangorous support, and then a distinct voice blaring out of the uproar, exclaiming, "Go on, rebs! Go at it! Fight each other, you copperheads!"

Rushing past him was a clutch of a dozen or so men who joined the horde of people converging on an open carriage in the middle of Pennsylvania Avenue. Uninterested at first, Stephen kept walking. But then he stopped dead still as he caught a glimpse of the back of one of the two women sitting in the carriage. The blonde hair hanging over her shoulders glimmered in the morning light like wheaten straw. That hair, he concluded without hesitation, could belong to only one woman. He quickly joined the others.

"All right, men, I said break it up!" He heard a thick, halting voice bark out a command in the middle of the swarm. "That's enough!"

"Hey, leave them alone," a second voice objected. "Let them fight if they want to."

"No!" a third objected vehemently. "That's John Wilkes Booth there."

"Who?"

"Booth, man—the actor."

"You people stand back," the first voice bore down. "On your way; this here's none of your business."

Inching closer to the eye of the storm, Stephen could see Rebecca Windfield in a blue dress and black hat and coat, clinging nervously to the side rails of a carriage being rocked back and forth by its excited horse. Hanging on beside her was Frances Seward, her face flushed and shining with the color of ripe cherries.

"Excuse me." Stephen pushed through the crowd. "May I get by, please?" Sliding his way through the cluster of bodies toward Rebecca, he was startled to hear Paddy O'Connor's voice suddenly boom out above the rest. "Take your hands off me, lad," he was growling. "I mean it!"

"I'm sorry, but you're coming with me, sir," said the policeman, pinning his arms behind him. "You started this—"

Stephen finally broke through the crowd into the open arena around the carriage. There, next to the front wheels of the chassis, was Paddy O'Connor, restrained by the thick, powerful arms of the policeman, scowling at a small man in an expensive black suit. John Wilkes Booth, for his part, was poised calmly in front of the carriage horse, eyeing O'Connor closely, adjusting his cravat, saying nothing.

The policeman's eye caught Stephen. "Watch it, sir," he cautioned. "You'd better stand back." He was a pan-faced, mountainous man, as bulky as Paddy, but still having to struggle to hold the Irishman down.

"It's all right, Officer," Stephen put forth boldly. "I know this man." He stepped up to O'Connor. "Paddy, what are you doing here?" he asked him. "I thought you were at the hotel."

"Sorry, Captain," he evaded, but relaxed a little. "I never made it."

"These two gents was fighting," the officer explained to Bedford. "And this Irishman here started it. So I've got to take him to jail."

"I told you, I ain't going to jail," Paddy quickly retorted. "I'm not leaving those ladies in the hands of that villain."

"Sir." Rebecca Windfield leaned toward Paddy from the carriage. "If you don't mind my saying so, Miss Seward and I are not in anyone's hands. And anyway, Mr. Booth is hardly a villain."

"I know what I'm doing, ma'am," Paddy mumbled.

"Well, knowing what you're doing isn't the issue—"

"Mr. O'Connor," Frances interrupted. "Becky is right. We're not in any danger. We appreciate your intentions, but we are quite all right. Really."

Paddy glanced at her, then dropped his eyes to the ground.

Stephen shifted his gaze from Booth, a dark and romantic figure with black, brooding eyes and a sad expression in his face, to the plain, blunt policeman. "Look, Officer—" he started.

"The name's Hainey, sir."

"Officer Hainey," he entreated, "if you will let me take charge of Sergeant O'Connor, then maybe we can forget this whole affair. I can promise you, there won't be any more trouble."

"Captain, you don't have to promise him anything on my account—"

"Let the officer respond, Sergeant," Stephen said firmly.

"Yes, sir."

The policeman finally let go of Paddy's arms and pushed his blue hat back on his head. "Well now, I don't see how I can do that, sir," he answered. "We can't very well allow fighting in the streets, can we? Especially when there are ladies involved."

"Yes, but there's no real damage done," Stephen argued. "You can see that no one's been injured."

The policeman rubbed his chin. "Well, that's true enough," he allowed. "Nobody seems to be hurting any. I don't see why I couldn't do that—"

"Just a minute, officer." Booth held up a hand. The thicket of curious people, now nearly a hundred strong, instantly fell silent. The actor made a display of buttoning his coat and tipping his hat at Bedford, before he spoke to the policeman. "I appreciate this gentleman's concern for his friend," he began. "However, since I was the one attacked, and not him, I think I should be allowed a word or two on the subject."

"Go ahead, Mr. Booth," the officer replied.

The actor nodded. "Now," he began, playing to the people around him, "naturally, I've been attacked by drama critics before, but never in the middle of Pennsylvania Avenue. . . ." The people closing in around him instantly erupted into laughter. "My first thought," he went on, "when I saw this man dashing out at me with fire in his eyes was, 'My God, he must have seen me in *Titus Andronicus*.'"

As he joked, the crowd became an audience. They stood paralyzed and attracted. Even Stephen could feel it. Booth's mere presence was exciting. His handsome looks and his clear, melodic voice set him apart and aloof from everyone else. And yet, those penetrating eyes of his seemed to reach out to whomever they fell upon, begging directly to that man or woman's personal undivided attention.

"Are you saying you want this man locked up, Mr. Booth?" the policeman finally cut through the rhetoric.

The actor played the scene as a Roman emperor being asked by a gladiator whether to spare a defeated Christian. He waited for his followers to offer a response.

They obliged. "Arrest him!" one screamed.

"Yeah—put him away!" another demanded.

Others noisily and insistently called out their own desires, then hushed instantly as Booth opened his mouth. "Officer," he decided, "I think the 'ayes' have it, don't you? You may as well do your duty."

"Yaay!" the people cheered. "Lock him up!"

Stephen stood silent for a few minutes, watching the talented actor work. How, he wondered, could a man conduct himself with such poise and grace at the same time he was hatching a depraved plot to murder four innocent human beings? He had a powerful driving compulsion to cry out to these adoring admirers around him that this beloved Hamlet of theirs was nothing more than a cutthroat assassin. But he kept still because he knew they would never believe him. After all, he didn't have a shred of proof.

"Mr. Booth," he addressed the actor when the noise had settled, "surely a gentleman like you wouldn't want to take advantage of a situation—"

"You have that backwards, sir," he interrupted. "Mr. O'Connor is the only situation here. And he took advantage of me."

"But there's no need to send him to jail," he contended.

"I'm sorry," he apologized. "There is nothing I can do about it."

Stephen knew now he would have to press. He couldn't let the police take Paddy away. Without him, he would have no chance at all of stopping Booth. "He had good reason to attack you, sir," he claimed to Booth.

The actor raised his eyebrows with curiosity. "What are you trying to say?" he asked.

The frosty, hostile stare of the crowd sent a chill down Stephen's spine, but he went on. "I'm trying to say that Paddy lost his head for a moment—just as any other jealous man would have."

The crowd began mumbling to each other at his words. The policeman frowned. "I didn't follow that," he puzzled. "Jealous of who?"

Stephen took a deep breath, then boldly flung out his assertion. "Of Miss Seward," he declared.

"*This* Miss Seward?" Hainey gasped. "The Secretary of State's daughter?"

"That's right."

"Well, I'll be," the officer marveled at the idea.

But Booth dismissed the notion with a shake of his head. "Ridiculous," he stated.

"Is it?" Stephen challenged. "Then why don't we ask the lady herself?"

"Because, sir," Booth replied indignantly, "I wouldn't embarrass the lady by asking her such a thing. No gentleman would," he added.

"Well, I don't happen to be no gentleman myself," the policeman broke in. "So maybe I'll ask her. Miss Seward . . ." he acknowledged her by cocking back his hat, "looks to me like you could settle this for us, once and for all. Do you know this Irish fellow here?"

Frances shifted her weight in the carriage seat. "Yes," she admitted, "I know him."

"Does that mean you're connected to him in some way?"

"Mr. Hainey, please—" She bowed her head and blushed.

"You know what I mean, ma'am," he said.

She glanced over at Paddy, then dropped her eyes to her feet. "I don't want you to . . . do it," she finally said in a low voice.

"Ma'am?" the policeman strained to hear.

"Would you please let him go, Mr. Hainey?" she spoke up. "I don't want him to go to jail."

The policeman scratched the wrinkles in his forehead with a thick index finger. "What about you, Mr. Booth?"

he asked. "You're the victim; you've got the last word on the subject."

Booth shrugged. "If she wants you to release him, then release him." He stepped toward the carriage. "I'm willing to forget the whole matter."

"So be it, then," Hainey pronounced. "You're free to go," he said to Paddy.

Booth climbed into the carriage, tugged down his buttoned coat, and took the reins from Rebecca. "Now, I'll say good morning to you all," he offered, and cracked the lines sharply against the horse's rump. The buggy jerked, lunged, and rolled away up the street.

The crowd on Pennysylvania Avenue rapidly disintegrated. Within seconds Stephen and Paddy were standing alone in the middle of the street. "Well, that was a close shave," Stephen sighed. "Reminds me of that night at Porter's Inn in Richmond—"

The Irishman looked straight at Bedford, with sad, round eyes. "I don't see why you had to shame the lass in public like that, Captain," he complained in a sullen voice.

Stephen frowned. "I had to do something to keep you out of jail," he explained. "And I couldn't very well tell them why you were so concerned about Booth. They would've clapped the irons on both of us."

"Well, I wish you hadn't done it that way, Captain Bedford," he said. "Frances Seward is just too fine a lady to shame in public."

"She'll recover," he said, a little too harshly.

"Yes, sir. Well, I guess I'll be seeing you, Captain." O'Connor turned away.

"Wait—where are you going?"

"I'm just going, Captain."

"Paddy!" He grabbed his thick arm and held him back.

"You're not running out on me, are you? Not after all we've been through. I need you."

O'Connor hesitated, then said, "I ain't running out on you. You're a good and proper lad, Captain, and I love you like a brother. I always will. But you just shouldn't have shamed Miss Seward like that."

Stephen started to defend himself, then decided it would be better to let the man go. He released his arm and watched him plod sadly down the street toward the hotel. Just as he veered to the left and vanished inside a clump of cherry trees, Stephen caught sight of Booth's carriage pulling to a halt on the edge of the street. Rebecca Windfield descended to the curb, glanced up at Booth, then swung around toward Bedford.

On the corner of Pennsylvania Avenue and Fifteenth Street, N.W., he waited anxiously for her to come to him. He felt his chest grow tight and his pulse quicken as she drew nearer. The closer she got to him, the faster and hotter his blood pumped through his veins. By the time she reached him, his face was as warm and flushed as Paddy's.

She paused three feet away. "I just wanted to tell you that I told Mr. Seward about the coded message you found," she said coolly. "But the man was so ill, I'm not sure it registered with him."

He tried to interpret her stiff manner. "I appreciate that, Rebecca," he responded formally. Then added: "But I'm not sure I know what it means."

"It means, Mr. Bedford," she said sternly, "that I have done what I promised you I would do. Now, I'm done with you—"

"Oh no, you're not." He thrust himself in front of her. "I'm not letting you get away that easily."

She bumped against him. "What is the matter with

you?'' She backed away quickly. "You ignore me in public and treat me like a harlot in private. Is this more of your Southern charm?''

"No. I just don't happen to approve of the people you go out in public with,'' he explained.

"You don't approve!'' she gasped. "Stephen, I declare, you are so . . . exasperating!''

"You told me yesterday that you and Booth were not friends,'' he reminded her. "And yet you're with him again today—''

"Will you please let me pass—''

"Becky, I have to know about Booth!'' He stood his ground. "Now. It's important.''

She glared at him, but made no attempt to move. "All right, Stephen,'' she bargained, "I will tell you about Mr. Booth. If you will tell me something first.''

"Anything you want to know.''

"Tell me why you would kiss me last night and totally ignore me this morning. And why you would stand in the middle of a . . . rabble and embarrass me, and Mr. Booth, and, of all people in the world, poor Fanny.''

"I did what I did to keep Paddy out of jail, Rebecca,'' he evaded.

"Well, I hope there's more to it than that.''

"There isn't,'' he lied.

She pressed her lips together. "I think I understand,'' she said, tears forming in her eyes.

"No, you don't,'' he denied.

"Please, Stephen—''

"You *don't* understand, Becký, damn it!'' he insisted. "If I just hadn't seen you with him again today, right after I told you about the note—''

A look of recognition flashed across her face. "Dear

God,'' she said softly. "You think John Wilkes Booth is part of this assassination scheme, don't you?''

"Becky—''

"And you also think that I'm—what, Stephen? The man's lover or something?''

"No, Becky,'' he averred. "But I do know I don't like the idea of your being with him.''

Her eyes glistened with tears. "You don't really believe he's involved in this, do you?'' she led him. "The idea is so preposterous!''

"Why is it so preposterous?'' he pressed. "Because he's handsome? Because he's a hero on the stage?''

"It just . . . is,'' she fumbled. "John Wilkes Booth is not only a great actor, Stephen, he's sensitive and intelligent—he just isn't capable of doing anything like that.''

"You're wrong,'' he stated bluntly. "He's not only capable of it; he will do it. Unless somebody stops him.''

She stood with her eyes locked on his. "Can you prove it?'' she asked him.

"That's what Edwin Stanton wanted to know,'' he groaned.

"Well, can you?''

"No, Rebecca,'' he answered wearily, "I can't prove it.''

"You just want me to accept this ghastly idea on faith. Is that it?''

He searched her eyes for a glint of understanding or encouragement, but he couldn't find any of either. But that didn't stop him. "What I want is for you to come with me to see Mr. Lincoln,'' he proposed.

Her eyes widened with surprise. "Why? To tell him that

John Wilkes Booth is plotting his murder? No, thank you."

"Becky, if nobody else is going to do anything about saving Mr. Lincoln, I have to."

She considered his words for a moment, then shook her head definitively. "No," she contended. "You wouldn't even get in to see him. The President doesn't have time to talk to people like us."

"Then he'll just have to make time. I'll break into his bedroom if I have to. One way or another, he's going to be told about this."

"Well, you can break in without me, sir," she declared. "I'm not going to bother a great man like Abraham Lincoln with a . . . fairy tale about John Wilkes Booth."

"Now look who's being exasperating," he accused. "You're so sure you understand the way of the world, you're willing to let it blow up under your nose rather than admitting you may be wrong."

"And you're not that way?" she charged.

"I'm trying not to be, but you make it very hard."

She looked at him angrily. "I hate Southern manners!" she snapped, and gathered up her skirts to go.

"Becky—"

"Mr. Booth is waiting for me," she announced. "I've got to go."

"Becky, come with me," he pleaded.

She hesitated a second, then began walking. "Good luck with the President," she said, leaving him alone on the edge of busy Pennsylvania Avenue.

# Chapter 11

With the anguishing image of the beautiful Rebecc
Windfield seated next to John Wilkes Booth in his carriag
flashing on and off in his mind, Stephen impatiently poke
his way through a temperance congregation bustling aroun
the entrance to the White House. He ignored both th
impassioned demands for him to stop his evil drinking an
the fervid requests of the angry ladies for him to join ther
in a chorus of "Come Home, Father." He squeezed throug
the tumult and charged up the white steps of the executiv
mansion.

It seemed to take forever to locate a person of authorit
in the herds of sombre-looking men in dark busines
suits huddling together inside the house. But finally h
discovered a homely clerk hidden behind a mammot

mahogany desk in the chamber outside the Cabinet Room.

"My name is Stephen Bedford," he announced hurriedly. "I need to see the President."

The pock-faced little clerk chuckled. "I reckon everybody needs to see him today." He gestured toward the fifty or so men standing about in long coats and top hats, chattering, arguing, and laughing at jokes as they waited. "You might as well take your place."

"How long will it be?" he inquired.

"I couldn't tell you that, Mr. Bedford," he answered. "But I will put your name on my list here."

"Thank you."

"You can wait in here, or you can come back later," he offered. "Makes no difference to me or the President."

"I'll wait," Stephen decided, taking out his watch. It was 10:35. "It won't be any later than noon, will it?" he asked hopefully.

"Probably not," the clerk agreed.


At 4:35 p.m. Stephen snapped the cover of his watch shut and crammed it down into his vest pocket. He had just spent the hardest, most anxious six hours of his life. He wasn't sure how much longer he could remain in this nest of vultures. Everyone wanted notice of some kind or other. He had seen government men, soldiers, temperance ladies, and reporters lump together and wait to be recognized. Even famous people drifted through. He had seen Matthew Brady arrive in the hall to announce the opening of his new exhibit of war photographs, highlighted by "a panorama of the taking of Richmond." The waiting had become unbearable; he would have to do something soon, or explode.

"General Grant!" one of the men called out to the darkhaired gentleman emerging with a covey of military aides from the Cabinet Room. At the sound of the name the ranks tightened around him. "General Grant—" the man nudged closer. "What's this we're hearing about Robert E. Lee? Is it true the man's going to go unpunished—after all he's done?"

"I hadn't heard that," Grant evaded.

"Yes, but is it true?"

"It's in the terms of the Appomattox parole, yes," he confirmed.

"But Lee was the North's greatest enemy!" the other man protested. "You don't really plan to let him go scot-free, do you?"

"General Lee was a soldier, sir," Grant replied stiffly. "And in fighting the Union Army, he was performing a soldier's job. I see no need to punish him for that."

"What does the President say about it? Does he agree with you?"

"I haven't discussed it with the President."

"General Grant—" A slender man in spectacles forced his way through. "My name is Davis, *Evening Star*," he grunted. "I understand that you and Mrs. Grant will be attending the President and Mrs. Lincoln tomorrow night. Is that correct?"

Grant started walking. "News travels fast in this town," he commented. "I've only been here a few hours and you people know everything."

"General, there is a rumor circulating that Mrs. Grant is—shall we say, disgruntled with Mrs. Lincoln."

"Well, I can assure you, there's nothing to that rumor."

He waved his hand from side to side. "It so happens, the ladies are the best of friends."

"Then you will be going with the President tomorrow night?"

"Yes, we will. We'll all be going to Ford's Theatre to see the play."

The Lieutenant General's words slit into Stephen's brain like sharp daggers. For the first time he could see how carefully Booth had planned his quadruple murder. It made his breath flutter. This general, a man who had guided thousands of men through a long and complex war, suddenly turned into nothing more than a puppet dangling by a cord—a marionette being placed at a certain time and place by his creator and destroyer, John Wilkes Booth. Both of them were headed directly for the trap: Grant and the man behind the closed doors . . . .

In a heartbeat Stephen Bedford dived into the crowd and smashed through to the great double doors of the Cabinet Room. With the hysterical shouts of the terrified clerk ringing behind him, he burst open the doors.

"Mr. Bedford!" the clerk snatched his collar.

But Stephen rattled it loose and rushed into the room. The two men poised in front of the huge map on the south wall immediately spun around toward him.

"What on earth—" Lincoln started.

"I'm sorry, Mr. President," the clerk quickly apologized. "I couldn't stop him."

"I had to speak to you, Mr. President," Bedford professed. "I'm not asking for much. Just give me six minutes. One minute for every hour I've stood outside waiting."

After taking time to compose himself, Lincoln scrunched his face and rubbed his bearded chin. "If you've been out

there for six hours," he said, "I can see why you're a
little uneasy. I've only been here two myself, and I already
have an aching back."

Stephen faced the clerk. "I waited all that time and he
wasn't even here!" he snapped.

"I didn't tell you where he was, Mr. Bedford," the
clerk said. "You just assumed it."

"It's all right, Thomas" Lincoln told him. "Go on back
to your duties. I'll give the man his six minutes." The
President turned to the shorter man. "Mr. Chase," he
said, "would you mind leaving us alone?"

The Chief Justice nodded agreeably and laid the map
pointer down on the conference table. After giving Bedford a close look, he excused himself and left the room.

"Now, sir," said Lincoln, settling his lanky frame down
into a chair, "what can I do for you?"

Stephen strode forth eagerly, sucked in a deep breath,
and proceeded to lay out for him the whole story, from
Massey's note in Arlington to his run-in with Booth on
Pennsylvania Avenue. To Bedford's great relief, the President received the threat of an assassination very seriously.
He held his long body erect, listened to the words
patiently, asked questions, and absorbed every detail Stephen could muster. When Bedford had finally finished, he
sat for a long time slumped forward in his chair, clenching
his teeth, rubbing his forehead, reflecting on what he had
heard.

At last he spoke. His voice was low and deliberately
modulated, but as crisp as autumn air. "It's strange that
John Wilkes Booth should be after my blood," he observed absently. "I mean, I would never have considered
him an enemy. Actually, ever since I saw him in *The*

*Marble Heart* at Ford's Theatre a couple of years ago, I've admired him. I even thought of inviting him for supper.''

For a time Stephen waited reverently while Lincoln stared blankly at the wall and scraped his wide, thin palm back and forth along the edge of the conference table. Then he broke the uncomfortable silence. "Mr. President?" he said. "You know, there isn't much time left. What are you going to do about this?''

Lincoln looked up at him. "What would you suggest I do, Mr. Bedford?'' he asked. "Arrest John Wilkes Booth?''

"Well, yes, sir, for a start—''

"And what would I charge him with?''

"I don't know, sir—anything. In a situation like this, what difference would it make what you charge him with?''

"Maybe none," he acknowledged. "But then, I wonder, what difference would it make if we did collar him and chuck him into jail? You said yourself John Wilkes Booth isn't going to kill anyone. Wouldn't his plan still be carried out?''

"Not if you forced him to talk," Stephen ventured. "Made him suffer a bit—''

"You have a lot to learn about radicals, Mr. Bedford." He smiled weakly. "They only talk when you don't want to hear them. And as for suffering—all that trouble does nothing but convince them their ideas are worth something after all.''

"But you can't sit back and let it happen!" Stephen kicked the table leg with his boot. "You can't let this cutthroat take your life!" He turned to Lincoln. "At least cancel your plans. Don't go to Ford's Theatre tomorrow night.''

"Staying at home tomorrow night would do no good," he replied in a calm, measured voice. "This is no different from a court trial. If I am to be murdered, merely changing locations isn't going to alter the outcome any."

"But it could give us time to find out who these assassins are."

Lincoln's face grimaced as he massaged his deep-set eyes with his thumb and forefinger. Then he pushed himself out of his chair. "You know, Mr. Bedford," he revealed as he lumbered toward the window, "I've had a feeling about this for a long time. In fact, I've even dreamed about it," he added, wiping the moisture off a pane of glass. "I'm not sure how it will happen, but I know for certain it will. There is nothing on this earth you or I or anyone else can do about it. In the course of things, apparently, some events must occur. And if this is one of those events, so be it."

Stephen wondered at the profound sympathy he was feeling for a man he had hated for so long. Where did that feeling come from? In this room Abraham Lincoln seemed as vulnerable and as perishable as any other frail human being. And yet, somehow, there was more to this man than to other men. Thriving somewhere in that homely human structure of his was more resolve and more wisdom and sense of purpose than he had thought possible in any one man. To his astonishment, Stephen Bedford believed he was in the presence not of a Yankee leader, or a Union politician, but of a great man.

"Mr. President," he offered shakily, "this country needs you now more than ever." He paused at the odd sound of his own words, then went on: "The South is not only down and beaten; it has been ripped apart. We're scared of this Reconstruction that's coming, Mr. Lincoln. We need you."

Lincoln turned around. "I'm touched to hear those words

coming from a Southerner, Mr. Bedford." He smiled warmly. "They mean more to me than you could ever know. But I'm afraid I'm not the one to help this nation bind its wounds. That she must do by herself. I've done my part; now the bickering factions that inevitably crawl up out of the aftermath of war must take their own turn at the wheel."

"You could control those factions, just as you've always controlled men like Speed and Chase and Greeley—"

"No," he corrected. "I've never controlled the ideals of men, Mr. Bedford. I can't do that. I can only remind them of the ideals they are losing sight of. During these long four years I have served a very clear and definite purpose: to keep the idea of a democratic Union in front of the people of this nation. Amidst all the agony I have tried to remind them that the preservation of the Union was the most vital of all their endeavors. Not because I wanted that, but because they did."

"Mr. President—"

Lincoln held up a hand, hesitated, and went on. "Among all the great nations on this earth, Mr. Bedford," he said, "Americans are the people who love freedom the most. To others, it's an idea; to us, it's our heritage. We are born to it and, by the Lord above, we hold it dear. If we, the very symbols of liberty, had allowed our country to destroy itself from within, then not merely a nation would have been lost in this conflict. The whole essence and spirit of democracy would have crumbled in the blood and dust of our civil war. And civilized man would have been flung back into his own history a thousand years."

"But you won that war, Mr. President," Stephen pointed out. "You're a hero."

His face remained warm and friendly, but rigid. "You're

very kind to say that, Mr. Bedford," he thanked him. "But people only need heroes when they have lost sight of their values for a time. When they finally realize what is important again, they no longer want a symbol to remind them what to believe in. It's then their heroes die."

Stephen felt a lump form in his throat. "But the people of this country still have faith in you," he argued. "They re-elected you."

"Oh, yes, they did," he conceded. "But only because our army was beginning to turn the tide and they were afraid of swapping their horse in the middle of the stream. The war is over now, though. If the election were held today, they'd be strapping the harness on another horse before the old one had a chance to leave the stall. And rightly so."

After a pause, Bedford slid around the table, toward Lincoln. "I understand what you're saying, Mr. President," he said, "but I can't let this happen. I just . . . can't."

"Then try as hard as you can not to let it happen, Mr. Bedford," he said simply. "Please. Do everything in your power to stop it. But for my part, I can do nothing. I must carry on as usual. I'm not going to cancel my plans, and I'm not going to walk around with armed guards knocking at my elbows."

"But, sir—"

"Do your job as you see it, Mr. Bedford," he said. "After that, we will have to stand aside and let the Almighty God do His."

Stephen started to speak again, but changed his mind. Lincoln was already lost in thought, staring vaguely out the window, contemplating, Bedford guessed, his own fate and the fate of the country he loved.

\* \* \*

An hour later, when he crossed the threshold of his quarters at the National Hotel, Stephen first noticed his friend Paddy O'Connor, perched on the edge of the bed, cleaning his Sharps breechloader. Then he saw the condition of the room. The place was a shambles; tables were overturned, a water pitcher lay shattered to pieces on the floor, the dresser mirror stood cracked like a spider web, and drawers had been yanked out and gutted.

He stepped into the room, shaking his head. "Looks like a train hit us," he noted. "What happened?"

"Robbers, I guess." The other man wiped the rifle barrel with an oily cloth. "They wrecked the room well enough, but the only thing they took was your sword."

Stephen set up a lamp table and scanned the room. "Who would go to this much trouble for a sword?" He frowned. "Not even a good sword. It doesn't make sense."

"Who knows, Captain?" Paddy said. "I've noticed the folks in Washington City ain't very friendly these days. Maybe this is their way of telling us to go back home."

"Uh-uh." He smacked a drawer shut. "There's more to it than that."

"Well, whatever there is to it," Paddy said as he slipped off the creaky bed, "I can't be hanging around here to find out. I've got some things to do."

"With a Sharps rifle?" he dug at him.

Paddy stopped and looked at him with hard, accusing eyes. "I've got to do something, Captain," he stated. "I can't be sitting around anymore."

"What do you think you can do with a rifle? The war's over, Paddy. You can't go around shooting people anymore—even people like John Wilkes Booth."

"I won't be shooting anybody, sir," he replied. "Not unless I have to." He hesitated, then went on: "Captain, I can't take any more of this waiting. I spent the whole day trying to find the lad with the glassy shoes, and I couldn't. Now, I've got to act.''

"What does that mean?"

O'Connor's face turned a bright shade of red. "It means I've got to protect somebody," he evaded.

"By somebody you mean Fanny Seward," Stephen surmised.

"That's right, Captain: Fanny Seward," he rebuked. "The lady you shamed in front of all those people on Pennsylvania Avenue this morning."

"Paddy, look—" Stephen stepped closer to the big Irishman. "Believe me, I know how you feel. I may feel the same way about Rebecca Windfield, I don't know. But you can't go park yourself in front of Frances Seward's door for the next twenty-four hours."

"Yes, I can," he said defiantly. "And I'm going to."

"Paddy—"

"I've got to be going, Captain."

"Damn it, man, will you listen to me!"

O'Connor clenched his teeth and stared at Bedford with steady, unblinking eyes. "Go ahead, Captain," he told him. "I'm listening."

Stephen swallowed. "Paddy, I talked to Mr. Lincoln this afternoon," he revealed. "I told him everything."

"Glad to hear it. What's he going to do about it?"

"He's not going to do anything. There's nothing he can do. That's why I need you. We have to make sure that these four men know about Booth's plot."

"Why do we have to do it? The President will tell the others, won't he?"

"No, he won't. Men like Lincoln and Johnson can't let themselves be worried about assassination threats. If they did, they wouldn't have time to accomplish anything. They can't be walking around the countryside surrounded by guns and swords or scurrying around from one government office to another every time they hear about a new plot. But we *know* this is for real. We must tell the others.''

O'Connor reflected a minute. ''Captain,'' he said, changing his tone, ''you know, I might have gotten this assassination business all mixed up when I told you about that meeting. I had been drinking, and I was squirreled away in a corner, so I couldn't hear much of what they were saying.''

''You heard enough.''

''What I mean is, isn't it possible these ain't the assassins in Massey's note? They could've been just talking. Remember, all that was on the message was part of the word *Seward*. Maybe we should stake ourselves out at the Seward house and wait for them.''

''Paddy, you don't believe that prattle. You know very well it's all the same plot.''

''I don't know, Captain.''

''You do know. All you want to do is save Fanny Seward!''

''Well, all right, suppose I do,'' he retorted with shame. ''Is that so wrong?''

''Yes, it is wrong—if that's all you do. Paddy, we've got to save these four men. Above all, we cannot let Abraham Lincoln die. I think I've finally been waking up these past two days. I believe I understand for the first time what that man has done for this country—the North and the South. And he must be allowed to guide us a while longer. If he's killed, Reconstruction is going to be nothing but a living hell for all of us.''

Paddy stood huge and unyielding, apparently unmoved. "Are you sure all this hobnobbing with the likes of Abraham Lincoln and Edwin Stanton ain't puffing you up, Captain—making you shove aside the little folks, like Fanny Seward?"

Stephen felt a rage of anger building, but he reminded himself why Paddy was acting so irrationally. He squeezed his nails into his palms to stay calm. "Your brain is addled, O'Connor," he charged. "That woman's got you turned inside out."

"Just answer me, Captain," he pressed.

"You're taking this shame to Fanny Seward too seriously, Sergeant. Women are a great deal tougher than they look. A little embarrassment on the street may look like the end of the world to a modest woman like Fanny Seward, but it's only one of a thousand little embarrassments—she'll live through it."

"You ain't answering me, Captain," Paddy persisted stubbornly.

"All right, Sergeant, I'll answer you," he yielded angrily. "If you're too damned smitten to see it yourself, I'll tell you. You can't let the love of a woman keep you from doing your duty to the rest of us. There's nothing wrong with wanting to protect Fanny Seward, Paddy, but for God's sake, remember who these men are. They are men who matter. They must not be murdered. Fanny wouldn't want that to happen, would she? You know she wouldn't!"

"All I know is, I never loved any woman before, and I'll not be letting any harm come to this one."

"Then go get her! Kidnap her! I don't give a damn what you do—but don't stand around protecting her while Abraham Lincoln, Andrew Johnson, and Ulysses S. Grant are cut down to their knees and this nation's government collapses.''

Paddy considered his words for a time, then lifted up his rifle. ''All I want is her, Captain,'' he swore. ''That's all I can think about tonight.''

''Then run over to that stuffy house and jerk her out and bring her here,'' he advised. ''She'll be safe here.''

He looked around the disheveled room. ''It doesn't look safe to me,'' he commented. ''Anyway, she wouldn't come.''

''Well, then make her come.''

O'Connor ambled toward the door. ''A fine lady like Fanny Seward would never come into a man's hotel room,'' he stated. ''Nothing could make her do that. It wouldn't be proper.''

''Paddy—''

''Good night, Captain.''

''Damn you, Sergeant. What do you want me to do— order you to stay?''

He paused a moment, smiled grimly, slapped his rifle upon his shoulder, and marched out of the room. Ten feet down the corridor, he turned around, faced Bedford at the door, and snapped his hand up for a salute. ''Captain,'' he said sharply.

Bedford returned the salute. ''Be careful, Sergeant,'' he warned.

''Yes, sir, I will,'' he said. ''You, too.'' And with those words, Paddy O'Connor popped down his hand, spun around on his heels, and shuffled on down the hall.

# Chapter 12

The sharp rapping at Stephen's door two hours later was loud and persistent. Stooping bare-chested over the wash basin, he fumbled for the towel on the rack beside the dresser and scrubbed it briskly against his wet face. "Just a minute!" he groaned, and flung the damp towel on the basin. In one flowing motion, he scooped his shirt off the bed, slipped his arms in, and dropped it down over his head.

"Stephen, will you let me in, please," a woman's voice called out frantically from behind the door. He recognized it instantly.

"Becky!" he exclaimed as he whipped open the door to reveal the pretty blonde woman in the hall. "What are you doing here?"

Without hesitation she charged in. "Stephen, you've got to do something," she breathed excitedly. After catching her breath, she added sadly, "You just have to."

He watched her fan her face with her hand. She was panting and her cheeks were flushed with color, as if she had been running. "Calm down," he told her.

"I can't calm down." She began to pace. "It's going to be horrible if you don't do something to help them. Frederick's too mule-headed to listen to a woman, and Fanny's too naive to believe anybody would ever do such a thing. They're all so . . . frustrating!"

"Becky, what are you talking about?"

"I'm talking about the Sewards, Stephen!" she cried. "Why else would I be here?"

He reached out to touch her, but at the last moment drew back his hand. "Will you please make sense?" he exacted. "What can I do about the Sewards?"

She stopped a few feet away from him. "Stephen, I'm really scared," she confided, grasping her shawl close to her neck. "I know now what you said is going to happen. But nobody in the house will listen to me. If you don't do something, I'm afraid they're all going to be killed."

He understood now. "Paddy showed up with his rifle, didn't he?" he asked her.

"It's not just Paddy," she answered. "It's Booth! Oh Lord, you were so right about him! All he was interested in today was finding out more details about the Seward house. It was ghastly. He was planning the murder with us sitting right there in the carriage with him!"

"I'm glad you know what kind of man he is, Becky."

She nervously brushed back a lock of hair from her forehead. "Stephen, will you come back with me?" she begged. "Will you come back and stay at the Seward house with us?"

"Paddy's already there, Rebecca," he reminded. "He's determined he's going to protect Frances."

"But Paddy is just one man with one gun. We need you. I know if you really tried, you could convince Frederick and Augustus of what this monster is going to do. Then you could stay with us all day tomorrow—"

"I can't do that, Becky," he regretted. "I can't spend all day in William Seward's house. I'd like to, but I can't."

"Why can't you!" She bristled. "Is it too much to ask, for a Southerner to risk his life for a family of Yankees?"

"Damn it, Rebecca, you know it's not that."

"Then what is it, Stephen? You act so interested—but you won't help me save my friends from being murdered."

He hesitated. "I can't be in two places at once, Becky," he explained. "I have to stay as close to Lincoln as I can tomorrow."

"Lincoln!" she blurted. "The President has people all around him all the time, but what does Fanny have? Or her brothers? Or me? Don't you think we need you more than he does?"

"Becky, you told me yourself—Abraham Lincoln is a great man. We all need him. I didn't think you would change your mind so easily."

"I haven't changed my mind," she denied quickly. "I still feel the same way about him. But my God, Stephen, I'm talking about people who have taken me into their house and treated me like a member of the family. I can't turn my back on them."

"And I can't turn my back on President Lincoln, Becky."

She stared angrily and hopelessly at him. "Is that all

you can say about it?'' she asked. "You simply won't do it?''

"I'm sorry,'' he apologized. "I won't.''

"Then I guess there's nothing else we can say to each other, is there?'' She started for the door.

"Becky, wait—'' He placed his hand on her shoulder.

"Wait for what, Stephen?'' She shook it off. "Why keep talking about it? If you don't care enough to do this, I certainly can't force you.''

"But I do care,'' he protested. "My God—I've never cared so much for anything or anybody in my life. All I have to do is think of you and I'm ready to explode.''

She shot him a puzzled look, paused, then whirled around quickly and raced for the door.

But he got there first, slapping his hand against it with a loud clap. "Becky, I love you,'' he professed.

"Please don't say that—''

He seized her hands in his. "I've got to say it,'' he asserted. "It's true. I love you more than I've ever thought I could love anyone. You know that as well as I do.''

"I know no such thing.'' She twisted her wrists.

"And I think you love me, too.''

"No, I don't!'' She wrenched her hands free. "Now will you please stand aside and let me go?'' she demanded. "Or do you want me to scream?''

"Becky,'' he pleaded as he reached for her.

"Stephen,'' she whimpered and tried to back away. "For God's sakes—'' She resisted, but he was too strong for her.

"I want you so much,'' he murmured as he pulled her close. The touch of her breasts against him started his chest start pounding and his stomach twisting into knots. He could feel his desire for her building swiftly now; it was surging up, ready to erupt at any second. As she turned her head, he caught the nape of her neck with one hand and gently lowered his mouth next to hers.

"No—" she moaned.

He stifled her words with a kiss. At first she fought him, then gradually her lips began to separate under his. Spurred by the warm moistness of her breath against his mouth, he boldly slipped his tongue in between her wet lips, and she closed them around it.

They kissed passionately for a moment, but then she squirmed in his arms. "Stephen, stop it!" she gasped.

"You do love me!" He held her close. "I can feel it!"

"I do not!" she denied. "I hate you!"

"Becky, I can't keep letting you run away from me."

"Stephen—" She strained against him. "Please let me go—I can't breathe!"

"I'll let you go when you tell me how you feel."

"You're hurting my neck—"

"Tell me!"

"All right!" she exploded. "I do! Now are you satisfied? Now will you let me go!"

"You do *what*, Rebecca? Say it!"

"Stephen—"

"Say it!"

"All right—I love you! Now will you—"

He kissed her again. Once more she tried to writhe away from him and pleaded with him to stop. Then, all of a sudden, she impulsively flung her arms around him and kissed him back. His mind spinning, Stephen peeled her shawl off her shoulders and dug his fingers into her hot, bare flesh.

"No, don't," she begged him. "Please—I mean it."

"Oh, Becky," he moved a hand between them and

pressed it against her bosom. "I love you so much—" He slid his palm across her heaving breasts, then trailed his fingers lightly across the smooth skin above the neckline of the dress.

"We shouldn't do this," she breathed as his fingers groped, then plunged toward her naked breast.

"Oh God, Becky—" His eyes closed and his mind began to spin wildly as he measured the firm, warm roundness of her breast with his hand and squeezed the hard, erect nipple between his fingers.

For an instant she seemed to give in completely to his touch, but when his lips touched hers again, she started shaking her head violently. With a surge of strength she shoved at him and managed to spring herself from his arms.

"Dear God, what am I doing!" She swallowed, her palm flat against her throat. "I must be crazy. Now, of all times—"

He reached for her again.

"No!" She quickly retreated. "Don't come near me." She stumbled back against the wall.

"Becky, I'm not going to hurt you."

She slid along the wood to escape him. "No, you're not," she vowed. "You're going to let me go through that door. Right now!"

He stepped toward her. "Becky, for God's sakes—we love each other!"

"I know that, Stephen," she assented. "That's why I have to get out of here."

Though swept up in the throes of passion, Stephen was suddenly struck by a sober thought as he looked at the beautiful woman cowering against the side of the dresser.

"Becky," he asked soberly, "am I frightening you? Are you afraid of me?"

She shook her head. "It's not you I'm afraid of," she declared. "It's the way I'm feeling. Oh, why did I come here alone? I should've known better than this. Why do I keep flouting the rules?"

He drew in a long, deep breath and blew it out. "Why don't you go home, Rebecca." He stepped aside. "Go back to the Seward house. Everybody will be all right; Paddy will look after you."

She nodded. "I believe it would be the best thing to do right now." She let out a breath of relief.

"Then maybe you'd better do it." He took another step back.

"Yes, I'd better." She brushed sharply past him. "While I still want to," she added as she flung open the door.

Stephen did nothing to stop her from sweeping through the doorway out into the hall. For a few seconds he stood near the threshold, taking in the fresh fragrance of her perfume lingering in the corridor. He imagined he could still feel the touch of her flesh, the roundness of her breast in his hand.

By the time he reached the window inside the room, Rebecca was climbing into her carriage on the street below. As he split the curtains and peered out, the black covered vehicle was lurching away from the National Hotel. A few heartbeats later it was fading out of sight down Pennsylvania Avenue, into the dark night.

# Chapter 13

Paddy O'Connor stood poised against the rough brick of the outside wall of the Seward house, holding his brawny body almost at military attention. He gripped the barrel of his Sharps rifle tightly and diverted his eyes from the concerned glance of the dark-haired young woman standing near him, on the front doorstep. The Irishman had felt awkward and out of place since he'd arrived there, but he hadn't minded that. All that mattered to him was that he was protecting Fanny Seward, the only woman he had ever loved.

"I do wish you didn't have to stay out here, Mr. O'Connor," Fanny was saying as she folded her arms across her chest. "The air is so damp."

"I like it damp," he mumbled.

"But don't you think you should come back in, at least for a little while?" she advised. "I'm sure Frederick wouldn't mind if you stayed a few minutes."

"There's nothing wrong with this, ma'am," he refused. "I've been in a lot worse weather than this, plenty of times."

"Well, I still feel terrible about it," she declared. "You come all the way over here to protect us and my ungrateful brother makes you stand outside. He can be so stuffy sometimes."

"He didn't make me, Miss Seward," he corrected. "He only asked me."

"To tell you the truth, I think you were much too polite to him. I think you should've broken his nose."

"I was tempted to do just that," Paddy confessed.

She shook her head resignedly. "My brothers think because I'm sick so much, my brain must be weak. They think I wouldn't know a good man if he bit me."

Paddy erupted into laughter.

"Oh, you know what I mean." She colored.

He laughed again, then caught himself, and the two instantly plunged themselves into a long, embarrassed silence.

Finally Frances broke it. "I know you're a good man, Mr. O'Connor," she complimented him. "And someday my brothers are going to know it, too."

"I just don't want you to get hurt, Miss Seward," he muttered. "Any of you," he added quickly.

"Well, I'm not as sure as you are about all this danger, Mr. O'Connor," she said, then smiled, "but with you here I am sure there's no need to worry about it."

Suddenly the front door to the house cracked open and a round face with thin hair and curly sideburns popped into view. "Frances, it's getting late," Frederick Seward stated firmly. "It's time for you to come in."

"In a minute," she stalled.

"I mean now, Frances," he insisted sternly. "There's rain in the air. If you don't come in now, you'll be sick for a—"

"All right, Frederick!" she cut him off. "I don't have to be told more than once."

He glowered at her. "Your tone of voice isn't becoming, Frances," he chastised. "Being around Rebecca Windfield is making you forget your manners."

"Frederick, will you go away, please?"

Seward crinkled his nose, threw Paddy a disapproving look, then slithered back into the house without a sound.

"Isn't he just awful?" She sighed. "And to think, most of the time, he's so sweet. But I don't know, every time I start liking someone, he and Augustus all of a sudden turn into big grizzly bears and start hovering over me."

"Am I someone you like?" Paddy asked. It was the boldest, bluntest question he had ever formed in his mind, and it took every ounce of his courage to ask it. But he had to know.

Fanny looked away sheepishly. "Do you honestly think I'd be standing out here in this dreadful night air if I didn't like you?"

"I didn't know." He shrugged.

"Well, now you do." She drew her arms closer to her body and shivered.

"Are you cold?" he asked her. "Do you want my coat?"

She shook her head. "I think I will go in," she decided. "Frederick's right; it is getting late."

"Yes, it is."

"But I wish I didn't have to leave you out here alone."

"I'll be fine," he assured her. "I can take care of myself."

As Fanny started to move toward the door, Paddy snapped up his rifle at a rustling sound coming from the trees across the street, near the executive mansion. He held the stock hard against his shoulder and his finger wrapped tightly around the trigger as a small, dark shape burst out of the trees, darted in and out of the shadows, and broke into the open street.

"Hold it!" Paddy hollered at him. "Stop right there!"

"Are you Mr. O'Connor?" a small voice returned out of the night.

"It's just a boy," Fanny said.

"What is it you want here, lad?" Paddy relaxed. "State your business."

The boy, eight or nine years old, in tan trousers and a blue muslin shirt and a straw hat cocked back away from his face, approached. "I got a letter for Mr. Paddy O'Connor," he announced. "Seward residence, across from the White House."

"Who's the letter from, lad?" Paddy lowered his rifle.

"Don't know, sir. Ain't none of my business. I'm just trying to earn a penny or two, that's all." He stepped up to Paddy and held out a white envelope.

The Irishman eyed the little boy closely, then took the letter over to one of the front windows. While the messenger scurried off into the darkness, he held it under the window light. He scanned the *Sgt. Paddy O'Connor, CSA* on the outside of the envelope. "I don't know who wrote this, but it's got my name on it," he reported to Fanny.

"Well, open it and find out what it is," she suggested anxiously.

After hesitating another moment, Paddy cracked open the envelope and slipped out the single sheet of paper. He carefully unfolded the page and tilted it to catch the light. With difficulty, he read the note aloud:

> Paddy. Come back to the Hotel. I have
> found Massey's M. Hurry. Capt. S. Bedford.

"Massey's M?" Frances echoed. "What does that mean?"

"It means the man who murdered Donald Massey," Paddy answered, coming back from the window. "He's the one I've been looking for ever since I got to Washington City. And while I've been standing around here waiting for something to happen," he reproached himself, "Captain Bedford's gone out and found him."

"I don't understand; why would Captain Bedford want you to go back to the hotel?"

"I guess he needs me," he replied simply. "And I've got to go help him. I walked out on him one time tonight; I won't do it again."

"Paddy?" she ventured, "I . . . don't know if I should ask this, but are you certain it was Captain Bedford who sent you that note?"

"What do you mean?" he puzzled.

"I don't know what I mean." She became flustered. "It's just a feeling I have. You didn't seem to recognize the handwriting—are you sure it's his?"

Paddy wrinkled his wide brow, unfolded the letter again, and squinted at the words on the page. "I don't know if it is or not," he admitted. "But who else could've written it?"

"Anybody could have written it, Paddy."

"Uh-uh." He shook his head. "Nobody else knows I'm here. It has to be from Captain Bedford."

"Anybody could know that, too," she pointed out.

"Maybe they could," he acknowledged, "but who else would know about Donald Massey being murdered? Nobody except maybe the Secretary of the War Department, and Mr. Edwin Stanton is not about to be sending a Confederate soldier any notes, I can tell you."

She considered his words for a moment, then said, "If you're determined to go," she decided, "I want to go with you."

"No!" he declared vehemently. "You'll not be going anywhere!"

"Paddy—"

"No. I'll put your brothers on you if I have to. You're not leaving this house tonight."

She looked at him closely. "At least I'm going to wait up for you," she yielded. "You can't stop me from doing that."

"It ain't necessary, Miss Seward."

"Call me Fanny. And it is necessary."

"Well, I guess I know better than to be arguing with a fine lady like yourself," he relented. "I'll be back before long," he promised.

"See that you do. Look, there's Becky." She noted the carriage arriving in front of the house. "She can keep me company."

Paddy watched Rebecca lay the reins down in the carriage seat and step out. "Will you do me a favor, Fanny?" he said, gulping on her name. "Don't tell anybody about this note. Captain Bedford doesn't want people to know about Donald Massey."

"Not even Becky?"

"Nobody."

As soon as Fanny agreed to his request, Paddy swung his weapon over his wide shoulder and strode briskly down the sidewalk toward the street. Pausing to tip his cap to Rebecca Windfield, he muttered an abrupt "good evening" and marched down Pennsylvania Avenue in double time.

"Where is he going in such a hurry?" Becky asked Frances at the doorstep.

"He's going to see Captain Bedford," she returned vaguely. Her eyes were fixed on Paddy, watching his every step.

"I thought he was going to protect us, Fanny."

"He was," she replied sadly.

Rebecca examined her friend closely in the dim light. "Is something wrong?" she asked her. "Your face is as white as chalk."

"I don't know, Becky," she answered worriedly. "I'm just cold, I guess."

"Well, let's go inside and get warm, for heaven's sakes."

Frances resisted until the Irishman had vanished into the darkness; then she reached up and wiped a tear off her cheek. "Becky," she sniffed, "I don't think he's coming back."

"Of course he is," she encouraged. "Don't you know the man is in love with you, Frances?"

"Oh, Becky—not in two days!"

"I don't care how many days it's been," she declared. "If you love someone, you love him. The amount of time you've known him doesn't make any difference."

"I wish I could believe that," she said wistfully.

"Well, you can believe it. Now come inside and let me make you some hot tea. You need to get rid of that chill."

"Becky, do you really think he'll be back?" she asked hopefully.

"If he said he will, then he will. Now come in before we both get sick."

Casting a final long look down the street, Fanny heaved a sigh, grasped Rebecca's extended hand, and turned reluctantly toward the door.


The one-hundred-and-sixty-foot-wide Pennsylvania Avenue sliced through the trees like a great dark and silent river,connecting the executive mansion to the domed Capitol building. There was a strange absence of traffic on the thoroughfare as Paddy headed southeastward toward the National Hotel. In the glowing circles cast by street lamps he could see the leaves of trees fanning in the breeze, but all around him there was nothing else but stillness. He could hear the regular shuffling of his own feet in the damp road, but nothing else. There was not even the usual sound of faraway horses and coaches in flight or the forlorn howls of a lonesome dog off in the distant night.

Halfway to the hotel he thought he heard the clumping of footsteps behind him, starting and stopping as he did. But it was no one. Then he detected the rasping cough of a man clearing his throat a hundred feet away. He stopped, held his breath, and listened intently. But just then a two-horse covered coach rattled noisily by and he lost the sound. After that he shook off his foolish suspicions, curled his finger around the trigger of his rifle, and hurried on down the street.

As he crossed Sixth Street to the entrance of the National Hotel, his eye caught on the lumpy figure of a man in black lurking in the shadows between two of the porch columns. Paddy hesitated at the door, thinking the man looked familiar, but then he decided he didn't recognize him after all.

But just as his fingers touched the cool brass doorknob, the man spoke. "Mr. O'Connor?" he murmured in a low voice. "Is that you?"

Paddy turned around. "That's right, lad," he responded. "I'm Paddy O'Connor."

The man crept slowly into the light; his long face was wrenched into a smile that was almost a smirk. "Mr. O'Connor—" He held out his hand. "How are you this evening?"

The Irishman frowned as he grasped the man's soft, limp hand. "I don't believe I know you, sir," he observed.

"No, of course you don't. My name is Mason Butler. I work for the War Department. I've been consulting with Captain Bedford all day, so naturally I know who you are."

"I was just going to go up to see Captain Bedford." He dropped the other man's hand.

Butler wiped his hand on his cheek. "I'm afraid that would be a useless gesture," he commented. "A waste of my time and your effort."

"What?"

"What I mean is, you won't find Captain Bedford in his room," he explained. "He left it over an hour ago."

Paddy raised his eyebrows. "How would you know that?" he asked suspiciously.

"It's my job to know that, Mr. O'Connor," he replied simply. "The captain came to the Department and asked for our help, and we're giving it to him."

Paddy hesitated. "All the same," he said, "I'll be going to check the room."

"Go ahead and check it; it won't do any good. I happen to know that Captain Bedford is with the man who murdered one of our secret investigators. I believe he was one of your countrymen."

"You mean Donald Massey."

"Ah, yes. Captain Bedford said you were well-informed."

"Where is the captain now?" Paddy asked, "Him and this murderer?"

"They're not far," Butler evaded. "He sent me to make sure you came, since you have a vested interest in the murderer. Of course, I have no idea what that means. I assume it's some kind of code between you two."

"I know what it means," Paddy said, unconsciously rubbing his arm.

"Then you wouldn't mind if I took you to them?" Butler offered. "As he requested?"

"You just lead the way," Paddy replied.

The Irishman followed Mason Butler off the porch and down Pennsylvania Avenue. After plodding deliberately along for ten minutes, the clerk suddenly turned to the right off the thoroughfare and headed into a clump of trees. "This way," he ordered gruffly.

"Where in the world are we going?" O'Connor wondered. He was confused. They had inched along the open street at a snail's pace, whereas now they were moving fast through the damp foliage.

"Not far," Mason repeated. "You see, the Department has decided to keep this man hidden for a while, until the other assassins are arrested. Captain Bedford is helping us."

They silently meandered through the tall trees to another street Paddy didn't recognize. Then, a hundred yards to the south, they entered Seaton Park. The Irishman was becoming impatient with traipsing endlessly through the wet grass and bushes, but he didn't complain. He kept looking ahead, assuming that at any instant he would see Stephen Bedford's tall, straight body leaning casually against an oak tree, waiting for him.

Then, in the middle of an isolated clearing, Butler reached out and stopped him with the back of a hand in the chest. "Look at this," he observed in an oily voice. "It's real quiet back here in the woods, isn't it, Mr. O'Connor?"

"Is this it?" Paddy looked around. "Where is he?"

"This is the quietest place in Washington City."

Paddy tightened his grasp on the Sharps rifle. "Where is Captain Bedford!" he demanded.

"Ah, yes, Captain Bedford. And Mr. Massey's murderer."

"Quit stalling, man," Paddy growled.

"Well, it looks like you've found me out, Sergeant," he chuckled. "You're quite correct; I have been stalling. You're a very smart man, Mr. O'Connor. You've already guessed what has happened to him, haven't you?"

"I'm not guessing anything." He grabbed the clerk's lapels and clamped them close around his neck. "But you're going to tell me what did happen to him, or I'll be splattering your brains all over these woods."

"Mason gagged. "That won't help your captain any, O'Connor."

"Speak up, lad! Where is he!" He drew Butler's flaccid body next to his. "I'm about to break your windpipe—"

"Let me go and I'll tell you," Butler tried to bargain.

"You'll tell me now," Paddy said, tightening his grip.

"All right, all right!" Butler yelped. "He's over there!"

"Where?"

"Over there by the pine tree." He gestured vaguely with his hand. "Now let go of my throat. I'm choking!"

"I don't see anything," said Paddy, searching the grass and bushes in the direction Butler was pointing. "Captain?" he called out tentatively. "Is that you?" He waited. "Captain Bedford! Are you there?"

"He can't hear you, O'Connor."

"You snake—"

"He can't hear you because he's dead, you idiot! Don't you understand? Your beloved Captain Bedford is dead."

"You're lying!" Paddy squeezed the lapels harder.

Mason choked. "No, I'm not lying—stop it, man!"

"You are!" Paddy cried desperately. "He can't be dead."

"Go see for yourself." Mason gulped. "Go on; do it!"

Paddy's breathing shortened and his heart began to palpitate as he let Butler pry his fingers loose from his coat. Feeling stunned, he dropped his hands and stared blankly at the dark pine tree. If Stephen Bedford were there, he told himself, then he was to blame for it. He had selfishly and callously walked out on the man who had once saved his life. And now that man was dead. How would he ever be able to live with that?

Forgetting about the clerk, Paddy stalked through the darkness toward the tree. His chin trembled and his eyes watered as the many images of Antietam flashed across his mind. He could see young Stephen Bedford, oblivious to his own peril, sweeping down from his horse and dragging him out of a blazing torrent of gunfire—risking his life for a man he didn't even know. . . .

As he neared the tree, the image faded as the moon broke away from a cloud and bathed the place in a pale, ghostly light. At the sight of a black wool blanket spread over a shape the size of a man, he came to a halt and traced the sign of the cross on his chest.

"St. Andrew, forgive me," he said thickly. "I'm the one to blame for this man's death."

A few steps closer, he saw the long, shiny Confederate army sword anchored deep in the ground in front of the blanket, like a headstone for a grave. Even in the bleary light he recognized the long, slender hilt and the hefty octagonal pummel of the weapon. There was no doubting it. The sword belonged to Captain Stephen Bedford.

Slowly, reverently, with tears flooding his eyes, he lumbered over to the blanket. After slashing another cross on his heart, he laid his rifle gently down in the loose pine straw beside the blanket and sank to his knees on the damp ground.

"God have mercy on him," he prayed softly. "Christ have mercy. Holy Mary, pray for him. All the holy angels and archangels, pray for him. Holy Abel, pray for him. . . ."

His body stiffened as the words of his prayer seemed to clog together inside his throat. He swallowed drily at the sound of Mason Butler's footsteps treading heavily on the leaves behind him. He could tell without looking that the clerk was headed his way. At least, he decided, the man was decent enough to pay his respects to Captain Bedford. Shutting his wet eyes, while Butler's ponderous steps thumped closer and closer, Paddy started moaning again his litany for the dead.

"All the choirs of the just, pray for him. Holy Abraham and Isaac, pray for him. St. John the Baptist, pray for him. St. Joseph, pray for him. . . ."

He paused as Butler's steps came near, making a softer

noise in the straw; then he felt the presence of the man near his shoulder.

"All the holy patriarchs and prophets, pray for him," he went on, "St. Peter, pray for him. . . ."

Now he opened his eyes in the darkness. As the moon burst through the clouds again and cast a gloomy light on the scene, he could make out the hem of Mason Butler's thick black coat inches away, above the dark trouser legs, above the highly polished boots in the pine straw. Paddy's pulse began to throb in his throat as he gaped at the shiny leather. He could actually see the glow of the moon reflected in the surface of Butler's boots. The realization came with a jolt. They were just as Massey had described them—boots as smooth and slick as glass!

In the frenzy of a single moment of panic, Paddy thrust his bulky frame with all his might toward his rifle, but came up inches short of the breech. His whole body suddenly convulsed in a violent spasm of pain as the razor-sharp blade of Mason Butler's long and narrow knife sliced into the back, between the ribs, and plunged deep into his lung. Paddy groaned and gasped for air as he crumpled to the ground.

"You stupid Irishman," Butler growled scornfully.

O'Connor clutched at the other man's leg, and got the toe of his shiny boot rammed fast and hard into his face.

After glowering at Paddy for a time, Butler let out a breath. "Do you want to see what you're dying for, Irishman?" He knelt down and grabbed the corner of the blanket in his fingers. "Look at this, you stupid reb. It's nothing!" he exclaimed as he snatched away the cloth. "Nothing but dirt and stick and pine straw!"

"Captain . . ." Paddy could not push out the burning words.

"That's right, O'Connor," he anticipated, "your captain's not dead after all. Not yet, anyway. But if the man is as dumb as you are, I certainly shouldn't have any trouble fixing that."

Paddy stretched out a hand. "Coward—I'll —"

"You're not going to do a thing, O'Connor," he retorted smugly. "Ever again." He raised his pear-shaped torso up to his feet and took two steps over to Paddy. With a loud grunt he jerked the knife blade out of his rib cage. He turned up his nose. "Jesus God, I've always hated touching bloody things. But I can't help it. You brought all this on yourself," he charged. "If you hadn't meddled in our plans, you'd still be alive this Saturday morning, wouldn't you?"

O'Connor strained every muscle in his body, but his limbs would not budge. He lay flat on his stomach with his face mashed into the ground, bleeding and helpless, paralyzed by an agonizing and consuming pain.

"Your meddling was for nothing, too, Irishman," he added. "John Wilkes Booth's plan is going to work despite it all. Abraham Lincoln and his cronies will be eliminated, and I will finally have the position and respect in the government I deserve. And you, my friend, will have died a perfectly useless death. So . . ."

Once more Butler raised the dripping knife over Paddy's back, closed his eyes, and with a tiny, guttural bark, he slammed the blade into his flesh again. Panting heavily, he worked it out, lifted it up again, and jabbed the unresisting body a third time. Cringing at the wetness on his fingertips, Butler wiped his hands and the blade on the Irishman's dry trouser leg and returned the knife to its place inside his vest.

He still had work to do. First he carefully gathered up

the straw and dirt he had used to represent Bedford's body and meticulously scattered it about the area. Then he spread the blanket out on the straw, within an inch of O'Connor's outstretched hands.

Surveying the scene, he scratched his chin thoughtfully and nodded his approval. It looked like an illicit love nest, he decided; exactly the effect he wanted. He blew a puff of moisture out into the cool, damp air and muttered, "Two more items, O'Connor, and it's over and done with."

Nauseated at the thought of touching Paddy's bleeding body, he tilted his head away and grimaced as he dug his fingers underneath and groped for a pocket. After two tries he located the one he wanted. He slipped out the note, supposedly from Bedford, which he had sent to Paddy, and crammed it into his own pocket.

"And now, the *coup de grâce*." He sighed as he snapped the Confederate sword out of the ground. Looming over the great, still shape on the straw, he hesitated to get his breath. Then, charging his lungs with the heavy night air, he raised high Bedford's cutlass with both hands on the hilt and, with one swift downward plunge, planted it with a thud into Paddy O'Connor's back.

With the moon now shrouded by the gathering gray clouds, Mason Butler had to half-feel his way back through the darkness to the street. But he found it easily enough. He had planned this murder brilliantly and precisely. Nothing could possibly go wrong now.

He had only a couple of regrets about the whole affair, he told himself as he strolled up Fourth Street toward his home. Planning such a clever crime was not a strain to a mind as well-trained and nimble as his, and executing a job as effectively as he had was actually a pleasure. Justifying the violence was no problem, either, for Paddy O'Connor and Stephen Bedford had placed themselves, of their own accord, squarely in the way of what he knew he deserved. But still, he decided, it was a pity that killing a man had to be such altogether exhausting work—and that touching a dying body was such a sickening thing to do.

# Chapter 14

For the twentieth time in four hours, Frances Seward pinched back the white linen curtains, peered hopefully through the panes of the front window, and saw nothing but the vague little circles of light around the street lamps in the gradually thickening mist of a cool spring night. Flicking the drapes together, she wheeled around toward the woman sitting quietly at the writing desk by the fireplace.

"How can you do that, Becky?" She started walking again.

"How can I do what?" She looked up.

Frances fidgeted with the collars of her gray blouse as she crossed the floor. "At a time like this," she answered, "how are you able to sit there quietly and calmly writing letters?"

"I'm not calmly doing anything, Fanny," Rebecca differed. "I'm as frightened as you are. But trying to write a letter home is better than watching you pace up and down all night."

Frances stopped and smiled weakly. "I'm sorry," she apologized. "I shouldn't take it out on you. It's my fault, not yours. I shouldn't have let him go."

"Oh, don't be silly. Since when does a woman *let* a man do anything? When a man really believes he has to do something, there's nothing any woman can do to stop him."

"Then I should have gone with him," she offered.

"And what good would that do? Don't you think he and Stephen can handle this themselves?"

"Oh, I don't know what to think," she confessed. "I'm just so tired of waiting—"

"Then go to bed!" a male voice intruded from the doorway of the parlor. Frederick Seward stepped forth, draped in a blue flannel dressing robe and holding a lighted candle in a brass dish in front of his waist. "Both of you," he added, not bothering to look at Rebecca.

"I'm not going to bed, Frederick," Fanny explained to her brother. "I promised Mr. O'Connor I would wait for him."

"I don't care what you promised Mr. O'Connor, Frances; you can't stay down here any longer. Two women should not be down here alone at this time of night."

"But he may be in trouble, Frederick—on account of us."

"He's in trouble, we're in trouble, the President's in trouble—if you ask me, Frances, you're losing your grip on your reason. All you need to do is let the men deal with such things and you tend to your sewing."

"Just how have you been dealing with it, Frederick?" Becky interrupted. "Or have I missed something?"

He looked at her steadily. "I'm handling it as any man would," he said. "By being reasonable."

"Men and reason aren't necessarily related, you know," she pointed out.

"I'm too tired to fence with you, Rebecca," he said coolly, then turned again to his sister, "Frances, if you and Rebecca must wait for this Southern soldier, then do it in Father's room. Even though he's resting well tonight, he still needs watching."

"Frederick—"

"Do as I say, Frances. It won't hurt you to sit with him. Now go on up there, both of you. I'll close up the house."

Upstairs, in William Seward's bedroom, Frances and Rebecca sat and dutifully watched over the sleeping man for an hour. By two o'clock Frances had again begun to pace and check the window every fifteen minutes or so. Becky tried to ease the tension with some hot tea, but by then Fanny was much too nervous to drink anything. The longer she waited, the more convinced she became that something terrible was happening to Paddy O'Connor.

At the fourth chime of the Secretary's old mantel clock Frances turned away from the window for the last time. By now Becky was curled asleep in the leather chair next to the bed and her father was resting comfortably. She could see no reason to wait any longer. She simply had to go find him.

Barely making a sound, Fanny left the room and crept softly down the hall to her own room. Within five minutes she had slipped on her hat, shawl, and greatcoat, and was quietly descending the stairs.

As she neared the front door, Bell, the old black servant, appeared out of the shadows. Frances was startled by the puffy-eyed and droopy face glaring at her in the light from his oil lamp. "Bell—you scared me half to death!" she chided him gently.

"Miss Frances, what do you mean, headed out that door this time of night?" he scolded. "Does your daddy know you're down here?"

"No, and don't you tell him, either," she ordered.

He shook his gray head from side to side. "This ain't like you, Miss Frances," he observed. "Going out in the wet air by yourself. You're too sick a girl to be doing such a—"

"Good night, Bell." She reached for the doorknob.

"You're gonna catch your death out there, Miss Frances," he warned. "Seems to me we got enough miseries in this house now, without you adding to it."

"Oh, be still, Bell. I feel all right. I'll be back in a few minutes. Now why don't you make yourself useful and go get the carriage for me?"

"Yessum," he nodded. "Only I don't know as it's such a good idea, Miss Frances."

"Do you want me to walk instead?" she threatened.

"Uh-uh, don't do that. I'll get it for you," he promised. "You just wait right there."

"Thank you, Bell."

"Yessum. Only I still say, it ain't right, you going off, this time of night. Seems to me, ever since Miss Rebecca Windfield come—"

"Bell—go on!" she told him. "Hurry!"

"Yessum. I'm on my way, now."

*　　　*　　　*

Thirty minutes later, a cold and shivering Frances Seward parked her carriage on Sixth Street and hurried into the lobby of the National Hotel. Just inside the door she stopped to catch her breath and to collect herself. Even though the big, deserted room was warm, her body continued to shake with the cold dampness that had begun to seep into her bones the moment she left home.

Trying to ignore the trembling, Frances headed across the bold red floral carpet to the front desk. The chubby little man behind the counter popped up out of his chair as she approached.

"Ma'am?" He eyed her curiously.

Frances swallowed, took a deep breath, and forced her question out. "Could I have the number of Mr. Bedford's room, please?" she asked.

"The *what*, ma'am?" He frowned.

"The name is Captain Stephen Bedford—"

"Aye, I know the man well enough, ma'am."

"Then may I have the number of his room?"

"Yes, ma'am, but I sure wouldn't mind knowing why you want it."

"Well, I mind," she retorted, and colored. "But I assure you, it is important."

"Well now, I should say the reputation of the hotel is important, too, ma'am," he informed her. "If you understand what I mean."

Frances hesitated, then gave in. "I'm actually looking for Mr. Bedford's friend Sergeant O'Connor," she admitted. "He was supposed to meet me somewhere, but he didn't show up."

"Paddy O'Connor, huh?" He brightened. "Now there's a fine lad, I can tell you. Big as a bull, but mind you, he wouldn't pinch a flea of a dog, if it hurt either one of them. Except I never knew him to keep company with a lady before.''

''Well, now you know.''

''Aye, that I do, ma'am. And I guess if your business is with Patrick O'Connor, it must be all right. If the big lad's here at all, he'll be up on the second floor. Room 26, it is.''

''Thank you,'' she said, relieved.

''Just don't be making a racket up there, ma'am,'' he cautioned. ''We've got plenty of people trying to sleep here.''

''I'll be very quiet,'' she promised and picked up her skirts and hurried toward the stairs.


A few minutes later, Stephen Bedford shielded a gaping yawn with an open palm, cracked open the door to his room, peeked around it, and discovered, of all people, the daughter of the Secretary of State.

''Miss Seward!'' He swung the door open. ''What are you doing here?''

Noticing his robe parted at the waist, she shamefully lowered her gaze. ''I'm sorry to get you out of bed, Mr. Bedford,'' she apologized, blushing.

''Never mind that—has something happened? Where's Paddy?''

''I don't know, Mr. Bedford,'' she replied. ''That's why I'm here.''

Stephen pushed his dark hair off his forehead. ''I didn't think anything short of another war could have budged him from your house tonight. When did he leave?''

"He left just after he got that message." She swallowed. "He said he was coming back, but he didn't."

Stephen raised his eyebrows. "What message are you talking about?" he asked her.

"The note you sent by messenger, ordering him to come here."

"I didn't send him a note, Miss Seward," he said.

"Oh, no—"

He held up a hand. "Now don't panic," he pleaded. "We don't yet if he's in any trouble."

"But if you didn't send him that note, who did? And what would they want with him?"

"I don't know, but we're certainly going to find out. Wait right here. I'll get dressed."

"Mr. Bedford, thank you—"

"I'll be out in five minutes," he told her and closed the door.


The search for Paddy O'Connor was time-consuming, exhausting, and extremely frustrating. As Stephen and Frances meandered ceaselessly through the empty streets of northwest Washington, he felt his concern for his friend slowly turn into apprehension, then into that nauseating sense of dread he had experienced in Ford's Theatre days before. But he kept searching. By dawn they had probed every niche and corner of the area between Judiciary Square and the Smithsonian Grounds, but hadn't found a trace of the man.

"Where could he be?" Fanny lamented. "We've looked everywhere."

"He's here somewhere, Frances." Stephen gazed up and down Missouri Avenue. "We just have to keep trying."

"Oh, what did they do to him?" she fretted. "What did they want with that sweet, gentle man?"

"Look," he said to her, "why don't you go home and let me do this? You look exhausted."

"I'm fine," she insisted.

"It may take a long time—"

"Mr. Bedford—what about the assassinations?" she interrupted. "Isn't today the day—"

"Yes, it is," he confirmed. "God help us, this damp, dreary day is the fourteenth of April."

"Does that mean you're going to give up looking for him?" she cried. "Mr. Bedford—you're not going to let them have him!"

"No, Frances," he assured her. "I'm not going to let them have him. Come on, let's look through the park again. I know you're tired, but if you want to keep it up, we'd better start moving."

She nodded her head and blotted her tears with a handkerchief. "You like him a great deal, don't you?" she asked, smiling fondly.

"Yep," he replied as he led her toward Fourth Street. "I like him a great deal."

Before they had walked a hundred yards, Stephen stopped cold. "Listen," he said to her. "Did you hear that?"

"No—what?"

"In the trees, over there. Hear it? It sounds like someone running."

"Where? I don't see anything."

"There he goes!"

"Is it Paddy?" She grabbed his wrist.

"Uh-uh," he answered, shaking his head. "He's too small." He could see a thin little man in a wide felt hat dodging trees, racing full speed for the open street. Ste-

phen burst down the road and quickly cut him off. "Whoa!
He thrust himself in the way. "Where are you headed i
such a hurry, friend?"

The man panted, swallowed, and struggled to speak
"Got to get the police," he gasped.

"Now what would you want with the police?"

"Found a man in there," he managed to say. "Somebod
shoved a sword in his back."

"Where!" He squeezed the man's biceps.

"Hey, stop that—"

"Tell me!"

"Let me go, now—"

"Where is he!"

"He's straight through there," the smaller man grunted

Instantly Stephen sprang into the trees, leaving France
Seward and the man behind him. He ran so fast his che
and side began to throb in pain as he crashed through th
woods. He ran blindly and frantically, slapping back th
low limbs, cracking twigs, ducking under wet leave
stumbling through the underbrush. He finally had to stop
to get his bearings. Where was he? Was he still moving i
the right direction? He sucked in a long breath and sta
gered through a heavy clump of beech trees and into
clearing.

There, on the other side of the open space, he saw
huge shape of a man lying near a blanket under a pine tre
He lay scrunched up in the straw, like a sleeping dog, wit
a sword rammed down into his spine. With a surge o
strength, Stephen vaulted through the grass to the spot.

"Paddy?" He dropped to his knees beside him. H
touched his shoulder lightly. "Paddy—Good God!"

The man in the pine straw managed to move his leg

slightly; then he slowly, painfully opened his eyes. "Captain," he moaned.

"Don't move," Stephen ordered.

The big man shook his head. "Can't . . ."

Stephen leaned over him and examined the wounds. "It looks pretty bad, Sergeant." He winced. "You've got three or four holes in you. But it was bad at Antietam, too, remember?"

He managed a nod.

"Well, if we made it there, we can make it here. All you have to do is hang on, old friend. The police are on their way; they'll be bringing a doctor with them."

"Captain?"

"Paddy, please don't try to talk."

"Captain—"

"Save your strength, man," he said firmly. "They'll be here soon."

"Got to . . ."

Stephen hesitated. "All right, damn it," he agreed. "What am I going to do with you? If you must talk, go ahead. Do it."

"Captain," he grimaced. "Sorry I ran out."

"You didn't run out."

"I should have stayed."

"Well, maybe you should have," said Stephen, trying to hold back the tears, "but then I've never heard of an Irishman who didn't have a stubborn streak in him as wide as the Shenandoah—"

"It was wrong, Captain," he strained.

"Just forget it ever happened, Paddy." He tried to speak forcibly. "Right or wrong, it doesn't matter now. All that matters is that you make it out of this cold, godforsaken place."

"Can't . . ."

"Damn it, Paddy, don't you die on me! We've got work to do, Sergeant."

O'Connor smiled weakly.

Stephen could see the life seeping out of the big Irishman's body. "Paddy," he tried to bolster him. "Listen to me. Frances Seward is coming. She'll be here any minute. Do you understand me?"

"Yes, sir."

He looked back into the woods, but there was no sign of Fanny Seward. He turned back to O'Connor. "Paddy, can you tell me who did this to you?" he asked.

He said with difficulty, "Same one."

"What do you mean?—the same man who killed Donald Massey? Is that what you're saying? The man with the glassy boots?"

"Yes."

"Who was he? Did you know him?"

"He . . . told me his name—but I . . . can't remember." He wrenched his face in agony.

"All right, Paddy, don't strain. We don't have to talk about it anymore. You just lie there and try to wait. The doctor will be here soon."

"Captain—"

"Just let it go, Sergeant. Save your strength."

Paddy closed his eyes.

"God in heaven," muttered Stephen as he sank back, "why did this have to happen?"

"Paddy!" Frances Seward suddenly appeared at the other end of the clearing.

At the sound of her voice, Stephen rose up, waited for her to struggle through the damp grass, then caught her in his arms. "Frances—"

"Oh my God, Stephen," she panted. "What's happened to him? We have to do something! We have to get him to the hospital—"

"Frances, there's nothing we can do," he said.

"Let me go!" She squirmed. "We can't just stand here! We have to help him!"

"Frances!" He shook her. "Listen to me. We can't help him."

"Oh, Stephen, no—" she cried, leaning toward the wounded man.

"He's not going to make it."

"Oh, dear God."

"He's just hurt too badly," he said tearfully. "He's lost . . . too much blood. I don't see how he's lived this long."

She closed her eyes, took a deep breath, and eased out of his arms. Kneeling beside Paddy, she lovingly placed his wide, thick hand between her palms, holding it as if it were something breakable. "Paddy?" she breathed softly, trying hard not to burst into tears.

He slowly opened his eyes, but said nothing.

"I got tired of waiting," she explained. "So I went chasing after you. I hope you don't mind."

Paddy's face remained rigid, twisted in pain.

"I slipped out of the house," she went on. "Can you believe that? I walked out. Not even Frederick knows where I am. Aren't you proud of me, Paddy?"

His big hand squeezed her fingers gently. "Miss Seward—" he murmured.

"I asked you to call me Fanny, remember?"

"Fanny." His mouth formed a weak smile.

Tears began to stream down her cheeks now. "That's better," she sniffed. "After all—"

"Fanny!" He gripped her hand tightly. "It hurts—"

"Be still now. It'll be better soon."

"I can't see—"

"Oh no, Paddy," she whimpered, "please don't die. Please don't leave me."

"I . . ."

"Oh God, no!" she cried. "Don't let him go! Don't take him away! Paddy O'Connor!" She wrung his hands frantically. "I love you. Do you understand me? I love you. Don't leave me—I love you!"

"Frances," Bedford's sombre voice called to her.

"Stephen, he won't answer me! His hand is cold. Paddy— say something to me! Paddy, I have to know—"

"He can't hear you, Frances," Stephen said. "He's gone." After a few moments he reached down and helped her up and held her in his arms again.

"Oh God, I loved him so much," she wept. "It all happened so fast, I never had a chance to tell him."

"I don't guess I did, either," he said sadly. "Paddy O'Connor was the best friend I ever had, and I never told him how I felt."

"But who could have done such a terrible thing?"

"I don't know, Fanny, but I'm going to find out. And when I do, I promise you, he'll pay for it."

As Frances lay her head against his shoulder, he heard a loud scuffle in the trees, then saw a force of a half-dozen men in blue uniforms tramping noisily toward them across the clearing. Within a few minutes they had surrounded them completely.

Pushing his way into view was a dark little man with sharp, homely features and deep-set black eyes. He announced in a raspy voice that he was Officer Isaac Harper of the Metropolitan Police. After a long, accusing look at

Stephen and Frances, he strolled over to Paddy's body and stooped over it.

"Nice homey little scene." He got up and brushed a slug of mud off his kneecap. "Tell me, lady," he said to Frances, "which one is it you're hugging there—the husband or the lover?"

"Now just a minute, Officer!" Stephen snapped.

"What's your name, sir?" Harper countered.

"Stephen Bedford," he answered. "And this is Frances Seward."

"Do tell. What about the one on the ground?" He motioned to Paddy's body with his head. "Who's he—*Mr.* Seward?"

"His name is Patrick O'Connor."

Harper rubbed his chin thoughtfully. "So let me see if I can work this out then. You caught this Patrick O'Connor with the lady here, on the blanket. Is that what happened?"

"No!"

"And to show the gent you mean business, you sneaked up on the poor bastard and planted that sword in his back."

"What are you talking about! I wouldn't hurt him. He was my friend!"

"So what? It's usually friends, not enemies, that end up killing each other over women. Harris, bring me that sword."

"Mr. Harper—" Frances sobbed.

"You don't look too well, ma'am," he told her. "You'd better let somebody take you home. The police will take care of everything from here on."

"But it didn't happen the way you said."

"That's exactly what I'd expect you to say in a situation like this, ma'am. Believe me, I've heard it before."

"Here it is, sir," the young man handed him the bloody sword.

Harper held it in front of his eyes. "Well now, that's a quality blade," he acknowledged. "Hard steel, good edge, proper balance. It's a rotten shame a weapon this fine has to be used for butchering up human beings." He turned toward Stephen. "Mr. Bedford," he said, "you wouldn't happen to know who this sword belongs to, would you?"

"Officer, if you'll just listen to me—"

"All I want to listen to is the answer to my question, Mr. Bedford."

"But I just found Paddy here—"

"Answer me! Do you know who owns this sword?"

"It was stolen from my—"

"Mr. Bedford," he said sternly, "I'm beginning to lose my patience. Is this your sword!"

"Yes, damn it!"

"Thank you. I appreciate the confession. All right, men, take him in."

"What do you mean, take me in! You can't believe I did this!"

"As a matter of fact, I believe exactly that. If you ask me, it all fits together neat as a puzzle. A classic love triangle."

"But I couldn't have—"

"We'll let the court decide what you could or couldn't do. Somebody take this lady home," he ordered. "She looks sick to me. And you, Mr. Stephen Bedford, you're going straight to jail, right this minute—for the murder of Patrick O'Connor."

Bound by heavy iron manacles, Stephen was led quietly out of the park, up Sixth Street and past the National

Hotel. The dreary damp streets were still sparse with people, but he did see one man he recognized. As the procession crossed Indiana Avenue, he caught a quick glimpse of the man from the War Department, leaning casually against a lamp post, watching them pass.

He thought of calling out to him, but then he decided it would be a waste of breath. Mason Butler was nothing but a powerless bureaucrat, after all. There was nothing such a man as that could do to help him.

No, he decided, as a policeman shoved him into a white building on Sixth Street, he would have to figure some way to get out of this dilemma himself. And soon—for the black morning had already arrived. And in the dawn of April 14, 1865, his closest friend had been murdered.

Stephen wondered who else would die this day.

# Chapter 15

Stephen Bedford was raging with anger. In the space of an hour the Metropolitan Police had slammed him into a room in the police court, carted him off to the county jail on Fourth Street, then whisked him down to the Old Penitentiary near the Government Arsenal. And, during that time, not one person had uttered a civil word to him.

He marched back and forth in the dark concrete cell, trying to control his emotions and collect his thoughts. The task was impossible. Painful images of Paddy's bleeding corpse burned fiercely in his brain. Thoughts of Rebecca excited his passions. Fear of the impending assassinations made his whole body tremble. He had to talk to someone, or go crazy.

"Guard!" he hollered through the barred window. He

yelled three more times before he heard the thumping of footsteps in the corridor.

"Yeah, what do you want?" The huge man stuck his piggish face close to the window.

"I want to see the chief of police," Stephen told him.

"Oh yeah?" The guard scratched his thick nose with a dirty finger. "Well, you can want and scream all day, and it still won't happen. Hell, I've never seen him myself."

"Then at least tell me why I'm being held here. Why won't you let me see anyone?"

"Because that's what they told me to do, that's why. That's the way it works."

"Look, I'm sure nobody would mind if I sent a note to someone."

"Oh yes, they would."

"Damn it, man," he fumed. "I've got things to do. People's lives are in danger. I can't spend the day here!"

"Looks like you're going to, though, doesn't it?"

"For God's sake, let me send one note. One sentence!"

The guard considered. "Who'd you send this note to?" he asked. "I mean, if I was to let you do it?"

"To Edwin Stanton, the Secretary of the War Department."

"That's a good one." He turned away. "Better than I expected."

"Wait a minute—don't go off!" Stephen called out.

"Look, mister," he said, turning around. "I ain't taking no note to Edwin Stanton, I don't care who it's from. He wouldn't let me in the door."

"Yes, he will. He'll want to see it."

"Yeah?" he said skeptically. "Why would he want to do that?"

"Because we're working on a case together. Mr. Stanton will want to know the police are keeping me hidden down here.''

"Well, sir, it so happèns, Mr. Stanton knows that already,'' the guard chuckled. "So let's have some quiet around here for a change.''

"Why do you say he knows I'm here?'' Stephen pressed.

"It's simple, mister. He knows you're here because he was the one who ordered you down here in the first place.''


While Bedford languished in his cell, a small, well-favored man in the front room of Booker & Stewart's on E Street shrugged on the coat of his immaculately tailored broadcloth suit and fished a quarter out of his pocket for the barber standing next to him.

"A good job, Thomas,'' Booth approved, stroking his cheek in the mirror. "Do you think it's close enough to last me through the play tonight at Ford's Theatre?''

"Oh, I guarantee it, Mr. Booth.'' The stout little man beamed. "I always say, when I shave 'em, they stay shaved.'' He took a step toward the other man in the shop. "What about you, sir?'' he asked him. "Are you satisfied with yours?''

"Sure, why not?'' the skinny man in the gray tweed coat mumbled indifferently. "A shave is a shave.''

"Yes, sir, I reckon that's true enough,'' he agreed amiably.

The thin man shot him a hard look, plucked his black derby off the wall rack, tugged it down on his head, and with a grunt stalked out of the barbershop.

Booth lingered a moment to compliment Thomas again, then stepped outside and began strolling down E Street.

Even though the low sky was thick with ominous-looking gray clouds, the actor's spirits were soaring. As he made his way through the noisy morning traffic, he could feel a sense of great excitement pumping through the blood in his veins. At last, it was here—the day that would change the course of human history. In less than twelve hours, his assassins would be striking down the oppressors. After years of frustration and guilt, John Wilkes Booth would finally have done his part for the grand and glorious cause of his beloved South.

A while later, in the kitchen of Mary Surratt's boarding house, he placed his cane and overcoat on the oak table, poured himself a cup of coffee from the pot on the stove, leaned against the wall, and waited. At 10:30, right on schedule, the skinny man from the barbershop split open the door and squeezed quietly into the room.

"That's a good disguise you're wearing, John," Booth complimented him over the cup. "You look very English. But you didn't bother to cover your face."

The slender man—John Harrison Surratt—whipped off his derby and tossed it on top of Booth's overcoat. In tweed he looked even more peculiar than usual, Booth thought. He owned a pointed chin, a sharp nose that sandwiched a bushy moustache curled at the ends, and a high, spacious forehead above tiny, angry eyes that were always shifting about in their sockets.

"It was good enough to get me past the barber unrecognized," he countered in a surly voice. "Now, I've had a long ride in from Canada," he changed the subject abruptly, "so why don't we get down to business? Tell me who you've lined up for the other three targets."

Booth set the coffee cup down on the stove. "My friend Mike O'Laughlin is responsible for Grant," he answered.

"We've already met this morning. He told me he's ready and eager."

Surratt laughed shortly. "Oh, he's eager enough," he conceded. "I just hope he's strong enough. Who's to take the Vice President?"

"George Atzerodt."

"George Atzerodt is a dumb German," Surratt sneered. "He has too little courage and he drinks too much liquor. Who else?"

Both was annoyed by Surratt's indignant attitude. "Lewis Powell and Davie Herold will take care of Seward," he said stiffly.

"A frustrated preacher's son and a half-wit." Surratt shook his head dejectedly. "God, I wish we could do better than that."

"Never mind, Surratt," Booth said, irritated. "They will do the job."

"Maybe they will." He pulled at his moustache. "And then again, maybe they won't. Let me tell you something, Wilkes. If anything goes wrong today—*anything*—I will pull out so fast, you won't see me leave. Is that agreed?"

"Nothing can go wrong," Booth stated confidently.

"Well, if something does, the government will suspect me right off. They know I'm a Confederate spy."

"They won't even think of you, John," he assured. "I'm going to spend the whole day making sure every bit of the evidence and suspicion points directly at me."

Surratt gnashed his teeth. "Well, if you want to risk hanging that badly—"

"I'm not going to hang," he interrupted. "I'll be arrested, and I will have my hour on the stage. Then I'll be released. All you need to worry about is taking care of the President."

"All right, if that's the way you want it. But I need a

favor from you, Wilkes. Instead of using a rifle, I want to hit him at close range. Which means I need to be able to sneak into his box.''

Booth frowned. "How are you going to do that? It's bolted from the inside.''

"I've worked it out. I'll jimmy the lock beforehand and bore a peep-hole in the door. All I need is ten minutes of privacy to do it in. Do you think you can cover for me while I'm at the theatre?''

Booth considered the idea, then nodded. "I can cover for you," he said. He checked his vest watch. "It's 10:37 now," he noted. "At 11:30 I'll be going into Ford's Theatre to pick up my mail. While I divert whoever is there, you can work on the box.''

"Good," Surratt snapped up his derby. "You just make sure to keep everybody out of my way, Wilkes.''

"I can hold an audience for ten minutes, Surratt," he commented. "I've made a living holding them for three hours at a time.''

"Sure you have," said Surratt, heading for the door, "but this is not play-acting, my friend. This is for real.''

At 11:30 Booth could feel his heart thumping as he saw John Harrison Surratt skulking into Ford's Theatre from the side entrance. He straightened his body and kept walking toward the crowd of men loitering near the front doors. He recognized Harry Ford, the manager of the theatre, Arnold Nelson, an actor, and a handful of faceless scene shifters, carpenters, and advance men. They would be his audience for a while.

"Well, look at this, gentlemen," remarked Harry Ford,

grinning at Booth. "There strides the handsomest man in the United States."

Booth adopted a mock-serious pose as he clacked his boots down on the planks. "And there, gentlemen," he riposted, pointing at Ford with his cane, "stands the most perceptive."

While the others broke into laughter, the actor sidled close to the door, in order to peer inside the building. He could see only one person in the theatre. "Davis!" he called out to him. "Would you bring me my mail, please!"

"Well now, you can't do without the *billets doux* a single day, can you, Wilkes?" Harry Ford chuckled. "You should see the letters this man gets," he bragged to the others. "The ladies love to bare their palpitating little hearts and pour out their heated desires to him."

"They don't bare their hearts, Harry," he corrected. "They open them."

"Either way," Arnold Nelson observed eagerly. "I'd sure be asking to help them do it."

"Mr. Nelson," Booth said after a nervous glance inside. "I never take advantage of these women. I read their letters, but I don't respond to them."

"Well, why don't you read one of them to us?" Nelson suggested. "I'd like to hear some of this passion."

Booth's throat tightened as he caught sight of the slender form of Surratt's body moving around up in the President's box. At that same moment, the stagehand Davis was charging blindly up the aisle with a letter. Fortunately, neither saw the other.

"Go ahead, Wilkes," Harry encouraged. "Read us a letter."

The clutch of men at the front doors pleaded louder when Davis appeared with an envelope in his hand. To keep their attention away from the inside, Booth came forward and sat on the steps. Then, as the others watched with irritation, he pretended to read silently. He laughed or exclaimed at the contents of the letter each time someone appeared to be losing interest. At exactly 11:40 he sprang up and abruptly crammed the note into his overcoat.

"I'm afraid it's too confidential, gentlemen," he said to the expectant men. "Sorry."

"Oh, come on, Booth," Harry Ford said. "Read us a few words anyway."

"All the lady did was quote Shakespeare," he lied.

"Well, tell us what she quoted then. That couldn't be confidential."

Booth pretended to consider, then make up his mind. "All right," he said. "Here's one: 'If you have tears, prepare to shed them now.' "

"What does that mean?" asked Nelson, licking his lips.

"I don't know, Mr. Nelson," Booth said. "The other one was: 'There are tears for his love, joy for his fortune, honor for his valor, and death for his ambition.' "

Nelson raised his eyebrows. "That's a mighty peculiar sentiment for a woman to be sending to John Wilkes Booth, isn't it?" he observed.

"Yes, I guess it is," Booth agreed. "Harry," he said, turning to the manager, "I hear you're putting on a fine play tonight."

"We're doing *Our American Cousin*," he responded. "Laura Keene should be great."

"Good; I'll be here."

"You may change your mind when I tell you the President and General Grant will be here, too," he said.

Wilkes looked straight at him. "All the more reason to come," he said simply.

"I hear they'll be placing General Lee in the box next to them," he joked.

"Let them place him where they want to," Booth declared grimly. "As long as they don't parade him in front of everyone."

"Now, Wilkes," replied Ford, holding up his hands, "I was only jesting."

"Well, Lincoln and Grant are not joking matters, Harry," he noted ominously. "Gentlemen," he announced to the others, "I'm supposed to have lunch with Mr. Coyle, so if you'll all excuse me . . ."

The rest of the morning went very smoothly for Booth. Over a lunch of steak and potatoes with the editor of *The National Intelligencer*, he discussed the political philosophy of Abraham Lincoln for a while, then hit him with an abrupt question.

"Have you ever wondered what would happen if Lincoln were killed?" Booth raised his coffee cup to his lips. "Would it really change anything?"

John Coyle, a sober, studious man, peeled off his spectacles and wiped the lenses clean on a table napkin. "I wouldn't even like to think about it," he muttered.

"Well, think about it anyway, John," Booth encouraged. "What would happen?"

"Well," he answered shakily, "naturally Vice President Johnson would take over. Though I hope to God nothing like that ever happens."

Booth sipped some of the steaming coffee. "You can't deny an event like that would be very profitable for the paper," he suggested.

"That kind of profit we can do without, Wilkes." He put on his glasses.

"Yes, but suppose Johnson did take over," Booth pressed. "What would happen if he were killed, too?"

"Then Secretary of State Seward would become the President." Coyle shifted in his seat. "But what's the point in knowing that?"

"Oh, there's no point, John," he replied coolly. "I'm just thinking out loud. And what if Seward were murdered?"

"Then we'd have absolute anarchy, Booth. The whole government would probably collapse."

"Would it really?" He smiled approvingly. "What an interesting idea."

"It's nonsense, that's what it is." Coyle laughed nervously. "Nothing like that could ever happen. Not these days."

Booth touched the corner of a napkin to his lips. "No, I guess it couldn't," he conceded. "It's just wishful thinking for a defeated Southerner, I suppose."

"Well, if you ask me, Wilkes," Coyle offered, "I think you've been acting in too many plays. Thank the Lord, political leaders aren't assassinated anymore. Lincoln may look like another Julius Caesar to some people—but this is a different time and place. They don't make Brutuses any more."

"No." Booth shook his head. "They don't, do they? At least, none we know of."

Leaving Coyle to puzzle over his words, Booth rented a horse at Pumphrey's Stables, then met with George Atzerodt and Davie Herold at the Kirkwood House, in the room above Vice President Johnson's apartment. As usual, Herold seemed happy and at ease, but Atzerodt was rattled.

"I'm afraid the Vice President saw me a while ago."

He took a swig from a bottle of whiskey. "I'm sure he did. I don't know if we ought to go on with this—"

"Get hold of yourself, George." Booth jerked the liquor out of his hands. "What does it matter if he did see you? He won't be alive to identify you, will he?"

"No, but still—"

"Look, men, everything's going like clockwork," he reassured them. "There's nothing to worry about. Surratt is in town and Mr. O'Laughlin is ready. Now, after you take care of the Vice President, George, the police will find this letter."

He sat down at the desk and scribbled out a note:

*Don't wish to disturb you, are you at home?*
       *J. Wilkes Booth*

"There," he said with satisfaction. "This will lead them straight to this room, which I rented under my name. What about the clues they'll find, George?" he asked.

Atzerodt hesitated, then went over to the coat rack, fumbled through a wool overcoat, and drew out a small black book. "This is the Ontario bank book in your name," he said to Booth. "And let's see . . ." He rummaged through another pocket. "This here's your momma's handkerchief."

Booth nodded. "It's all set then. So you see, you have nothing to fear, George. All the evidence will point to me. You'll be sleeping on a cot in Maryland when I'm arrested."

"Yessir," he said doubtfully. "I sure hope so."

"Then you can drink all the whiskey you want to," Booth told him.

After a quick visit to Lewis Powell at the Herndon House at one o'clock, the actor turned his attention to promoting the public letter he planned to have his friend John Matthews publish in *The National Intelligencer*. The notice would seem to be a confession of the assassination, but would actually be an announcement of his retirement from the stage.

By 4:30 p.m. he had advertised the proposed letter to nearly two dozen people, from the stagehands at Ford's Theatre and his drinking cronies at Grillo's Restaurant to the owner of Pumphrey's Stables and the clerk at the National Hotel.

Now, as he climbed down from his rented mare on Pennsylvania Avenue, he braced himself for the tall, handsome John Matthews sauntering toward him. Booth felt so confident now that he didn't even bother to hold back his smiles. After all, the great plan was working to perfection. Every step of the way he was manipulating his real-life actors exactly as he had desired, precisely according to his brilliant plot. What he couldn't know at this moment was that an event was about to occur that, in the space of a few minutes, would forever alter the outcome of his plan—and the course of American history.

"Good afternoon, Wilkes," John Matthews greeted him with a handshake. "I expected to find you crying, and look at you—grinning like a cat."

"I feel good today, John," he explained.

"Then you must not have seen them bringing in General Lee's officers a while ago," he concluded.

"Oh, I saw them well enough," Booth responded. "But it seems rather silly to moan over it. After all, I don't even have a country anymore."

Matthews frowned. "I can never tell when you're acting, Booth," he said seriously.

"Well, never mind, John. I was wondering, since I'm

leaving town later tonight, would you mind taking this letter by the *Intelligencer* for me? I would appreciate it."

"What is it?" he asked, taking the envelope.

"It's an announcement," he answered. "But don't read it until tomorrow."

"I won't," he said and then, with a distracted look, began turning his head. "That's odd," he said.

"What's odd?" Booth asked him.

"That carriage going there. I could have sworn that was General and Mrs. Grant."

"Where!"

"There—going down Pennsylvania," he pointed. "In the carriage loaded with luggage. They must be leaving town already."

"They can't be!" Booth exclaimed.

"But they are. They're headed straight for the railway station."

"Damn—this is terrible. Are you sure it was Grant?"

"Well, I heard he was supposed to come to the theatre this evening, but I'm sure that's who it was."

Without a word Booth leaped aboard his horse. Digging his heels into the bay mare's flanks, he galloped full speed past the carriage, then pulled up and wheeled around. Guiding the mare slowly back down the avenue, he trotted slowly toward the buggy. His heart was pounding as he leaned over to peer into it.

After it had passed, he sat dazed in the saddle. For a moment he felt lost and confused. Everything had changed. Suddenly his perfect plan had a crack in it, for the man sitting straight and erect in the carriage headed out of town was indeed General Ulysses S. Grant.

\*    \*    \*

Stephen Bedford paced furiously back and forth in his cell until he could take no more. He whisked up his untouched dinner plate and flung it with all his might against the door. The tin dish clanged against the metal door and gobs of potatoes and gravy splattered against the wall.

"Guard!" he shouted through the porthole and kicked the door.

"What is it, now?" The big jailer ambled over to the door. "Don't you ever relax?"

"It's five o'clock!" Stephen boomed. "I've got to get out of here!"

"Well, good luck, mister."

"Look, there are only five hours to go. I've been here all day—isn't that enough!"

"It seems like it's been longer than one day to me," the guard commented. "I never heard such grumbling and yelling in my life."

"This is insane! Let me out of here! I haven't done anything. God knows, I wouldn't kill my best friend!"

"Why don't you hush up for a change, mister?" the guard advised. "Why don't you find yourself a nice corner over there and sit down and read your letter, or something?"

"Read what letter?" Stephen demanded.

"You know, the letter from Mr. Stanton."

"What are you saying? I haven't gotten any letter from Edwin Stanton!"

"Is that a fact? I guess I forgot to give it to you then."

Stephen wanted to reach through the bars and dig his fingers into the guard's throat, but he gritted his teeth and forced himself to remain calm. "Well," he said, simmering with anger, "could you give it to me now?"

"Sure I could; that's what I'm here for. Let's see here

. . .'' He searched his pockets. ''I believe I had it in here somewhere—yeah, see . . .'' He held it up. ''This is it: *Edwin Stanton, Department of War.*''

As soon as a corner of the envelope jutted through the bars, Stephen reached up and snatched it. Then he opened it and read eagerly:

> *Mr. Bedford: Please be advised that while the evidence against you in the death of Mr. O'Connor is meagre and unsubstantiated, I have asked the police to keep you in the Old Penitentiary a while longer—until tomorrow morning, at least. This is a formality. By that time, we should have the real culprit behind bars.*

Stephen looked away and took a deep breath. He forced himself to read the rest.

> *As to the assassination attempt, I assure you I am taking it very seriously. I asked Mr. Lincoln at the cabinet meeting this morning not to go to Ford's Theatre, but he positively refuses to stay home. I managed to talk Gen. Grant into leaving town, hoping that would dissuade the President, but that ploy didn't work. He is determined to go, and without escort. My hands are tied. All we can do is hope that you were mistaken about the plot, or that the plans of your would-be assassins, for some reason, have exploded in their faces.*
>
> E. Stanton.

# Chapter 16

"Close the door, Wilkes," John Harrison Surratt croaked at Booth from his bedroom in his mother's boarding house. "I don't want the other boarders to know I'm here." He cracked open the carpetbag on the bed and spun around toward the dresser.

Booth came in and closed the door softly behind him. For a moment he stood with his back pressed against the birch wood, watching Surratt rifle hurriedly through his dresser drawers. "You're not really going to walk out on us, are you, John?" he asked gravely. "After all the planning we've done?"

The other man strode back to the bed and crammed a white shirt into the carpetbag. "I told you I'd leave if anything went wrong," he explained. "Well, now I'm doing it."

"But nothing has gone wrong," Booth denied. "Michael O'Laughlin is on the train at this very minute. At ten o'clock tonight, he'll step into Grant's car and shoot him."

Surratt looked at him with cold, shifting eyes. "That's too much of a risk for me to take, Wilkes," he claimed. "Without you there to pat his head, O'Laughlin will probably wind up shooting himself in the leg or something. And when they take him off screaming to the police, I want to be as far away from Washington City as I can get."

"Look, John," he advanced, "I'm counting on you to make this plan work. You know how the others are. They'll do what they're told, but they need an example to follow. What do you think they'll do if you leave?"

Surratt shrugged his shoulders. "Why find out, Wilkes?" he said. "Why don't you just give it up? Forget this assassination plot of yours and go back to Baltimore."

"I can't do that." Booth shook his head. "I need to do this. It matters a great deal to me."

"Well, do it without me." He returned to the dresser. "Because all that matters to me right now is a fast horse and an open road."

"You mistake me, Surratt," Booth said seriously. "I'm not asking you to stay—I'm telling you."

"And I'm paying you no attention." He dug down into the drawer.

"John—" Booth's tone changed.

Surratt turned his head and met the business end of a Derringer pistol pointed at his chest. "Now what the devil is that for?" he grumbled.

"It's for you, John," Booth answered coldly. "I'm not going to let you walk out on me like this. I'll put a bullet in your head, first."

"Come on, Booth, you're acting. Put that thing away before you hurt somebody."

"I'm not acting." He gnashed his teeth. "I don't want to hurt you, but I mean what I say. If you make one move toward that door, I swear to God, I'll shoot you."

"You must be crazy," Surratt charged. "You're not going to shoot me down in my own mother's house!"

"I don't care where you are; I'm not letting you ruin my plans."

Surratt hesitated. "Tell me this, Wilkes: what's that little pop gun of yours going to do to me? It may stop me from going, but will it make me kill someone when I don't want to? Do you think anything can make a man do that?"

"I'll do whatever it takes to make my plan work," Booth said.

Surratt studied him for a moment. "Well, it doesn't matter, because you don't have the courage to shoot me anyway," he declared finally. "You've played the parts of heroes so long, you think you are one. Well, I happen to know people, Mr. Actor, and I'm telling you, John Wilkes Booth is no hero."

"You're pushing your luck, Surratt," Booth swore.

Surratt's eyes shot back and forth from the actor to the pistol shaking in his fist. Then, making a show of ignoring both of them, he gathered a leather vest, a pair of black wool trousers, a muffler, and two pairs of socks out of the drawer. "I was wrong—you're not crazy." He brushed past him and stuffed the clothes into his bag. "You're just weak."

"It doesn't take much strength to squeeze this trigger." Booth pulled back the hammer of the Derringer. The faint click of the metal sent a chill down his spine.

"Maybe not," Surratt said, "but it takes more nerve

than you've got." He buttoned up the carpetbag, grasped the handle, and slid it off the bed.

"Don't take another step, John!" Booth warned.

"Climb back on your stage, actor. Real life's too tough for you."

"Surratt!" He raised the Derringer to eye-level.

The other man froze for a second, then abruptly wheeled around toward the door. "Good night, Wilkes." He yanked it open. "And good luck to you. I'll be reading the papers to see how it turns out."

"Surratt—damn it!"

The loud thumping sound of the door slamming behind John Harrison Surratt echoed in the room and sent a shudder straight through Booth's body. Easing down on the mattress, he wrapped his arms around his chest and tried to forget what he had just done—or failed to do. He knew this was no time to reproach himself; it was time to think. He had to adjust the plan, had to find a replacement for Surratt—immediately.

He stood up, began pacing back and forth across the room. When his eyes accidentally lit on a pair of Surratt's shiny boots propped up in a corner, it suddenly came to him what he had to do.


The stout, cherry-faced woman in the lighted doorway of the big house on K Street greeted him with a perplexed look, then smiled tentatively. "I'm afraid Mason is eating supper at the moment, Mr. Booth," she apologized. "But I suppose if you'd like to wait—"

"Thank you," he accepted. "Tell him I must see him now. It's urgent."

Only minutes later Mason Butler slipped into the plush new library where the actor was waiting. He entered with a scowl on his big face. "Just what the hell do you think you're doing, Booth?" he snarled. "Of all times to come to my home—"

"Get your hat and coat, Mason," Wilkes ordered. "We've got work to do."

"I'm not going anywhere," he sneered.

"Yes, you are. You and I are going to a play tonight."

"I don't like parlor jokes, sir."

"I assure you, Mason, I am not joking. We are going to Ford's Theatre."

Butler glanced back at the door, came forward two steps, and said in a whisper, "What are you trying to do, Booth? Get us all hanged?"

"Surratt has backed out," Booth interrupted. "We're going to have to change our plans. Right now."

"Well go ahead and change them; I don't care. You don't need my help to do that."

"I'm afraid we do."

"Look here, Booth," Butler said angrily, "I've done my part."

"And you've done it very well, Mason," he complimented. "Now you're going to do a little more. I'm sorry, but I'm not going to give you the chance to refuse. None of us has a choice."

"You're trying to railroad me, Booth," Mason accused. "Now that something's gone wrong, you think you can drag me into this plot of yours."

"You're already in the plot, Butler," he reminded. "You killed Massey, didn't you?"

"Not so loud—my wife and children are in the dining room across the hall."

"And then you killed the Irishman—"

"Shut up, damn you! You can't barge into my home and talk to me like this!"

"Do you want me to say it louder?" he threatened. "Believe me, I'm desperate enough to shout it if I have to. I'll tell you wife where you get the money to pay for this fine house of yours. How much is it I'm giving you to take care of O'Connor—"

Butler sneered. "You weasel—"

"Mrs. Butler!" Booth yelled toward the door.

"All right, stop it." He held up a hand. "Don't . . . tell her. I'll do what you say. Tell me where to meet you."

"Uh-uh; you're coming with me now. We don't have time to sit around and wait for you to finish your supper."

Butler rubbed his chin. "I'll have to explain to my wife," he said.

"Well, go explain." Booth snapped out his watch. "But make it fast. We only have a little more than two hours to go."


It was just after eight o'clock when little Davie Herold shrank away from the open door and let the actor and Butler into Lewis Powell's room in the Herndon House. As Booth stepped over the threshold and penetrated the bluish cloud of dense smoke, his nostrils burned with the stifling odor of cheap whiskey and bad cigars drifting from the card table where George Atzerodt sat drinking and smoking. But his eyes followed the tall and gaunt Powell, who was stalking back and forth across the hook rug, with his hands rattling the change in his pockets.

"Good evening, gentlemen," Booth greeted them.

"What's going on, Wilkes?" Powell came to a halt. "Where have you been? We've been waiting for an hour."

Booth came out of his overcoat. "I've been talking to John Harrison Surratt," he answered. "I've had to make some adjustments in the plan."

"What kind of adjustments?" Powell glared at him suspiciously. "All we need to do is do it and get it over with. This hanging around is driving me crazy, Booth. I don't know if I can wait another two hours."

The actor flung his coat on the bed. "We have things to talk about, Lewis," he declared. "Surratt has decided to back out."

"I knew it!" Powell exploded. "I told you we couldn't depend on that worm. John Harrison Surratt would betray his own mother if he had half a chance."

"Forget Surratt; he doesn't matter," Booth said calmly. "We have an understudy to take his place."

"Now wait a minute, Booth," Mason Butler anticipated. "If you're talking about me, you can think again. I'm not taking anybody's place."

"We settled this at the beginning, Mason," he reminded.

"Yes, but God damn, man, I've done enough! I'm not going to ruin my career with a pot shot at Abraham Lincoln."

"Listen to this mole, would you?" Powell asserted. "Watch him pull the dirt in after him. He's a coward to the end. He's worse than Surratt."

"Why don't you just worry about yourself, Powell," Booth told him.

"Yeah, myself and Dimwit Davie over there." He gestured with his head at Herold. "That is, if you still want him to tag along with me over to the Seward house."

"We will all do our jobs according to the plan, Lewis," Booth stated flatly. "With no further changes."

"Ah!" he grunted defiantly, turned his back, and strode toward the window.

Butler stirred uneasily. "I don't like this, Booth," he fretted. "Look at these men—drinking, pacing up and down, cowering in a corner. They're falling apart."

"It's nothing but stage fright," said Booth, dismissing the idea. "I've seen it a thousand times."

"Well, I don't want any part of this 'stage fright,'" Butler announced with disgust. "I'm going home."

"Not till you agree to do your job," the actor informed him.

"This isn't going to work, Booth," Butler pleaded.

"It will work!" Booth insisted. "I've planned it to the last detail."

"Well then, let it work without me," he declared and headed for the door.

Booth instantly sprang across the room and snapped Atzerodt's whiskey bottle out of his hands. "Butler!" he yelled and hurled the bottle as hard as he could at the door. It crashed against the facing with a deafening shatter and glass and whiskey exploded everywhere.

For an instant the four men stood silent, staring at the amber-colored liquid dripping slowly down the white walls to the slivers of glass scattered about the oak floor. Then the actor grabbed Butler's shoulder and yanked him back.

"Now," he said to him in a cold, sober voice, "you will do this, Mason, or you will be hanged for the murder of Donald Massey. Which will it be?"

"Look, Booth—"

"Which will it be, damn it!"

Butler clenched his teeth. "What do I do?" he growled.

"That's better." Booth sighed. "At ten o'clock, you will proceed to a particular curtain in Ford's Theatre, pick up a rifle that will be there waiting for you, and you will use that rifle to assassinate President Lincoln.''

"That's all?"

"Yes. That's all."

Butler glanced at the other four men, then turned toward the door. "You'd better know what the hell you're doing, Booth," he mumbled as he left the room.

The actor looked around at the men he had chosen for his assassins. I hope to God I do, too, he thought. Then, to shore up his courage, he sprang to the door and looked out. "You can believe it, Butler!" he called to the clerk. "I know exactly what I'm doing."

An hour later he was jerking back on the reins, pulling his snorting bay mare to a stumbling halt in the middle of Tenth Street. The sight of the President's long black carriage, sitting empty and unattended in front of the lighted building, sent a cold shiver up his spine. It was as if Abraham Lincoln were willingly following his plan. The great man had come to Ford's Theatre this night in order to meet the destiny John Wilkes Booth had created for him. Feeling a sense of power surging inside him, he pricked his spurs into his horse's flanks and spurted toward F Street.

In the alley behind the theatre, he whipped his leg over the mare's rump and slid off the saddle, directly in front of the rear entrance doorway. "Spangler!" he called through the open door. "Ned Spangler! I need someone to hold my horse."

Minutes later, a small, eager-faced young man in a Union cap stuck his head out the door. Booth knew him as Peanuts Burroughs, a playbill distributor for the theatre.

"Ned told me to do it, Mr. Booth." He held his hand out for the reins.

"Hold her tight; she's skittish." The actor handed him the leather and stepped briskly into the building. In the wings he located a worried-looking man in a rumpled and collarless blue shirt. He was huffing and sweating as he hoisted up a scene panel with a rope.

"Ned," said Booth, drawing close to him. "Are you ready to help me?"

"Oh yes, sir," he answered. He strained to raise the panel another three feet. Then he tied off the rope and motioned for the actor to follow him to a dark corner.

"What has happened?" Booth asked anxiously.

"Well, first off, Mr. Lincoln arrived late," Spangler reported in a low voice. "They had to start the play without him."

"As long as he made it," Booth noted.

"Yes, sir. When he walked in, the audience stood up and applauded, and the orchestra played 'Hail to the Chief'—"

"I don't care anything about that. Tell me about Butler—and the rifle."

"Well, the Sharps is behind the curtain, Mr. Booth. But I haven't seen Mr. Butler yet."

Booth's face grew rigid. "What do you mean, you haven't seen him?" he said, holding his voice down. "He is out there, isn't he?"

"Well, yes. I mean, he's supposed to be out there. It's just that I haven't seen him, Mr. Booth. I looked, but it was crowded. Then I had to go back to changing scenes."

"All right, never mind." Booth swallowed drily, he was trying to calm himself, but his pulse was racing. "He's here," he said in a confident voice. "He has to be

Now remember, at ten o'clock, the instant you hear the rifle go off—''

"I know; I turn off the gaslights."

"That's right. It's all you have to do, Ned. But it's crucial. Be sure you do it."

"Oh, I will do it, Mr. Booth," he promised. "Don't worry."

Booth nodded, patted the other man's shoulder, and eased back over to the wings. Out front, he could see Laura Keene strutting back and forth, delivering her lines over the head of Henry Hawk, almost directly to the bearded man in Box 8 above the stage. He strained to see Butler in the audience, but he couldn't find him.

Trying to shake off his fear, he rushed out the rear entrance and hurried around to the front of the theatre. If Butler were in the audience, he reasoned, he would certainly come out with the others at the first act intermission.

"Well, good evening there, Wilkes," Arnold Nelson, the actor, waved a lighted cigar at him. "Out early for a smoke?" he asked, coming up to him.

"A drink, actually," Booth returned, gazing about.

"That's a topnotch play Laura's doing in there," Nelson commented. "Funnier than Ben Jonson, don't you think?"

Booth's attention was fixed on the doors cracking open and the crowd spewing forth. "Yes, I guess it is," he agreed abstractly.

"Do you think the President will come out for a breather?" Nelson asked cheerfully. "Mix with the common folk a while, maybe?"

"What?" Booth said. "Oh, yes, I'm sure he'll be out soon." While he appeared calm, his eyes were frantically searching through the hundreds of faces in the crowd.

"If you ask me, Wilkes," continued Nelson, sucking on his cigar, "Laura's already got old Honest Abe in the palm of her hand. Or somewhere thereabouts." He chuckled through the smoke.

"Who's with him in the box tonight, Arnold?" Booth asked, his eyes constantly scanning the flow of people.

"With who—Lincoln? Oh, that's young Major Rathbone and Senator Harris's daughter Clare. And Mrs. Lincoln, of course."

"Four of them," he mumbled absently.

"What's that?"

"Nothing. Excuse me, Arnold." Booth moved away.

"Hey, Wilkes, it's going to get even better when Laura really warms up," he called after him. "Wait and see."

Booth shoved his way breathlessly through a tangle of arms and legs toward the theatre. He could feel himself getting closer and closer to the edge of panic. A terrible, ghastly idea kept buzzing in his brain. If Butler didn't show up, then the other assassinations would mean nothing! The three deaths John Wilkes Booth had arranged and paid for would become three cold-blooded . . . murders!

He was near distraction when he finally spotted the clerk, slinking away from the others, shrouding himself in a shadow in the alley. Greatly relieved, but still excited, Booth struggled to him through a mass of overdressed and chattering people.

"Did you find the rifle?" he asked him, making sure no one could hear.

"Yeah, I found it," he answered, fidgeting with his tie. "It was just where you said it would be."

"Then there's no problem," Booth said hopefully.

"I still don't like this, Booth," Butler complained. "There are too many people here."

"Pay no attention to them," he instructed. "When you shoot, their eyes will be on the stage. And I will be drinking a whiskey-and-water in front of twenty witnesses at the Star Saloon—"

"What!" Butler gasped. "I thought you were going to be in the box next to Lincoln!"

"Now calm down, Mason. That was before Grant left town. I can't sit up there now, not alone. I need witnesses."

"I don't know, Booth." He shook his head skeptically.

"You don't have to know, Mason. All you have to do is aim and shoot. Everything else is taken care of."

A few minutes later the big doors banged open and the crowd began to shift back toward the theatre. "Go on," he urged the clerk. "Go back in and stand close to that curtain. And remember what will be happening in three other places at the precise moment you squeeze the trigger."

# Chapter 17

Perched on the edge of his cot in the dim light of a cold, damp cell, Stephen Bedford thought he heard a woman laugh. He jumped up, pressed his face against the window of the door, and peered out. All he could see was the long, empty corridor and an oil lamp fastened to the smudgy concrete wall at the end of it.

He raised his watch to catch some of the light. It was 9:32. Was he already too late? he wondered. Were these four great men, like Paddy O'Connor, already lying dead somewhere?

Again he heard sounds drifting down the barren hallway— a seductive little giggle followed by a hard, crude guffaw. He was stunned. The man's laugh he recognized as the guard's. The woman's voice sounded like that of Rebecca Windfield.

Then another shock: splashing into view around the corner of the corridor now was Becky herself, decked out in a scarlet satin dress, trimmed with pink ostrich feathers and cut so low at the neck that half her bosom was bare. She strode along the hall in black net stockings, tying strands of her long blonde hair into a red velvet ribbon.

"You just can't imagine how much I appreciate this, Mr. Haywood," she cooed at he guard as they neared the cell. "But Miss Keene wouldn't have it any other way. She insists this Mr. Bedford is the man who—well, you know, did *that* to her."

"Yeah, I know, but listen, call me Bob, all right?" He grinned. "Remember?"

"Oh, well, of course I remember." She brushed her breasts against his arm as she strolled past him. "Who could forget the name of a big handsome man like you? But first names are intimate, aren't they? And you know what they say about actresses—it takes a mighty long time and a fancy carriage to bring us around."

"Well, listen, I don't have the carriage, but I've sure got plenty of time. That's all you do have down here."

"You're sweet."

"Yes, ma'am." He blushed.

Rebecca stopped a few feet from Bedford, but didn't appear to notice him. "Do you know what, Bob?" She turned to the guard. "I'm really scared. I know it's silly, but after what Miss Kenne said this man did to her . . ."

Stephen stood next to the door in a stupor, amazed to see Becky allowing the guard to reach down and touch the bare skin of her neck with his long index finger.

"Oh, you'll be all right," the guard muttered. "You just let out a holler if he gives you any trouble. I'll fix him."

"Would you really?" She touched his finger with hers. "You wouldn't let anything happen to me?"

He took her finger in his hand and squeezed it. "No, ma'am," he breathed. "Nothing. Not unless I'm the one who does it."

"Well, we'll just have to see about that later, Bob," she teased. "Won't we?"

"Yes, ma'am," he replied eagerly. "We sure will. Now you hurry up in there, all right? I'll be right here, waiting." He gave her a sly, licentious wink as he crammed the big key into the lock.

"Why, thank you, sir," she purred coyly at him and waited for the door to swing open. Then, in a flurry of scarlet satin, she swept past him into the cell. Before Stephen could speak, she was squeezing his arm and tugging him off to a dark corner, out of sight of the guard peeping in through the window.

They spoke in fast, excited whispers.

"Becky, what are you doing here?" he demanded. "Look at you—"

"I thought if you took me for an actress, he might, too."

"But where did you get that dress—"

"I got it from Miss Keene," she answered. "Now forget how I look and listen to me."

"But why are you going to all this trouble, Becky? Why bother—"

"Stephen, will you listen, please? I'm scared. I didn't know what else to do. Fanny's so heartsick she's just wandering around the house—"

"Becky," he interrupted, "they're not going to let me out of here just because you want them to."

"Oh yes, they will," she stated confidently. She leaned against him and began whispering into his ear.

He listened to her for a moment, then shook his head. "Uh-uh," he said. "It won't work."

"Stephen—"

"I don't know."

"Well, we have to do something!"

He glanced at the door. The guard was gone. "He wouldn't believe it," he said.

"Stephen, he'll believe anything!"

He considered her words. After hesitating, he took a deep breath. Then, all of a sudden, he clasped her body against his. Just as abruptly, he kissed her. "Oh God, I want you," he said aloud.

For a moment she caught her breath. "Stephen, what are you doing!" she burst out and tried to turn away. But her jerked her back and began planting wild, passionate kisses all over her face.

As she tried to squirm out of his arms, he stroked her left breast, clutched at it hungrily, and thrust her back against the concrete wall. "Be quiet!" he commanded. "And be still!"

"Stephen, please don't. Oh, God . . ."

He covered her body with his. "You asked for this, lady," he growled. "Strutting around with half your chest bare."

"Stop it!" she screamed. "Take your hands off me! Bob! Bob!"

"Hey!" The guard stuck his face against the bars. "What's all the racket? What's going on in there?"

"Oh, Bob, help me! Make him take his hands off me!"

"All right, mister!" He strained to see around the corner. "Leave the lady alone, do you hear me?"

"Mind your own business." Stephen snatched the hem of her skirt and lifted it up to her waist. "I'll take care of this."

"I said, Leave her alone!" the huge guard roared.

"I'll leave her alone—after I'm through with her," Bedford chuckled.

"Bob, do something!"

"I'm coming, ma'am," Bob yelled. "Hold on!"

The instant the key clanked noisily in the lock, Stephen broke away from Rebecca, ducked under the casement, and waited in a crouch for the door to open. As soon as the guard pulled it and stepped in, Bedford rose up and rammed his boot straight into the man's groin. "Sorry," he grunted.

"Oh—goddamn it—" The guard automatically reached for the spot, dropping the keys to the floor.

As he bent over, Stephen raised his clasped hands over his head and crashed them down against the jailer's neck with a heavy thud. The big man crumbled to the floor under the blow.

"Let's go, Becky." He scooped the keys off the floor. "Hurry, while he's still down!"

"Is he all right?"

"Come on, Becky, let's go!" He yanked her out.

They scrambled through the door before the guard could pick himself off the floor. "Stephen—he's coming!" Becky warned.

Bedford was busy fumbling with the keys. "Damn it—which one is it?" he fretted.

"Stephen—"

"Close the door, Becky!" he yelled.

"Oh Lord!" She froze as she saw the guard charging the door.

"You lying little vixen!" the man fumed at her. "I'm gonna break your neck!"

But just before he reached them, Stephen grabbed the bars and pushed the door shut with a loud, echoing slam. "Try to keep it closed," he told her. "I think I have the right key."

"I can't hold it, Stephen. He's pushing against it. Help me!"

He held the bars with one hand and juggled the key ring with the other. "I've almost got it, Becky," he panted. "There—" he stuck it into the lock. "Damn! I can't turn it!"

"Oh, Stephen."

"Hold it closed, Becky. Push hard!"

"Nobody's gonna make a fool out of me." The guard banged his fists against the door.

"Stephen, we can't keep it closed long enough!"

"Yes, we can. Just keep pushing. All I need is one second to turn the key."

"I'm getting tired."

"We've almost got it—" He made a final heave and twisted the key. The metallic sound of a lock snapping shut made every nerve in his body relax—for a second. Then he grabbed Becky's hand and headed out. "Come on," he said. "Run!"

"Hey!" the guard boomed. "Somebody get me out of here! The prisoner's escaped!"

His voice became thinner as they raced around a corner. Then, as they hustled up a flight of steps and slipped into the second floor corridor, it faded altogether into the damp walls of the Old Pentitentiary.

"You were very good," Stephen complimented Rebecca as they climbed into her open carriage.

"So were you," she returned. "Too good." She pressed her palm against her left breast.

"Sorry—but you said to make it look real." He popped the reins over the horse's rump and the carriage bolted forward.

"Well, it was so real it was scary," she told him. "You don't see *that* in the theatres."

Bedford took out his watch and held it next to the running light on the side of the carriage. "It's 9:45," he said. "I was in there for over twelve hours."

"I tried to get you released, Stephen," she apologized. "But nobody in authority would listen to me. I finally tried to see Mr. Lincoln himself, but I couldn't even get close."

Stephen cracked the whip over the horse's head and closed his eyes and listened to the thumping of her shoes in the dirt. As he thought of Paddy curled up on the cold, damp ground, bleeding, dying, he imagined he could hear his own heart beating in his chest. How perishable human life was.

"Stephen?" Becky said in a low voice. "We will make it, won't we? We will save Mr. Seward and Fanny?"

He smiled to comfort her, but he let the words of her plaintive question sweep away into the black night like leaves in a windstorm. There was no need to speak now. He had no answers for her. All he and Rebecca could do now was to keep looking ahead, and hope they would be in time.

Ten minutes later, while they were racing through the streets of Washington, and John Wilkes Booth stood drinking and waiting at the Star Saloon near Ford's Theatre, two men in overcoats and hats led their rented horses under an oak tree down the street from the Seward residence across from Lafayette Square.

"That's it." Davie Herold pointed at the house from the shadows.

"That's a big place," Lewis Powell commented. "Where do you figure the old man's bedroom is? On the third floor?"

"I don't know," Davie shrugged.

"You don't ever know, do you, Herold?" he said scornfully. "All your head does is separate your ears. Well, here," he said, disgusted, "give me that bottle of medicine. You stay with the horses. I'll go in there alone."

"No," Davie resisted.

"You little idiot—" Powell plucked out a long, bone-handled Bowie knife with one hand and gripped the back of Davie's neck with the other. "Now you listen to me," he sneered as he tucked the point of the glistening blade just inside Herold's nostrils. "One good push and your brains will start spewing out of this nose like water out of a pump."

"Lewis—"

"All you have to do is resist." He slid the blade inside the nose another quarter of an inch. "Just resist, and in she goes."

Gasping for breath, Herold fumbled into his coat for the medicine for a minute and finally handed it to Powell.

"Ah!" Lewis snapped it out of his hand and eased the point of the knife out. "That's a good boy, Davie. Now, all you have to do to earn your money is stay here out of sight while I do the work. Do you understand that?"

"Yes—"

"Good. Because this is a job for a man, not a moron."

Minutes later, with his coat carefully buttoned to shield the Colt revolver and Bowie knife behind his belt, Powell rapped sharply once, twice, three times on the door. He patted the bulge in the wool material and braced himself as the doorknob rattled. The instant the wood moved, he kicked it in with the heel of his boot and pushed into the house.

"I've got some medicine for the Secretary of State," he announced loudly, his eyes following the line of the stairway leading to the bedrooms. "I'm supposed to deliver it in person." He lunged toward the stairs.

"Sir—wait!" the servant Bell called out to him. "You can't go up there!"

"I'm betting his room is on the third floor," Powell muttered. He shoved Bell aside and headed straight across the floor.

"Mr. Frederick!" Bell hollered up the stairs. "Mr. Frederick, come quick! Somebody's in the house!"

With the servant's frenzied shouts ringing in his ears, Powell leaped up the steps two at a time, all the way to the third floor landing. At that point he ran into a small man with thick, curly sideburns.

"What in the hell is going on?" Frederick Seward demanded. "Bell—who is this man!"

"I couldn't stop him, Mr. Frederick." Bell came puffing up the stairs. "He just kept coming."

"I've got some medicine here for the Secretary," Powell told Frederick. "It's from Dr. Verdi."

Frederick eyed him suspiciously. "Well, give it to me, sir," he extended his hand. "I'll see that he gets it."

Powell shook his head. "I'm supposed to give it to him personally," he stated flatly.

"Well, I'm sorry; you can't do that."

"Oh, stand aside, you little snipe."

"Look, sir, Mr. Seward is my father. If you can't leave that package with me, then you needn't bother to leave it at all. Is that clear?"

Powell clenched his teeth and glared angrily at Seward for a few moments, then turned around and looked down the stairs.

Thinking he was about to leave, Bell asked him politely to be quiet going down the steps.

But Powell had no intention of going. With round, glaring white eyes, he split open his coat and snatched the slick maroon handle of the Colt revolver and pulled it out. But at the sound of someone rushing up the walk outside, he froze. He listened through the open front door to the footsteps scuffing across the concrete, then clacking on the oak floor inside. Then he saw a tall young man in a gray suit rushing into the foyer below.

Stephen Bedford came to a stop and looked up. "Frederick! Look out!" he called up to the Secretary's son. "He has a gun!"

As the servant dropped to his knees, Bedford sprinted up the stairs toward the man with the gun. With a wild, dazed look on his face, Powell raised the revolver and held it straight in front of his eyes. Holding his breath for the shot, he aimed the barrel at the new intruder and squeezed the trigger.

As the gun went off, the windows of the old house rattled. And a cloud of white smoke exploded into the air. The tremendous impact of the bullet crashing into Bedford's flesh propelled his body backwards down the steps, to the floor. He was digging his fingers into the searing pain in his shoulder and trying to get to his feet when Rebecca Windfield caught up to him.

"Stephen!" she cried and dropped down beside him. "Oh, God—"

"Get out of here, Becky," he ordered.

"Stephen, you're hurt—"

"Becky, damn it!"

The noise and confusion were rattling Powell's brain. But one idea he held on to: he was there to assassinate William Seward. He didn't care who wanted to get in his way; he was going to do just that. Spinning toward Frederick Seward, he lifted the colt, aimed the black barrel directly at the man's heart and pulled the trigger. But the pistol jammed. Frustrated, he squeezed again. Nothing happened; the hammer wouldn't budge.

"You son-of-a-bitch!" he snarled at the gun. Then, with a low growl, he savagely smashed the heavy butt of the pistol straight down into the center of Frederick's head. The skull bone cracked like a nutshell, and Seward toppled helplessly to the floor. For good measure, Powell stooped over the writhing man and hammered one more punishing blow into the bleeding wound.

"Murder! Murder!" the terrified servant yelled as he scrambled down the stairs. "Someone help us, please! Murder in the house!"

Powell watched Bell scurry past Rebecca and Stephen and burst out into the yard. He held out the bloody pistol and gaped stupidly at it. The thing was useless steel now. He would have to use his knife.

Bounding up to the third floor, he saw a black Union soldier breaking out of a room to his right. Booth had told him Seward kept such a person for a nurse; he quickly concluded the room was Seward's. He headed for it.

"What is this?" the soldier shouted as Powell approached him. "Who fired that shot?"

"Get out of my way, boy." Lewis shoved his way in, swishing at the soldier with his knife. After a close miss, he struck skin and cut a gash just above the brow. As the soldier faltered, Powell stuck his hand into his face and shoved him back against the wall.

Suddenly, a young woman was running toward him out of nowhere, flinging her whole body against him, shrieking, "No, no," and flailing wildly at him with her open palms.

"Get away from me, girl!" He pushed at her.

"I won't let you do it—" Fanny Seward swung her arms hysterically.

"Go away!" Powell slammed his elbow into her bosom and sent her reeling across the room.

With those two out of the way, he could focus his mind on the old gray-haired man curled up in the bed. He looked ridiculous to Powell, propped up against the headboard and trembling like a frightened child under the sheets. "It's your turn now, Mr. Seward," he informed him. "Say your prayers, old man."

Too scared to speak, the Secretary shook his head pleadingly, then drew his knees against his chest and covered his face with his bony arms.

Powell stepped silently to the bed.

As his thigh touched the edge of the thick, high matress, he heard a shuffling sound behind him, then felt the soldier's fingers clutching madly at his coat. Fanny Seward was back again, too, grabbing convulsively at him.

"Stop it!" she cried. "Stop it! Somebody help us! Augustus—help us!"

Sweeping them back again, Powell stretched his long frame over the bed, raised his weapon, and brought it down at Seward's face with a loud grunt. The Secretary turned his face to the side and the razor-sharp blade sliced through his cheek as if it were cutting a loaf of bread. As he groaned in agony and tried to protect the wound, Powell slashed at him again and opened a long and bloody gash beneath his ear. Seward now began to roll back and forth across the bed, trying to avoid the knife. Powell jabbed awkwardly at the moving target, sticking one hole after another into the mattress as he missed.

At last Powell sprang himself completely free of Fanny and the soldier. Like a wild animal pouncing on its prey, he hopped up on the bed and straddled Seward's body. Eagerly, he grabbed a mat of gray hair between his fingers and yanked back the man's head, tightening the skin of the neck like the cover of a drum.

Panting with fatigue, Lewis aimed for the jugular vein and slashed down with the dripping blade of the Bowie knife. To his surprise, the edge of the blade struck a hidden sheet of metal under the collar of his nightgown. He had clanked into the steel brace used to set the neck and jawbone broken in his carriage accident a few days earlier. Angrily Powell snapped the blade away, carving into the sagging flesh of the Secretary's neck as the knife came up.

At the same moment, a thin, bearded man in a blue officer's uniform appeared in the doorway. Without a word Major Augustus Seward exploded into the room and clamped his powerful fingers down on Powell's shoulders. With a mighty heave, he and the black soldier together managed to drag the assassin off the bed and send him crashing to the floor.

But Powell rose up instantly. Grabbing a medicine bottle from the nightstand, he began to pound the hard glass into the heads of both his opponents. The soldier stumbled under a direct hit to the eye and skidded across the floor; the officer staggered back against the door.

"God, I've gone mad!" Powell gasped. He stared unbelievingly at the bloody sight on the bed: Seward's small skeleton lay quivering in the blood-saturated sheets. The man was spitting up gore as he fought for breath. "I'm mad, I'm mad!" He shook his head. "I must be!"

From his left, Augustus suddenly charged again, but Lewis mechanically sent him back with a quick rip into his chin from one sweeping blow of the blade. Then he felt a compulsion to run. Charging out of the room and down the steps, he found a confused-looking man at the front of the stairway holding a stack of messages for the Secretary in his trembling hands.

"Move!" Powell ordered.

"What?"

"I said move, you idiot! Can't you see I'm mad!"

"Where is Mr. Seward—" the messenger blurted, but buckled as Powell rammed his Bowie knife deep into his side.

Powell hurled the bleeding man over the rail and jumped down to the first floor. "I'm mad," he screamed as he dashed out the door. "I'm mad!"

# Chapter 18

"Bartender—bring me a rye whiskey!" Booth called out to the owner of the Star Saloon. He drummed his fingers nervously on the dark walnut bar while the bartender coasted over and poured out his drink. "My watch has stopped, Peter," he said shakily. "What time do you have?"

"I don't know, but I reckon it's about ten or so," he answered. He set the bottle down and stuffed the cork back into the neck with a loud squeak. To confirm his guess, he pulled out his watch. "Yep," he said. "That's right. I've got one minute after."

Booth nodded, and gulped down the strong whiskey in one shot. With the hotness of the liquor still burning his throat, he took a deep breath and braced himself for the alarm in the streets. The explosion of human voices was bound to come at any second. Someone would be bursting out of the theatre shrieking hysterically, 'The President is dead! Lincoln is dead!'

"Give me another one, Peter," he ordered. As the glass filled up, he listened intently for the screams of terror and confusion outside the theatre. But the room, the theatre, the whole city was as still and silent as a corpse.

"Would you like some water with that, Mr. Booth?" the bartender asked casually.

"No," Booth said with a shake of his head. "Look, Peter, are you sure about that time?" he asked. "It seems earlier than that to me."

"No, that's the right time, all right," he replied nonchalantly. "Say, what's the rush, anyway? You wouldn't be meeting one of those fine ladies I'm always hearing about, would you?" He winked.

"No. Not tonight." Booth stared at the whiskey.

"Well, if you do, I wouldn't mind you saying a hello for old Peter Taltavul while you're at it." He grinned. "You just holler if you want another drink," he said as he drifted down the bar to another customer.

Booth raised the glass to his lips, swallowed down the warm, harsh liquid, and lowered the empty container gently to the counter. With his eyes closed, he wrapped his fingers around the glass, gripped it tightly, and counted the seconds. Sixty. Fifty-nine. Fifty-eight. Fifty-seven.

Why wasn't it happening? Why wasn't he hearing the cries of death in the night?

"Peter!" he yelled down the bar. "What time is it now?"

The bartender hesitated, then flipped out his watch. "It's 10:02, Mr. Booth," he replied. "Going on 10:03."

The numbers scorched into his brain. He knew now that something had to have gone wrong! Slapping two quarters down on the bar, he stormed out of the saloon and headed for Ford's Theatre. Passing by the President's carriage, he leaped upon the planks in front of the building and ducked inside the front door. Immediately he heard the audience roar with laughter at the play.

When he saw Ned Spangler off to his left, he quickly motioned for him to come over. "What's wrong, Ned?" he whispered to him. "What's holding him up? Why hasn't he shot?"

"I don't know, Mr. Booth," he answered worriedly. "I've been standing here waiting to turn off the gaslights, but he hasn't even moved!"

"I'll see if I can find him," Booth said. "Meanwhile, you keep an eye on the stage clock. Keep me posted on the time."

"Yessir."

The actor slipped quietly through the theatre doors and scanned the audience. To his right he could see the great man in his balcony box. He was leaning over the arm of his private rocking chair, smiling as he whispered something into Henry Rathbone's ear. Below the President's box, on the stage, Henry Hawk was booming out his 'American Cousin' lines to Laura Keene in an affected rural accent. In front of the big platform sat the spectators in the dim light, totally engrossed in the play. He searched the dark sea of faces for a minute or two, but he could not see Mason Butler.

Where was he?

As the audience erupted again, Booth shut the noise out with the door. Too nervous to stand there any longer, he stalked out of the building. Out in the cool air, he noticed a dark cloud passing in front of the bright moon. The sombre appearance of the sky sent a chill through him. He buttoned his coat to the neck and looked back at the theatre building.

What was Butler waiting for? Why hadn't he fired the shot?

He waited. Time and motion seemed to freeze. The dark, still streets looked like the evil paths of a ghostly city. The only motion he felt was his own pulsating heart, thumping in his chest, beating faster and faster with each passing second.

"It's 10:07, Mr. Booth," said Spangler, sticking his head out the door. "What are we going to do?"

Just as he was about to answer, he caught sight of a big, dark-suited man slithering out of the other door. Without hesitation he sprinted briskly across the planks and thrust himself in his path.

"Butler!" He grabbed his arm. "What are you doing!"

"Take your hands off me." Mason snapped loose. "And keep your voice down," he whispered. "You're not acting in a play here."

"What are you doing out here!" Booth said excitedly. He was trying to control his temper. Since there were people loitering nearby, he wouldn't let himself explode in anger.

"I'm going home, Booth," the other man answered. "This plan of yours smells. I don't want any part of it. I was crazy to agree to do it in the first place."

"But you *must* do it!"

"Get out of my way." The clerk started to go.

"Mason—" Booth blocked him. "What do I have to do to convince you? You can't back out. It'll ruin everything!"

"It won't work, Booth."

"It will work! If you follow the plan—"

"Oh, to hell with your plan. It's stupid."

"Mason, listen to me," the actor pleaded desperately. "If Lincoln doesn't die, then the other deaths will mean nothing. Don't you understand? We'll be nothing but murderers!"

"So what?"

"For God's sake, man—"

"Look, Booth. If you want Abraham Lincoln dead, then go in there and shoot him yourself. I'm leaving."

"You're a coward, Butler!" he accused.

"That's not me you're talking about," Mason said coolly. "It's you. You don't have the courage to shoot him. You're like every other actor in the world. You can't do anything but talk."

"I've put everything I have into this, Mason—"

"Then it's left up to you to do it, all by yourself. Go ahead—try it. Get yourself caught."

"If I am caught, remember this: I'll bring you down with me, Butler. I swear to that."

"Mr. Booth?" Spangler came out of the theatre. "It's ten minutes past ten."

"Which means," Butler noted, "it's probably too late for anybody to do it, anyway. So if you gentlemen will excuse me . . ." He tugged the lapels of his coat together, bowed his head, and marched away.

"Mr. Booth?" Spangler eyed him curiously. "Are you all right?"

"Get out of here, Ned," he ordered. "I'm going to do it myself. I don't care what happens."

"Mr. Booth, you don't know how to use a gun—"

"I know enough. Mason was right. I have been taking

the coward's way, trying to get other people to carry out my plan.''

''Mr. Booth—''

''Go on, Ned,'' he urged. ''Get as far away from this place as you can.''

Spangler hesitated a moment, then struck off for a dark alley down the street.

After the scene shifter had disappeared into the darkness, Booth pushed through the front door again. Inside the theatre, at the foot of the steps leading up to the balcony, he paused. As the audience snickered at one of Laura Keene's saucy lines, he decided it would be insane to kill Lincoln now. All he had was a single-shot .44-calibre Derringer in his vest pocket and the Bowie knife his brother had given him tucked down in his boot. If he were to try it, it would have to be done within a range of two or three feet. That close to the target, he would never be able to escape.

But then he thought of the other assassins: Azterodt and Powell and O'Laughlin. By now they had done their parts; each had killed his man. Without the shelter of his plan, they would be arrested and convicted. How could he let them hang for carrying out his orders? Seven useless deaths would be on his head. It would be too much to live with.

No. He had no choice. It had to be done—now. As he climbed swiftly up the stairs, he roughed out a new plan. He would gun down the President in his box, at close range. Then, when Ned cut the lights, he would leap down to the stage and grope his way to the rear entrance and escape into the night. He was very familiar with the layout of the theatre. It could work—

''Excuse me, sir,'' a policeman startled him at the top of the steps. ''I'm afraid no one's allowed past this point.''

From the first time in his life, Booth's voice failed him. He could only swallow and cough in reply.

"Sir?" The policeman looked at him askance.

The actor thought quickly. He pulled out one of his visiting cards and handed it to the policeman.

"Ah, Mr. Booth," he said, reading the ornate signature. "I thought it was you."

"I . . . have a box down the hall," he said.

'Yessir, I know. It's Number Seven, isn't it?''

Booth nodded.

"Well, you better hurry if you want to see much of the play, Mr. Booth," he advised. "They're already in the second act."

"Yes, thank you."

The policeman moved aside and John Wilkes Booth stepped into the long, narrow hallway leading to the President's box. The two or three yards down the corridor seemed to take forever to walk. But he finally reached the closed door of Box 8. Lincoln was near, he told himself—no more than a breath away.

As he passed his right hand inside his coat and wrapped his trembling fingers around the warm, slick walnut handle of the Derringer, a strange and eerie sound went off in his head. For a moment he thought he heard the crack of a pistol in the air, above his left ear; then the mewling cries of women seemed to seep out of the walls and ceiling—

A gasp of breath later, though, all he could hear was Henry Hawk blustering out a comic line down on the stage below and the audience responding to it with peals of laughter. He shut his eyes and charged his lungs with air. His frightened mind was playing tricks with his senses. To do this great deed, he would have to control his fear and dread.

Feeling a dry constriction in his throat, he drew out the pistol from behind his belt. With the sensation of the gun still bulging against his stomach, he pushed the corrugated hammer back with his left thumb. Then he lowered himself to his knees, to peer through the hole Surratt had bored that morning.

Through the opening in the thin wood, he could see Clara Harris in the farthest corner of the box, poised very properly in a maroon velvet chair; to her left, on the sofa, was Major Rathbone. Next to him, Mrs. Lincoln was holding herself erect in a cane chair beside the President. They all sat like statues in a museum, rapt in the action of the play.

Booth got to his feet, sucked in a long, deep breath, released it haltingly, and placed the flat of his hand against the door. Once again, somewhere in the recesses of his mind, he heard a single shot exploding and echoing— followed by the sobs and sighs of heartbroken mourners all around. To shake away the fantasy, he looked down at the barrel of the Derringer. The hard reality of the steel object he was gripping in his fist made him quiver.

Could he actually do it? Was John Wilkes Booth, actor, capable of shooting down a man in cold blood?

He didn't know. But he knew he had to try. At any moment the audience would begin to agitate excitedly with the news of the deaths of Johnson, Seward, and Grant. When that happened, his great opportunity to bring the corrupt Union government to its knees in one grand and dramatic blow for freedom would be lost forever. He had to act now.

Moving softly and deftly, he shoved the door in a ways and slipped his body quietly through the crack, into the cool little box. Rathbone, his fiancée, and Mrs. Lincoln were laughing at the buffoonery of Henry Hawk below; the President was leaning his head over the railing, to catch a better view of the actors.

No one in the box saw him take his three steps forward and pause a foot behind Lincoln's walnut rocking chair. And, in the turmoil of the noisy performance, no one heard the wheezing of his lungs as he raised the Derringer to the level of Lincoln's head. In a low voice Booth timidly spoke his name. Getting no response, he said again in a louder voice, "Mr. President?"

As Abraham Lincoln, still grinning at Henry's antics, spun his body around, Booth felt the end of the barrel bump against his head. He nestled it into a mat of the President's hair, just behind the left ear, and curled his index finger around the curved metal in the guard—

"God save the country!" he proclaimed and squeezed the trigger.

Out of an ear-splitting crack and a choking blast of white smoke, the soft-lead, .44-calibre bullet burst with a low-sounding *thump* into Lincoln's skull. In a single beat of his heart, the leaden slug burrowed deep into bone and muscle, drilled straight through the compact tissues of the brain, and lodged itself in a soft little mass of shattered cartilage, just above the right eye.

All of a sudden, with one quick snap of his finger, he had turned the man he'd seen as the great oppressor of the South into nothing more than a limp and useless mass of flesh slumping in a chair. Dropping the smoking pistol to the floor, Booth dug his fingers into the President's coat and yanked him out of the way. He looked at the others in the box. Clara Harris and Mrs. Lincoln were covering their faces in terror and squealing hysterically; Major Rathbone was edging toward him with fire in his eyes.

"You maniac!" the officer barked. "What have you done!"

Booth could hear behind him, below the box, the audience stirring in confusion. Someone was shouting, "Look up there—in the President's box!"

"What's he doing!" another cried.

"God help us! Someone's shot the President!"

Excited and desperate, Booth reached down to his boot and jerked out his Bowie knife. "Get out of the way, Major," he threatened with it. "I'll use this, too."

"You maniac! I'll tear you apart!"

"No, Henry—don't!" His fiancé clutched madly at his coat. "Don't go near him, please!"

"Let me go, Clara! The man's a murderer!"

"No!" She tugged at him, but he managed to pull away.

As he pounced, the actor retreated two steps and swished the blade back and forth through the air to ward him off. "Stay away from me!" he warned. But Rathbone inched forward until the two men close enough to touch. Booth slashed the knife at the other man's chest; the major shielded his heart with his left arm and caught the ripping edge of the blade in the flesh beneath his elbow.

"Henry!" Clare Harris clasped his other arm and pulled him away.

Booth turned from Rathbone to the man he had shot. He was lying unconscious in Mary Lincoln's arms. "Somebody help me, please!" she was crying as she cradled his head. "He's dying. He's dying!"

For an instant he felt compelled to explain to her his deed. But there was no time. He sprang to the railing and looked down. All eyes in the audience were fixed on him.

Why hadn't Spangler turned off the lights? Why had everything gone wrong?

"Look!" a shout rang out from below. "There he is—on the railing!"

"Villain! Murderer!"

"Look out, he's going to jump!"

As the actor climbed over the railing, the bleeding Rathbone broke away from Clara's grip and pinched the corner of his coat. Knocked off balance, Booth rolled over the iron and snagged his right spur in the flag of the Treasury Guard fastened to the railing. Then down ten feet he fell to the stage below, his left leg twisting and crunching under the weight of his body as he crashed to the floor.

With a burning, agonizing pain rippling up and down his leg and hip, Booth struggled to his feet. In front of the stunned and silent audience, he raised his bloody Bowie knife above his head. *"Sic semper tyrannis!"* he shouted and started to hobble off to the left of the stage.

By now the audience was a chaotic mass of movement, confusion, and noise. "Somebody do something!" a woman screeched. "He's killed the President! Can't somebody stop him?"

"Hang him! Hang him!" another yelled.

"Burn the theatre!" a soldier hollered. "Kill all the rebels!"

Suddenly, a gray man in black hopped on the stage. "Stop that man!" he shouted, pointing at Booth. "Stop him! I know him! That's John Wilkes Booth!"

With a fiery pain throbbing through the muscles of his leg with each step, the actor staggered breathlessly into the wings. Just past the curtain, William Withers, the orchestra leader, was standing bewildered in his path.

"Move!" Booth commanded. "Let me pass!"

"Wilkes—"

"I said, Let me pass!" Booth slashed madly at his breast with the knife. The blade slit through his vest and shirt. As Withers wheeled around, the actor whacked the flat side of the knife into the back of his neck and sent him to the floor.

"My God, William—" he stared at the musician sprawled on the floor. He wanted to pause, but couldn't; the audience was converging on the stage behind him, now and one man was in pursuit. He had to run.

He stumbled awkwardkly down a dark passageway, turned a corner, and crashed headlong into another body in the way. As he automatically raised his blade to strike him down, the other man snapped hold of his wrist.

"Mr. Booth!" he shouted. "It's me—Ned Spangler!"

"Ned!"

"Mr. Booth—we forgot the lights!" he cried in tears. "When you told me to leave, we forgot we had to turn off the lights!"

"Let me get by, Ned." He shoved him away.

"Oh Lord, Mr. Booth, I'm sorry!"

"Keep them away from me, Ned," he cried and pushed his way toward the rear entrance. At his back he could hear his pursuer, huffing toward him, alerting everyone, "Stop him! Stop him! That's John Wilkes Booth!" He had to move faster than he ever had, despite the broken leg—

Crashing through the rear door, he discovered Peanuts Burroughs sitting on a box next to the wall in the alley and holding the bay mare by the reins.

"Mr. Booth!" He jumped up. "What's wrong? What happened!"

"Give me my horse!" He plucked the reins out of his hand and flipped them over the horse's head.

"But you're hurt—" Peanuts grabbed the bit. "You can't even walk. You're in no shape to ride a horse."

But Booth thrust his torso over the saddle and swung his leg over the hindquarters of the frightened horse. "Let go of my horse, Burroughs!" He reached down and whacked the other man's temple with the handle of the knife. When Burroughs let go of the bit, the mare began snorting wildly and twisting around the alley in circles.

"Booth!" his pursuer cried as he burst out of the theatre door. Pausing only for a moment, he raced across the alley, yelling "Stop!"—and hurled his body toward the spinning horse.

Just as he bumped against her flanks, Booth straightened the reins and spurred his horse away from him and out of the alley, down F Street and toward the Capitol. Giving the frightened mare her head, he grasped a handful of mane in his fist and tried to stay in the saddle.

Wheeling down Sixth Street from Pennsylvania Avenue, he finally managed to cram his left boot into the flopping stirrup. When he caught sight of the Navy Yard bridge a while later, he reined the horse down to a walk and tried hard to pull his thoughts and emotions together. To get past the sentry, he was going to have to act as if he were out for nothing more than a casual ride.

"Good evening, Sergeant," Booth tried to speak warmly to the stocky young man braced stiffly in front of the crossbar to the bridge. His words sounded forced and hollow to him, but he remained poised in the saddle.

"What's your name, sir?" The sentry ceremoniously crossed his chest with his rifle.

"The name is Booth, Sergeant," he answered. "May pass, please?"

The guard eyed the bay mare closely. "Looks like

you've been riding her pretty hard there, Mr. Booth,'' he noted. ''You must be in a hurry.''

''Of course I'm in a hurry,'' he replied quickly. ''It's half-past-ten and I'm not home yet. Who wouldn't be?''

''Would you mind telling me where your home is, Mr. Booth?''

''I live in . . . Charles County,'' he said. ''Now would you let me by? I have people waiting there for me.''

''In town or in the country?'' The sentry touched the sweaty mare with the tips of his fingers. ''I don't remember seeing you cross before.''

''I live close to Beantown, Sergeant,'' he stated with a tone of impatience. ''And if you don't mind, I'm anxious to get there.''

''Yes, sir. I was wondering if you knew nobody's supposed to cross this bridge after nine o'clock.''

''All I know is, I've been waiting half the night for the moon to come out so that I could see to ride home. And now you're standing in front of the bridge, blocking my way. Now tell me, why would you want to keep a gentleman from his home at this time of night?''

The sentry scratched his chin thoughtfully. ''Well,'' he decided, ''you do look like a gentleman, it's true. I suppose it'll be all right, this one time.''

''Thank you, Sergeant. You're very kind.''

While Booth listened apprehensively in the silent night for the sound of pursuing hoofbeats behind him, the sentry very deliberately slid the wooden crossbar to the side. Then, at last, Booth was nodding congenially at him and trotting the mare across the rickety old bridge into Maryland. Once out of sight of the guard, he ran her up to full speed and headed down Bryantown Road.

He was following John Harrison Surratt's escape route:

south to John Lloyd's tavern at Surrattsville for supplies, then north to Baltimore on the Port Tobacco Road. But he knew he would never make it that far with a broken leg. After the tavern stop, he would go south a few miles, to the home of Dr. Samuel Mudd. Since the doctor was a staunch Southerner, he would probably jump at the chance to do what he could for the assassin of Abraham Lincoln.

A mile farther down the road he yanked back on the reins and brought the mare to a stop. His leg was on fire, and his mind was burning and swarming with a mad confusion of images and sounds. In the pale glow of the moonlight on the dirt road, he slumped over the pommel of his saddle and wrenched his face in pain.

As he lay with his cheek against the mane and his palm on the warm, moist neck, the gruesome reality of what he had just done suddenly exploded in his mind. In one terrible revulsion, he relived the scene. He felt the heft of the Derringer in his fist, the stinging backlash of the detonating bullet, the splatter of splintered bone and mangled flesh and hair on his trembling fingers.

In a spasm of pain Booth bent over low and emptied his stomach. As the liquid splashed in the dirt below, the horse started. Booth stretched and vomited again. But it didn't help. His body was cold, nauseous, covered with a clammy sweat. He would never be able to shake the sickening truth of what he had done. John Wilkes Booth had committed a murder—and for that ghastly act against man and God, he knew he was damned forever.

Gripping his churning stomach with both hands, he dropped his face into the thick coarse hair of the mane and waited for the other assassins to come.

# Chapter 19

Feeling woozy, Stephen Bedford gradually became aware of a tall, strong man with fluffy whiskers helping him to his feet, then of a noisy rabble scurrying wildly around him in the Seward house. As his mind cleared, he heard the frantic movement of a crowd buzzing with restless excitement outside the front door.

"You'll be all right," the man assured him. "The bullet went straight through. Here—" He quickly wrapped a cloth around his shoulder and tied it tight. "This will stop the bleeding."

"Thank you." Stephen found his balance. "I appreciate it."

The man turned to the servant of the Seward house. "Which floor is Dr. Verdi on?" he asked him.

"He went up to three, with Mr. William." He pointed up the stairs.

"How many are wounded, Bell?"

"There's wounded people all over the house, Dr. Barnes," he answered. "Half a dozen, maybe. That man just plain went crazy, cutting up everybody he could reach."

"Well, call me if I'm needed down here," he said and headed up the steps.

As Bell started to leave, Bedford grabbed his arm. "Bell," he asked him, "where's Becky?"

"Sir?"

"Where is Miss Windfield?" She was standing right here, not ten minutes ago."

The servant's eyes fell to the floor. "She's gone, Mr. Bedford," he said.

"Well, I can see that. Where did she go?"

Before he could answer, the big front door banged open and slammed against the facing as Edward Stanton and a handful of men in expensive dark suits stormed in.

"Where is Mr. Seward?" Stanton demanded of Bell.

"He's right up there," Bell replied and slipped away into the congested foyer.

As the Secretary of War started for the stairway, he stopped with his eye on Stephen. "What are you doing here, Bedford?" he said. Without waiting for an answer, he growled, "Never mind. I'll get to you later."

"Mr. Stanton—what about the President!" Stephen asked. "Is he all right?"

"Of course he's all right," he countered. "He's at Ford's Theatre, where he's supposed to be. Thank God."

"But if someone tried to assassinate Mr. Seward—"

"That's enough, Bedford," he cut him off. "Those

people out there are ready to panic now. Don't encourage them.''

''Mr. Secretary?'' someone bellowed from the top of the stairs down to Stanton. ''Mr. Seward is asking for you.''

''How does he look?''

''He looks bad, sir.''

''All right, I'm coming. Thomas, Coolidge,'' he ordered two men, ''I want you to keep that door closed. Don't let another soul into this house unless I say so.''

''Mr. Stanton—''

''I said later, Bedford.'' He clambered up the stairs.

Stephen waited until Stanton and three other men had reached the first landing, then he turned and plowed his way through a mass of people in order to reach Bell, retreating across the room.

''William,'' he struggled to reach the servant. ''You didn't answer me.''

Bell swallowed as Bedford spun him around. ''I'm sorry, Mr. Bedford,'' he apologized. ''But Miss Windfield went with them.''

''Went with who!''

''The killers!''

''What! Now look here, Bell—''

''There wasn't anything I could do about it, Mr. Bedford. There were these two killers together in front of the house. The one with the knife and another one. And Miss Windfield was with them. Then they split up.''

''Bell, if you're lying to me—''

''No, sir, I swear I'm not lying. She rode off with one of them. Plain as day I saw it.''

''All right. Which way did they go?''

"It looked to me like they were going south, Mr. Bedford."

Stephen released Bell's arm and forced his way to the front door. When he stepped outside, he met the frightening mass of some two hundred people, pushing and shoving loudly and violently toward the Seward house. He searched their faces in vain for Rebecca. In the few minutes he had been nearly unconscious, the woman he loved had completely disappeared into the night. Was she Booth's hostage, he wondered, or had she gone of her own free will? He struggled to put that thought out of his mind.

Suddenly a man on a black horse thundered through Lafayette Park, came to an abrupt halt, and bounded to the street. Frantically he began gouging his way through the crowd toward the house.

"Let me through!" he yelled in a panic. "I have a message for Mr. Stanton!"

"Hey, look out!" Someone rammed his chest with an elbow.

"Yeah, watch where you're going, sport—"

Still he pressed on. "I've got to see Mr. Stanton!" he cried desperately. "It's terrible! It's terrible!"

After a minute he had dug his way to the front door. At that point Stephen Bedford reached out and grabbed him. "Hold it!" He squeezed his arms. "What is it? Is it the President?" he demanded.

The man nodded his head, gulping for breath. Then he gasped, "The President's been shot!" he wailed. "God help us all. Abraham Lincoln is dying!'

An hour later Stephen stood in the midst of an agitated throng of people outside William Peterson's house on

Tenth Street, where Lincoln had been taken. At this moment the crowd was holding still, rumbling quietly as they waited for news of the President. But he could feel the crisp night air teeming with their anger and outrage at what had happened. They appeared ready to erupt at any moment, at any provocation.

"They're saying the one who shot the President was John Wilkes Booth," a man next to Stephen commented. "But they don't know who killed the Sewards," he added.

Bedford recognized him as the clerk at the National Hotel. "Nobody killed the Sewards, O'Leary," he corrected. "They're badly injured, but they're alive."

"Well, Captain Bedford," he acknowledged, "I didn't know that was you. Tell me, what do you make of all this coldblooded killing? It fairly scares a man to his soul, don't it, sir? And to think the lad was right there in my hotel, not more than a few hours ago. It's all like an ungodly dream, isn't it?"

"Yes, it is," Stephen agreed.

"And now I hear they're going to murder the Cabinet, and then blow up the Capitol. Saints in heaven, sir, it looks like the whole world's coming apart."

Stephen nodded, not bothering to correct the rumors. He kept his eyes glued on the front steps of the Peterson house. Any second now someone would be coming out to make an announcement.

O'Leary gazed restlessly around the crowd. "Where's old Patrick O'Connor, Captain?" he asked. "Haven't seen him at all today."

Stephen looked at him. "Paddy's dead, O'Leary," he said.

"Patrick O'Connor dead? Now that can't be, Captain,"

he said unbelievingly. "What on earth could kill that big ox?"

"Not what, O'Leary—who. Paddy was murdered last night."

"Mother of God!" He crossed himself. "What is going on in this place, Captain? Is the world coming to an end? Where is it all leading?"

"I wish I knew, O'Leary."

Suddenly a hush fell over the crowd as a bulky, well-dressed man in a tall hat appeared on the balcony of the second floor. He stared at them with a glum face, then very slowly peeled off the hat.

"Ladies and gentlemen," he spoke reverently, "a bulletin will be published later with the details of this calamity. In the meantime, Mr. Stanton wants me to make this statement: The President has been shot in the head by the actor John Wilkes Booth. A large calibre bullet is now lodged in his brain. According to his attending surgeons, there is absolutely no hope of recovery."

A woman cried out in grief. Others followed.

"Damn Booth!" a man cursed. "Damn his black soul!"

"And damn the South, too!" another yelled. "They did it to him!"

"Why don't you go after him?" a woman wailed. "Hunt them down! Get them before they get us!"

"She's right, men—we're all in danger."

"Let's go get them then!"

"Find your horses and let's ride. Death to Booth and the other assassins!"

While the excited, confused mob began to splinter away from the house in a hundred different directions, Stephen turned south, toward Pennsylvania Avenue. After only a few steps he bumped into a big man in a black three-piece suit.

"Well, if it isn't Mr. Bedford." Mason Butler stood with his arms crossed, grinning widely. "Escaped from jail."

"I'm sorry, Mr. Butler, I don't have time to talk—" Stephen tried to sidestep him.

But Mason cut him off. "You'd better make time, Bedford," he said. "That police officer standing over there is waiting for my signal to have you arrested and taken back to your cell."

Stephen glanced at the policeman, then sighed resignedly. "What do you want, Butler?" he asked. "I've got to go—"

"You're not going anywhere, Captain," he stated as he held up a finger. "Nobody can leave the city. All exits have been blocked. There is no way out."

"I'll find a way."

"I want you to stop and look at these people around you, Captain," he advised. "There's blood in their eyes. They want somebody to hang. I believe a Confederate officer that murdered his best friend will do as well as any."

Stephen clenched his teeth. "I didn't murder Paddy," he stated flatly. "Mr. Stanton knows that."

"At the moment he's forgotten you exist, so I have charge here. One word from me and you're back in jail. On the other hand, one word to these people here and you're staggering up the gallows with a rope around your neck."

"Just what are you getting at, Butler?"

Mason rubbed his chin thoughtfully. "Mr. Stanton is sending a detachment of federal troops out tomorrow morning,'' he said. ''Since he's assigned me to this case, I expect to be prominent in that detachment. I want you to ride with us.''

''Why?''

''Let's say I respect your instincts. After all, you did predict this would happen.''

''That's not the reason.''

He laughed shortly. ''No, there is something else. Mr. Stanton is offering nearly $100,000 reward for Booth and his cronies. Unfortunately, as an employee of the War Department, I'm not allowed to collect that reward—''

''I don't give a damn about any reward, Butler!''

''Yes, but I do. You see, after all this, when I run for a public office, I will need a great deal of campaign money.''

''And you want me to collect this reward and give it to you,'' he guessed.

''Let's say we will share it, Captain.''

Bedford gripped his fists until his knuckles turned white. ''I wouldn't share a match with you, Butler.''

''Think about it, Captain.''

''I don't have to think about it.''

''You're proud and stupid, Bedford,'' Butler said angrily. ''You deserve to waste your life in a cell.''

An instant after Butler raised his hand, Bedford felt four hard hands clamp down his arms. He twisted to get loose, but the two officers were too strong to budge. ''Butler—'' he threatened.

''Take him away,'' Mason ordered. ''And don't tell anybody where he is.''

''Wait a minute!'' Bedford grunted.

''Are you agreeing to the proposition, Captain?'' Mason pressed.

''How can you think of money—''

"Are you *agreeing!*"

"All right, damn it. I agree," Stephen said, thinking that perhaps, after all, this might be his best chance to find Becky. At the moment it seemed wisest not to mention her to Mason Butler.

Butler nodded for the soldiers to let him go. "Now we can track down this vile creature Booth and shoot him like an animal," he said to Bedford. "I never knew the man, of course, but I happen to believe that no coldblooded murderer has any justification for living."

"He won't be shot down," Stephen declared. "He'll be brought back and tried for his crime. In a court of law he will reveal every person involved in this assassination plot, and they'll be tried, too."

Butler swallowed hard and shifted his weight. "We all want justice," he offered shakily. "But first things first. The posse forms at dawn, Mr. Bedford. In front of the War Department."

"I'll be there."

"In the meantime, if you try to leave town—"

"I've agreed to your proposition, Butler," he declared, walking away. "I said I would be there, and I will."

He started for the National Hotel. There, away from the chaos of these two attempted assassinations, maybe he could shut out the horror of the past two days and rest—

But even as that thought occured to him, he knew he wouldn't be able to sleep this night. Instead, he would spend some of the long, dark hours mourning the death of a friend and the passing of a great man.

The rest of the time he would be thinking of Rebecca Windfield.

\*     \*     \*

When Becky's stolen horse thundered to a stop in front of John Wilkes Booth outside the tavern at Surattsville an hour later, the actor shot her a cold, ruthless look.

"What the devil are you doing here?" he demanded. "And why are you dressed like that?"

"I didn't ask to come, Mr. Booth," she retorted, "so I didn't get to choose what to wear."

Davie Herold spoke up as he slipped down from his horse. "Lewis told me to bring her," he explained. "He said take her for a hostage, so I did."

"And where is Lewis?" Booth asked, his eyes still on Rebecca.

David shrugged. "We got separated," he answered. "He must've got lost or something."

Booth turned his head toward Herold and winced under a wave of pain. "Well, let's forget Lewis Powell," he said. "Go inside and get the supplies. I'll watch her."

Becky sat shivering in the cool night air as Booth took the reins of her horse and Davie scampered away into the tavern. After a time, she ventured in a shaky voice, "Is what he said true? Did you really have President Lincoln shot?"

"No," he answered. "It didn't work out that way. I shot him myself."

"Dear God!"

"I don't expect a Northerner to understand."

"I understand that you ended a man's life. A great man—"

"Abraham Lincoln was a tyrant, Miss Windfield," Booth said wearily. "Tyrants must be assassinated."

"You can't really believe that ridiculous idea justifies murder!"

"It was not a murder. It was an assassination." He

wrapped the reins around his fist. "There is no similarity between the two acts."

As the moon glided out from behind a cloud, she got a better look at him. His face looked twisted in anger in the ghostly light; a mere glance at it made her shudder. Only a short time ago he had been so calm and poised and handsome. It was strange how long ago that seemed.

"Just what do you intend to do with me?" she asked him.

"I don't know," he replied sharply. "I can't think clearly with this pain. We'll just wait for Davie."

Minutes later Herold raced out of the tavern with a rifle and whiskey, grabbed Rebecca's reins, and hopped aboard his horse. Then, with Booth leading the way, the three riders broke off the main road and headed down a winding path into the dark forest. After four torturous hours of galloping in and out of the shadows of trees, they finally drew up in front of a rambling white farmhouse.

Huffing and groaning, Booth slid off the mare, supporting himself with a hard grip on the mane. "Get down, Miss Windfield," he told her.

"What is this place?" she resisted.

"It's a doctor's house," he said. "Now please, get down."

Encouraged by the thought of seeing someone other than these two men, Becky climbed down and straightened the hem of her red satin dress.

He eyed her suspiciously. "If you're thinking of appealing to these people for help," he warned her, "remember this: once they know who we are, they automatically become accessories to a crime. In the eyes of the law, they will be traitors."

She nodded.

"And if you try to escape, we will have to shoot every person we meet, in order to cover our trail. Do you understand?"

"I can't believe you're the same person I talked to in that hotel room." She regarded him curiously. "How could anyone so sensitive be capable of doing what you've done?"

"Give me a hand, Davie," he ordered, ignoring her.

"If you really believed that what you did was justifiable," she pressed, "you wouldn't be slinking through the woods in the dark, would you? You'd stand up and be proud of it."

"I am proud of it!" he blurted. But his words sounded sad and empty to her.

At the door they were met by a tall, stern-looking man with a high forehead, thin, curly grayish hair, and a full black moustache and goatee. "Come in," he said solemnly and backed up a few steps.

"My name is Harris, Dr. Mudd," Davie announced. "This here's Mr. Boyd—"

"I don't need to know your names." He helped David drag Booth over to the sofa.

"My horse fell," Booth grimaced. "We were on our way—"

"I will ask you not to tell me anything else." Mudd knelt on the floor to examine the injury. "You're a patient, and I'm going to treat you. That's all any of us has to know. Here, help me get him upstairs. This leg is badly swollen; I'll have to cut his foot out of the boot."

"Well, get on with it, Doctor," Booth moaned. "I can't take much more of this pain. I think the bone has already cut through the flesh."

"It probably has." He raised the actor to his feet. "You should've had it tended to immediately."

As the doctor and Herold carted Booth up the stairs, they passed a small compact woman in a pale blue sleeping cap and night robe. Her eyes followed the men for a moment, then she looked down disapprovingly at Rebecca's low-cut dress.

"Are you with them?" she said drily.

Becky's breath quickened. In a heartbeat she could explain to this woman who they were and what had happened. But then she remembered what Booth had told her. She had no right to drag an innocent person into this terrible business. After thinking about it, she swallowed and nodded.

"Well," the woman said coldly, "it's no concern of mine." She came slowly down the steps. "I'll have to make a fire," she said. "He looks like he'll be here awhile."

"Mrs. Mudd," Becky said to her, "this isn't what you think."

"I don't want to hear about it, Miss," she brushed past her on the way to the fireplace. "I'll help my husband mend your bodies as best he can. Your eternal souls are your own affair."

"Mrs. Mudd—"

"That's all I have to say on the matter," she declared.

Becky started to respond, then plopped down helplessly at the table and watched the woman jiggle the warm coals in the fireplace with a poker. Although she had been riding all night, she was too excited and apprehensive to feel tired. Her mind swirled with images of that tall madman furiously wreaking havoc in the Seward house, shooting Stephen, pounding the pistol into Frederick's head. . . .

She tried to think of other things, but nothing helped.

She kept wondering: Was Stephen all right? Did he know where she was? Would he be coming after her? Or was he dead, too, like Lincoln, and was Seward, was Fanny?

As the long day passed, Rebecca was constantly on the verge of telling Mrs. Mudd who they were. Once she had a perfect chance. While Booth slept upstairs, Herold and the doctor left the house in search of a carriage. She and the older woman were left alone in the kitchen. But each time Becky started to tell her, she recoiled in fear.

Finally, at dusk, while Mrs. Mudd was out gathering another load of wood for the cookstove, Becky stole upstairs and wrote a note:

> *Mrs. Mudd, Please alert the authorities that the man your husband has attended to has* shot *the President. Tell them I overheard him say that we would be continuing south, into Virginia.*
> *Respectfully, R. Windfield.*

As she reached the first floor with the folded note clutched in her fist, Davie Herold crashed through the front door into the living room.

"Federal troops!" he shouted. "We've got to get out of here!"

While Herold was clambering noisily up the stairs, Becky rushed over to the doctor's wife at the stove. "Mrs. Mudd—" She held out the note. "Take this, please."

"Whatever that is, I don't want it." She shook her head.

"You can read it after we've gone. That way, you'll be safe."

"I'll be safe if I never read anything you've written, young lady."

"Then at least show it to the federal troops when they come!"

The woman paused, then wiped her hands on her apron and, at last, took the message. At that moment Herold and Booth came hobbling down the steps.

"Come on," Herold said to Becky, "let's go. They're already at Bryantown."

Following the two men, Becky tried to catch Mrs. Mudd's eye one last time, but she was busy shoving a thick piece of pine into the stove. On the threshold of the door, she looked back. Her heart sank in her chest like a ball of lead at what she saw.

Mrs. Samuel Mudd was stooped over the stove, peering into the open fire door. After staring at the popping flames for a moment, she very calmly pitched Rebecca's note into the fire, rose up, and slammed the iron door shut with a loud and resounding clank.

# Chapter 20

By the time the federal troops led by Lieutenant Alexander
Lovett and Special Officer Mason Butler reached the white
frame farmhouse south of Bryantown, Stephen felt very
discouraged. In three hard days of tracking, the only person they had arrested was the owner of a tavern Davie
Herold had visited on the night of the assassination. And
they had found no trace of Rebecca.

But when he overheard the tall, gloomy-looking man
inside the farmhouse say to Lieutenant Lovett that he was
a doctor, he felt a sudden spark of hope. He slid down off
his horse, tied him to the hitching post, and hurried into
the house. He found Dr. Samuel Mudd sitting uneasily on
the sofa, surrounded by Lovett, Butler, and six armed
cavalrymen.

"Did he see Booth!" Stephen asked Lovett.

The short, box-shaped officer glowered at him. "Why don't you let me do this, Bedford," he rebuffed him. "You interfered enough, back there at the tavern."

"I'm sorry, Lieutenant," Stephen apologized. "Go ahead."

"Thank you," Lovett responded coolly. Swaggering a little, he glanced over at Mason Butler, who stood watching silently, then at the frightened man on the couch. "Now, sir," he addressed him, "do you happen to know an actor by the name of John Wilkes Booth?"

"I don't think so," Mudd replied calmly. "I believe I've heard of an actor named Edwin Booth, but not John Wilkes."

"Doctor—" Stephen broke in. "Booth's leg was broken; he must have come here!"

"Bedford, what did I tell you!" Lovett warned.

"Well, why don't you ask him pointblank?"

"I was just about to do that, Bedford," he admonished. "If you'll stay out of it."

"All right, I'm out of it. Ask him."

He gave Stephen a long, critical look, then turned back to the physician. "Now, sir," he began, "have you treated a man with a broken leg recently? Say, in the last four days maybe?"

"No. Not in a month, at least."

"Are you sure about that?"

"Positive. You can check my records if you wish."

"No, I guess there's no need for that. He must have gone somwhere else. I'm sorry we bothered you—"

"Just a minute." Mason Butler stepped forth. He rubbed his chin, cast his eyes around the room at the small woman who stood next to the cookstove, wringing her hands, then at her husband. "Doctor," he began, "all we're trying to do here is find the lunatic who shot down and killed our beloved President. If we discover later that you have lied to us today, we will come back and arrest you for treason. And, in all probability, we will hang you."

"No!" Mrs. Mudd gasped. "You can't do that! He hasn't done anything!

"On the other hand," Butler continued, "if you tell us the truth, right now, we will not even arrest you."

"Now look here, Mason," Lovett broke in. "Don't go making promises to the man—"

"I give you my solemn word on that, sir," Mason swore to Mudd. "And the word of the United States Government as well."

Mudd gnashed his teeth as he weighed Butler's offer in his mind. Finally, after squirming on the edge of the sofa for a few minutes, he gave in. He confessed that he had let two men into the house, treated one of them, and then watched them go on the evening of the fifteenth.

"Is that all?" Mason waited. "Are you telling me the man was not John Wilkes Booth?"

"I can't say if he was or not. I never asked him his name."

"But you knew him!"

"No."

"You're lying, Doctor," Butler accused. "Which means you are going to hang with the rest of John Wilkes Booth's conspirators."

"Samuel, please—" his wife blurted.

"Be quiet, woman."

"Tell them what they want to know!"

"I have told them."

"But they're going to arrest you—"

"No, they're not. Now be still."

Butler turned sharply to the woman. "The man was Booth, wasn't he?" he quickly made his pitch. "Admit it, and both of you will remain free."

"Don't do it, Emma—"

She kept her eyes on Butler. "There's a boot in the bedroom upstairs," she told him. "He was wearing it that night."

"I'll get it," said Lovett as he rushed for the stairway. A few minutes later he returned, carrying a mud-covered black boot. It had been slit cleanly down the middle, from top to heel. "Looks like he had to cut it off his foot," he surmised.

Butler stepped closer to the surgeon. "Is that the boot worn by the man you treated?"

"Yes," he admitted, and shot his wife a cold look, "that's it."

"See if there's a name inside, Lovett," Butler ordered.

Every eye in the room fixed on the lieutenant as he peeled down the top of the boot and held the flap next to the glow of the oil lamp. After squinting at it, he nodded. "Yeah, looks like there is a name in here. It's . . . . J. Wilkes. That's our man, all right."

"Good," Butler said. "Sergeant," he commanded the man next to the door, "place Dr. Mudd under arrest for high treason."

"No!" Mrs. Mudd screamed. "You promised! I took you on your honor—"

"Now what can a traitor like you know about honor, ma'am?" he scolded her. "No decent human being would ever comfort a miserable cutthroat like John Wilkes Booth."

"Please don't take him away!" she cried. "He didn't know what the man had done!"

Butler ignored her plea. "We'll send him back to Washington," he informed Lovett. "After we've asked him a few more questions."

The lieutenant hesitated, clenching his teeth in disapproval, but then sounded the order to take the surgeon away.

While the rest of the group attended to the doctor, Stephen remained inside alone with his wife. He waited until he could hear the scrambling of the cavalry mounting their horses outside. Then he came forward.

"Mrs. Mudd," he said in a low voice, "there was a woman with Booth and and Herold. A beautiful woman in a theatrical dress . . ."

She eyed him blankly, with a stern, rigid face. "I have said too much already," she told him.

"Please, I have to know. She was here, wasn't she?"

"You have my husband, sir. What else do you want? Why are you trying to trick me again?"

"Mrs. Mudd, believe me, I'm not trying to trick you. I don't like Mason Butler's methods any more than you do—"

"Maybe you'd just better go, sir."

"Mrs. Mudd, please."

"Why don't you leave me alone!" she cried pitifully. "Can't you see I can't help you? Look at what I've done by trying to help my husband."

He hated to push, but he had to. "Will you at least tell me in what direction they were headed?" he asked. "It would save me days of hunting."

She wrestled with his request for a while, then shook her head. "I couldn't say," she responded.

He blew a breath of air through his teeth. "Well," he said with resignation, "I appreciate your talking to me anyway, Mrs. Mudd."

"Did I have a choice?" she retorted.

He let the sharp comment pass. "I would like to tell you," he said, "that the lady who was with Booth and Herold is named Rebecca Windfield. She happens to be the woman I'm going to marry."

"Well, that's no business of mine."

"No. I guess it isn't. I guess I just wanted to say it to someone." He walked to the door and turned around toward her. "I'll do everything I can for your husband," he promised. "But I'm afraid I have no power in Washington. And the country's too outraged at this murder to be lenient."

"We'll survive it," she stated bluntly.

"I'm sure you will," he said sadly as he opened the door.

"Sir?" she called out to him.

He turned around and waited.

"If it helps any," she muttered, "I think your Rebecca Windfield will survive, too."

"Are you telling me she was here?"

"I'm telling you nothing," she corrected. "And that is all I will ever say on the subject. Now, for God's sake, will you go? My husband is on his way to Washington, and I have a great many things to do."

Leaving the woman tearfully cramming wood into the cookstove, Stephen paused outside on the slick white porch to think about what she had said, then marched straight to his horse. Even in the midst of all this violence and sadness and insanity, he could feel hopeful now. Mrs. Mudd had given him a hint that he was on the right track to finding Rebecca.

And right now, he decided as he shoved his boot

into his stirrup and swung his leg up, that hint was all he needed to keep going.


While Stephen and the federal troops frantically combed the Maryland countryside for the fugitives, Rebecca, Booth, and Herold were holed up in a swamp to the south, near the Potomac River. After spending a night at a plantation owned by a man named Cox, they had been escorted by a servant to an old Confederate spy hideout deep in the pine thicket.

Left with her captors in the obscure little clearing, Becky couldn't help but shiver at what she saw. The dark, cold place looked positively evil with its slimy bogs and vapory sloughs. The tangled vines and underbrush seemed to be crawling all around her. The crooked limbs of the tall pine trees were like giant fingers groping toward her.

But then a hulking man named Thomas Jones broached the camp and stood before them with a heavy bundle in his arms. He had been sent by Cox with a supply of food and newspapers for the great liberator of the South, John Wilkes Booth. The actor responded eagerly to what he had brought. He raised himself up out of his blankets, grabbed one of the papers, and began to read it excitedly.

But his face turned sour as he scanned the printed sheets. "The *Intelligencer* didn't print the letter I gave to John Matthews," he compained. "Now people can only wonder why we did it."

"That's a Union paper you're reading there, Mr. Booth," Jones consoled. "People I know don't pay any attention to it anyway."

"Listen to this," said Booth as he folded the paper to read. "They're already beginning to slander my family.

This man claims I must be mad because my father was insane. Damn him! *I* did it, not my father!''

"It's only one man's words, Mr. Booth."

The actor whacked the paper with the back of his hand. "And where is the news of the others?" he asked. "It should be all over the front page."

"What others?" Jones wondered.

"The other assassinations? Johnson, Grant, Seward—"

"There weren't any other assassinations," he said calmly. "Mr. Seward was wounded all right, but they're saying now he's going to recover. And nothing at all happened to Grant and Johnson."

Booth stared at him in disbelief. "Then I'm all alone in this," he said grimly. "My conspirators have left me in a swamp, with nothing but a boy and a woman for company. I am doomed."

After that Booth acted like a man waiting for death to come. Wrapped to the neck in his woolen blankets, he lay curled up against a tree, staring vacantly for hours on end at the gray sky, grimacing once in a while, but seldom bothering to speak. As time passed, he grew restless and despondent. He lived only to read the latest papers Jones brought each morning and to scribble in his diary in the afternoon after he had gone.

As soon as the reporters began to repeat themselves on the subject of Booth, he became more absorbed in his own writing. It seemed to be an important ritual to him. He was almost childish about it, for while he was made a show of writing in the book, he was extremely secretive about it if Davie or Rebecca happen to ask him about it. Then, on their third day in the thicket, he called Rebecca over and asked her to listen to him read a portion of the diary.

"It's dated April 14," he said, holding up the little

book at a reading angle. "Even though I've been writing and rewriting the same passage for three days now."

She nodded and listened quietly while he read with a carefully controlled passion his description of the murder of Lincoln.

*"I can never repent it,"* he continued, quoting his own words with a profound sadness, *"though we hated to kill. Our country owed all her trouble to him, and God simply made me the instrument of his punishment—"*

"You don't believe that," she charged.

"What?"

"You can't believe you're going to be forgiven for this murder, just by claiming God made you do it. Let a preacher's daughter tell you something, sir. No matter what you write or say about the Almighty, you can never undo what has already been done. If you have committed a crime against Him, you will suffer for it."

"They haven't caught me yet, have they?" he retorted limply.

"No, but look at you. What kind of holy mission do you think you're on, curled up in a wet blanket in this terrible place? Do you think this is being an instrument of God?"

He looked at her in bewilderment. "Just what would you have me do, Miss Windfield?" he asked her.

"I'd have you give yourself up, Mr. Booth," she answered. "You shot the President—now go back to Washington and pay for it."

"That would be a very hard thing to do," he remarked.

"Of course it would. It's much easier to sit here day after day and write justifications for what you did in that little book of yours."

He smiled weakly. "You have a fiery tongue, Rebecca,"

he said. "I think from now on, I'll keep my writing to myself."

He said practically nothing to her after that. Sometimes, though, during those long and tedious hours, she would catch him staring curiously at her. But then, every time, he would quickly look away. Finally, on the morning of the twenty-first, he flung off his blankets and struggled with his stiff leg over to her. She was standing next to the hollow tree used by the Confederate spies as a letter drop.

"Miss Windfield—" He held out his diary in a quavering fist. "I would like for you to read this."

"I don't want to read it," she stated firmly, shaking her head. "It would only make me angry."

"It may not be what you think," he said mysteriously and tossed it into the hollow tree. "It's not as self-centered as the first entry."

She waited until he had hobbled away on the crutch Dr. Mudd had given him; then she took out the diary. Her eyes skipped over the first paragraph, and lit on the second:

> *April 16, Sunday, the Ides. The beautiful woman named Rebecca is a Northerner. She is my Accuser. She is a strange and disturbing light in a dark and dismal swamp. I must resist what her eyes are beaming.*
>
> *They make me wonder, was I wrong about the Union? Did I imagine a country of evil oppressors where only vital souls like hers lived?*
>
> *If I believe that, I cannot live with what I have done.*

The next section centered on her again:

*April 17. Rebecca Windfield is the Woman of the Well. I am a tired Crusader, about to drink of the water of Everlasting Life. . . .*

Startled by the powerful effect she somehow was having on this sad, troubled man, she flipped the page to the next day:

*Tonight I shuddered like a mewling child under Rebecca's accusing look. It is as hard as tempered steel. "What hast thou done?" it says to me. Is that to be the cry of the land? Have I forsaken everything I love merely to cower under the haunting glance of a gentle woman?*

She read the final entry with a mounting sense of excitement, mixed with relief, as Booth revealed a decision:

*April 20. We are all restless, tired, and weak. I am resolved to wait in this hell no longer. Rebecca and Davie have been my torches in this sunless, abandoned mire. Now they will gude me back to the scene of the act—and perhaps to peace.*

Her heart began pounding hard in her chest. Somehow her presence had convinced John Wilkes Booth to give himself up! Now they would soon be back in Washington. If only Stephen were there, waiting for her. She would throw herself into his arms and never let go.

But just as she pressed the thin pages of the diary together in her hands, she heard a crashing noise and wheeled around to see William Jones rushing headlong into the camp.

"Mr. Booth!" he called out. "I've got good news! You can leave now, if you hurry!"

"What do you mean?" Booth emerged from the trees.

Jones paused to catch his breath. "I just . . . heard that the federal troops have started pulling out," he panted. "They're on their way down to St. Mary's County. This is the best chance you'll ever have to get out of this swamp and back to civilization."

Booth sighed. "I was about to give myself up," he admitted, glancing at Becky.

"No—don't do that! Don't give up now," Jones urged. "All you have to do is reach Virginia. The people down there will help you. All of them."

Booth hesitated, then looked at Herold. "What about you, Davie?" he asked. "Do you want to try it?"

Herold shrugged his shoulders. "I'll try anything you say, Mr. Booth," he answered. "You're the boss."

Booth smiled warmly at the other man's blind loyalty, then reminded Jones that they would have to cross the river.

"The river's no problem," he returned. "There's a boat tied and ready. A few sweeps of the oars and you folks will be trotting free and clear across good old Virginia soil."

Booth looked at Rebecca, then pulled himself painfully across the clearing to her. "May I have that back?" He motioned for the diary. "It looks like I may be using it again."

She stared straight at him. "You're not really going to keep on running?" she asked.

"Not running, Miss Windfield," he said harshly. "Simply moving."

"But it's pointless," she argued. "They won't stop till they find us."

"Nobody will find us with all of Virginia helping us," Booth declared and, with that, plucked the diary out of her hands.

"Mr. Booth, please listen to me—"

"Save your breath, Miss Windfield," he said, then headed toward the big farmer. "Let's go, Jones," he said. "How far is that boat?"

"It's no more than a couple of miles," Jones answered. "You'll be strolling through Virginia before you know it, without a care in the world."

Jones uttered that prediction with confidence, but to Rebecca's dismay, it didn't work out that way. Once she and Booth and Herold were settled into Jones' flat-bottom fishing boat and gliding over the dark waters of the Potomac, the woods around them suddenly began to teem with federal troops. Stilled by Booth's hard grasp on her shoulder, she sat in the damp hull and listened to the sounds of soldiers moving about in groups to her right and left. They were sloshing noisily through the brush and mumbling incoherently in the trees or calling out to each other across the invisible sloughs. Once, catching a glimpse of a glowing torch in the woods, she started to raise up and yell out—but Booth quickly clamped his hand on her mouth.

"One little grunt and we're all dead, Miss Windfield." He dug his fingers into her flesh. "And you'll be the first to go. Do you understand?"

She nodded her head at his question.

"I've never hurt a woman," he whispered. "But until a few days ago, I had never killed a man. So please, don't try me."

She was too scared to try him. As the sky lightened, she

noticed that the personality of John Wilkes Booth had started to change before her eyes. His air of quiet grace and poise was gone now, as if it had dissolved in the damp fog lingering over the river. The long, agonizing days on the run were transforming him into a frightened, desperate man. Now, as he led them to the shore and into the Virginia woods, he began to complain endlessly about his swollen leg, to curse his pursuers under his breath, and to refer to Rebecca and Davie caustically as his "two burdens" in the forest.

And when he discovered that the people of Virginia were either indifferent or hostile, instead of friendly or helpful, his mood became sour and even offensive. After a doctor steadfastly refused to help him, he sent a freedman to him with a bitter, accusing note.

*I was sick, tired, with a broken limb,* he wrote to him, *and in need of medical assistance. I would not have turned a dog away from my door in such a plight.* Inside the folded paper he included five dollars for the food the doctor gave them—*on account of the reluctant manner in which it was bestowed.*

That evening he crashed into a tenant farmer's cabin and forced the terrified black man to put them up for the night. The next day, at knife point, the man carried them down to Port Conway, to catch the ferry to Port Royal.

When they reached the Rappahannock River, Booth clenched his fists and braced himself for a trio of hard-looking Confederate soldiers on horseback, galloping toward the ferry landing together. As soon as they pulled their horses to a stop, the actor adopted a rigid, determined look on his rough, bearded face, snapped Herold's revolver out of his trembling hands, and leveled it at the men dismounting.

"I guess you men know who I am." He leaned hard on his crutch while he cocked the revolver.

The tallest of the three young men nodded quickly. "You must be the man all these blue bellies are looking for," he surmised.

"That's right. I'm John Wilkes Booth, the man who killed Lincoln. And I'm worth $175,000 to any man who can take me in."

"Well, you can take it easy there, Mr. Booth." The tall man held up his hands. "We've just finished a long war with the yanks. We wouldn't cotton much to taking any of their blood money right now. You're safe with us." He went ahead and introduced himself as M.B. Ruggles of Mosby's command. The other two men, Alvin Bainbridge and Willie Jett, were of the 9th Calvary Regiment of Virginia.

Booth scrutinized them for a moment, then said cautiously. "Where are you men headed?"

"As a matter of fact, Mr. Booth," said Willie Jett stepping up, "we was riding down to Bowling Green for a little harmless àmusement, if you get my meaning." Leering at Rebecca, he added, "Which I'm sure you do, if this one's any sign."

Becky felt a chill run up her back as this stocky, gap-toothed man ogled her. She felt compelled to fold her arms across her chest and draw closer to Davie Herold.

"Can you find us a place to stay across the river?" Booth asked, ignoring his words.

Jett kept looking at Becky. "Sure we can, can't we, Alvin?" He nudged Bainbridge with his elbow. "We've got friends and neighbors all over Virginia."

Booth regarded them suspiciously, but went on. "We would greatly appreciate your help," he said formally.

Jett watched Rebecca as he scratched his thin nose with

his index finger. "That must be how you get fancy ladies like this, Mort?" he smirked. "You talk real smooth, like a gentleman."

"You'll have to overlook Willie," Ruggles apologized to Booth. "He's been away from women a long time. But he don't mean anything by it."

Booth gave the Confederate soldiers a stern look, but assured them he wasn't offended. Becky, on the other hand, was ready to run. These three men frightened her more than John Wilkes Booth ever had—especially the one they called Willie Jett.

All the way through the thick forests of Caroline County, Rebecca could feel his constant, lustful stare on the back of her neck. When they reached the farm of a Richard Garrett, Jett instructed the others to remain at the entrance gate while he took Rebecca and Booth in.

"I'll be coming back for you later," he whispered to her as they approached the house.

"What?" she said, stunned by his words.

"I've got some arrangements to make in Bowling Green," he said. "Meanwhile, you keep that stove of yours burning, all right?"

Before she could respond, he had climbed down from his horse and was stalking up to the porch of the old rambling farmhouse. By the time she had dismounted, he was introducing Booth to the Garrett family as a wounded Confederate soldier named Boyd. Rebecca was his sister Ruth. After Garrett finally agreed to lodge them in his house for a few days, Jett promptly leaped back on his horse and left them at the door.

For the next few hours Becky witnessed the revival of John Wilkes Booth. Warmed by the friendliness of the Garrett family, the actor slipped back into his old charm-

ing ways. At lunch he talked fluently about the war wit
the father and discussed the latest Paris fashions with th
lady of the house. In the afternoon he quoted Shelley an
Keats to Mrs. Garrett's sister, Miss Holloway, and prac
ticed shooting a revolver with the three sons. He had foun
a moment of peace, as he won the family's hearts.

Then, while they were eating supper, an excited neigh
bor came by and reported to the gathering that Mr. Lincol
had been shot. "And that evil John Wilkes Booth i
hiding out right here in Virginia," he informed them.

Becky could feel a tension begin to build in the room a
soon as the man left. Garrett looked suspiciously at Boot
with his gray head cocked.

"What this Booth has done is bad for the South," h
mumbled as he broke his hot bread. "Real bad. It'll g
hard on us now. Don't you think so, Mr. Boyd?"

Becky could see the pain wrenching in Booth's face a
he answered, "Maybe so."

"No maybe about it," Garrett huffed. "Now that we'r
down, the yanks will stomp us into the ground. All becaus
of that weasel John Wilkes Booth."

Becky swallowed drily as the actor clenched his teeth
though he remained outwardly calm. She ached to speak
but she was afraid that someone would get hurt if she did

"Poppa, what about that reward?" eighteen-year-ol
Bill Garrett offered. "It's over a hundred thousand dollars.

"It'd be worth it to be able to hang that low-life Booth,"
the farmer said hotly.

"Well, he'd better not come my way," the son boastec
"because I need that money."

Booth nervously cleared his throat. "Do you mean you'
betray a fellow Southerner for a handful of Yankee dollars?"

"Let's just say he'd better not come around here any time soon," Bill hinted.

After that Booth's charm and confidence began to unravel from his personality like rotten threads from an old shirt. He started peering apprehensively over his shoulder at any movement and jumping at every unfamiliar sound. He acted bitter, resentful, and defensive. "No one understands what I did," he complained to Herold when he joined him at the farm, "but I don't care. I did the right thing."

It was to escape Booth's annoying ways that Rebecca volunteered to fetch the afternoon water from the well behind the house. While she stood turning the windlass, she suddenly felt a hand gripping her shoulder. She was so startled that she let go of the crank and dropped the oaken water bucket into the well with a splash.

"Afternoon, Miss *Boyd*," Willie Jett chuckled as he massaged her neck with his short, stubby fingers. "I told you I'd be back, didn't I?"

She jerked her shoulder from him. "Excuse me," she replied coldly and started to go.

"Hey, hold on there, Missy!" He grabbed her wrist and twisted her arm back. "Remember, you're not in the North anymore. Down here you don't walk away from folks while they're talking to you."

"Are you pretending to be a Southern gentleman, Mr. Jett?" she snapped.

"Watch that sassing, girl," he warned. "I'm liable to start breaking something."

She winced as he yanked a numbing pain into her elbow.

"Now that I got your attention," he said, "I want you

to listen real close. I got it all arranged for us in Bowling Green. Do you get my meaning?''

''I have no idea what you're talking about,'' she said as he relaxed his hold.

''Then I'll spell it out for you,'' he told her. ''I've hired a place for us. You and me, all night long. Do you follow that?''

''You're insane,'' she gasped.

''Oh, no—I'm smart,'' he smirked. ''See, the yanks may have won the war, but it's Willie Jett's who's going to get the spoils.''

''What makes you think I would ever agree to such a thing?'' she asked, appalled.

''It's simple,'' he replied. ''If you don't, I'll tell the blue bellies where to find you and Mr. John Wilkes Booth. You folks won't have time to spit. They'll be on you like fleas on a dog.''

''Will you let me go—'' she insisted.

''You're not listening, Missy,'' he cautioned.

''Let me go!'' she cried.

''Hush up, girl,'' he snarled as he pulled her against his thick chest and pinned her arms behind her body. ''Think it over. Either you do it with me or I'll tell them all about you. Which will it be?''

Becky struggled as hard as she could to squirm out of his brawny arms, but it was useless. For the first time in her life she felt utterly helpless. She had always assumed she could handle any man with a few sharp words and a hard, determined gaze. How naive she had been to believe that!

''Say it, Rebecca,'' Jett grunted as he held her arms with one hand and groped at her breasts with the other. ''Say the word.''

"NO!"

"Now that ain't the right one." He squeezed. "Try another."

"Stop it!" She shoved at him.

"It's too late for that now, Missy—"

"Jett!" a clear, strong voice suddenly rang out. "Let her go!" Booth ordered, aiming down the long black barrel of a .45 calibre revolver.

As soon as she felt the soldier's grasp loosen, Rebecca slipped away from him. Panting wildly, she backed away from the well and nearer to Booth.

Jett pursed his lips. "Are you planning on using that thing, Booth?" he asked defiantly.

"Yes, I am." Booth cocked the pistol. "I can't trust you, so I have to use it."

"Well then, get on with it, man."

Booth hesitated; the pistol shook in his hand.

"Can't you do it, Booth!" he laughed. "Or are you yellow?"

"I can do it—"

A wide grin crossed Jett's face. "You don't have the guts," he declared. "Just as I thought: the great John Wilkes Booth is nothing but a sniveling coward. I knew you couldn't look a man in the eye and kill him."

"I can—"

"Then do it, coward," Jett taunted. "Shoot me!"

"If you don't stop—"

"You're going to have to do it in the back, coward," he said and started walking. "Because I'm leaving."

Booth followed the back of Jett's head with the pistol barrel as the Confederate soldier descended the hill. For a long, tense moment he held the gun straight out in front of him. When Jett reached his horse at the bottom of the incline, he lowered it to his side.

"He'll probably be telling the federal troops where we are," Booth said weakly. "We'd better find another place."

Rebecca drew in a deep breath and nodded.

He turned toward her. "I'm sorry this had to happen," he said. "What was once a noble idea somehow has turned us into vile things in the sight of everyone. It's robbed us of all our dignity. Even a scoundrel like Willie Jett believes he can force himself on you."

"If you feel that way, why don't you give up?" she urged him. "We could reach them before he does."

"No." He shook his head. "I'm not giving up."

"But if you believe it was wrong—"

"I didn't say I believed it was wrong, Rebecca," he corrected her. "I still believe I was meant to kill Abraham Lincoln. The man deserved to die."

"My God—can't you see yet what a terrible thing it was? You see how people feel about it. Even loyal Southerners like the Garretts—"

"Then it's they who are wrong. And we have to get away from them. One of the Garrett boys told me about a tobacco barn nearby. We can stay there tonight."

"But surely you realize that everybody is after us now? There's no one to support you."

"Then I'll fight them alone," he said calmly. "And I'll fight them to the end." He slid the revolver behind his belt. "And as God is my witness, Rebecca, they'll never take me alive."

# Chapter 21

"Answer me, damn it!" Mason Butler barked at the young man standing in front of the ferryboat on the Rappahannock. "Did he or did he not cross this river?"

The cowering little black man kept his eyes low, shrugged his shoulders, and said nothing.

Butler took a step closer. "You were here, weren't you?" he growled. "You couldn't very well miss him."

"No sir," he muttered. "I reckon not."

"Look here, you rascal. Admit you took John Wilkes Booth across this river and be done with it."

"I don't know nothing about it." He shook his head. "I just run the boat."

"All right, boy—" Butler reached out and snatched him by the collar. "Either you tell me about Booth, or so help me, I'm going to drown you."

"Mason—" Stephen advanced.

"Stay out of this, Bedford," he warned. "I'm through listening to liars. They're protecting him!"

"Abusing this man isn't going to accomplish anything."

"Let's just see if it does," he said. With a hard snap he jerked the black man down to the muddy water line. "Now then—" He cupped his big right hand on top of his head. "Talk!"

"I don't know nothing."

"I said talk, damn you!" Butler shoved him down to his knees and plunked his head into the cloudy water.

Instantly Stephen pounced. In one sweeping motion he knocked Butler's hand away, reached down, and clamped hold of the ferryman's shirt. With a great heave he hoisted him out of the water. The dripping man clung desperately to Stephen's arms and shoulders while he gasped for air.

"You could've killed him," Stephen fumed at Butler as the frightened man broke away and staggered back on the shore.

"I ought to kill you instead," Mason grumbled.

"What did you say?" Stephen faced him.

"All you've done for a week is get in my way, Bedford. You're worse than that bull-headed Irishman. . ."

Stephen looked at him, stunned. "Are you talking about Paddy?" he managed to ask.

"Forget it. I wasn't talking about anybody in particular," he fumbled.

"What do you know about Paddy O'Connor?" Stephen insisted.

"I don't know anything about him." Butler backed up. "All I want to do is get Booth. Isn't that why we're all here? We all want the man who killed our President?"

"You know something, don't you?" Stephen pressed.

"I remember now—you were on the street that morning they arrested me for Paddy's murder. What were you doing out so early, Mason?"

"Don't come any closer." Butler suddenly whipped a Colt revolver out of his coat pocket. "Lovett!" he hollered at the officer standing ten feet away, in front of his troops. "This man is threatening me—arrest him!"

The lieutenant furrowed his high brow with a frown.

"Didn't you hear me, Lovett?" Mason fidgeted. "I'm ordering you to put Stephen Bedford under arrest!"

"I'm not arresting anybody, Butler." Lovett reached into his pocket.

"You traitor! All of you are traitors!"

Lovett advanced toward the river, holding a piece of folded paper in his gloved fist. "This just came by messenger." He offered it to Butler. "It's from Mr. Stanton. He's sending Colonel Baker down to Virginia. Someone reported seeing Booth below Fredericksburg."

Still managing to hold his pistol steady, Mason snapped the paper out of Lovett's hand. His long face twisted into a scowl as he read it.

"If Stanton's sending down the head of the War Department detectives, they must know exactly where Booth is," Lovett reasoned. "From now on it looks like it's Baker's show."

"Oh no, it isn't!" Butler angrily wadded up the paper in his fist. "Not if I get there first."

"Don't you understand—he's calling us back," Lovett explained. "We're not going anywhere."

"Nobody's stopping me from crossing this river," Butler declared and flung the ball of paper into the river. Standing ankle-deep in the mud, he glowered at the officer, at Stephen, then at everyone else. Finally he pointed his gun at the black man kneeling on the ground, still panting.

"You!" he ordered. "Get up and come over here."

"Sir?"

"You heard me. Get up!"

"Yessir." He obeyed the command.

"Take me across the river," Butler said as he led his horse on the scow. "And be quick about it."

"Yessir."

"Now all of you cowards can turn tail and run home if you want to," he scolded the others as the boat shoved off. "I'm going to find that villain by myself. John Wilkes Booth shot and killed our beloved President, and by God, I'm going to make sure he pays for it!"

Stephen felt his muscles tighten his whole body as his eyes followed the scow through the currents. He felt like diving in after him, but with Butler still holding the revolver at the boatman's temple, he was afraid to make a move.

"Let him go, Bedford," Lovett advised from his saddle as the troops mounted their horse. "What harm can he do?"

"Mason Butler is a frightened man," Stephen observed as he watched the boat inch closer to Port Royal. "Something is driving him. And it's not patriotism."

"He's probably jealous of Baker being given the glory," Lovett offered.

"No, he's not after glory. He's desperate."

"Well, anyway, we'll be heading back now," Lovett said. "Are you coming along?"

"No, I think I'll go on," Stephen said.

"Whatever you say. Personally, I'll be just as happy to read about it in the papers."

As the troops stormed back through the brush, Stephen stood and stroked his horse's velvety nose and stared across the river. The figures in the scow were getting smaller now, but he could see that Butler still held his captive at gunpoint. Then he did something else. It sent a violent jolt through Stephen's body to see it.

As the wide boat vibrated in the waves, the clerk bent down and wiped the mud off his boots with a handkerchief. Suddenly Stephen's mind began to yoke things together. Why hadn't he noticed before? For the past week Butler had somehow always managed to keep his boots bright and shiny. Of course—this was the man Donald Massey had identified before he died. It was Butler who murdered Massey!

But why? His thoughts raced. They both worked in the War Department. Massey must have discovered that Butler was part of the assassination plot and was killed to keep it quiet. Now Butler would have to do the same to Booth!

A pain shot through his heart as that conclusion led to the next one: Paddy had stumbled upon the plot, too, and Butler had found out and murdered him.

Stephen closed his eyes as the image of Paddy O'Connor flashed before him. The big man's heavy frame lay twisted into a knot in the pine needles, warped with the pain of a Confederate sword stuck in his back. He could see Fanny Seward leaning low over the sergeant, weeping.

"Oh no Paddy," she had cried, "please don't die. Please don't leave me."

Then, as the big Irishman cried out that he couldn't see and sighed one last agonizing breath, she had burst into hysterical tears. But there was nothing to be done for the best and most loyal friend a man ever had. Paddy O'Connor was dead.

Wiping his watery eyes, Stephen climbed aboard his horse and headed him toward the river. The scow had landed on the opposite shore by now, and Mason Butler had vanished into woods. Stephen reined the animal down to the water's edge, stopped, and sucked in a long, deep breath. "I swear I'll get him for you, Paddy," he vowed and kicked his spurs into the horse's flanks.

In a mighty burst of strength, the stallion dug his hooves into the mud and thrust his huge body away from the bank and, with a wild and glorious splash, plunged straight into the churning currents of the Rappahannock River.

Several hours later, in the Garrett tobacco barn, Becky curled her back against the tattered cushion of an old discarded Victorian sofa and tried very hard to doze. But she was too frightened to sleep. She had a cold, empty feeling that something terrible was about to happen. She sensed it in the way the shadowy figure of John Wilkes Booth was hobbling restlessly back and forth across the floor on his crutch. Once he'd been a fine, poised actor who had commanded a thousand eyes when he strode confidently across the stage. Now he looked diminished and unimportant, like a common hunted fugitive, doomed to die.

"Mr. Booth!" Davie Herold whispered excitedly from his lookout position near the door. "Listen—somebody's out there!"

At his words, Rebecca held her breath and strained to hear. At first, all she could detect was Booth's painful, labored breathing; then, somewhere beyond the walls, she heard a deep, low voice call out to another in the distance.

"That's old man Garrett's voice, Mr. Booth," Davie said nervously. "I recognize it."

"Be quiet, Davie," Booth told him. "Maybe he won't tell them where we are."

Her heart pulsating, Becky raised herself quietly up from the sofa. The instant her shoes touched the dirt floor of the barn, she heard another voice floating in the darkness outside. Then two more. Pressing a palm against her chest, she tried to calm herself. But there were dozens of them now, and the thrashing sounds of men marching toward them through the woods.

"Oh, Lord," Herold fretted. "It's the troops—they're coming after us!"

Propped on his crutch, Booth cocked his carbine. "Let them come," he scoffed. "I'm ready for them."

Herold stepped back from the door. "I just heard Willie Jett's voice out there. He betrayed us—he told them where we were! It's because of her!"

Booth looked towards Rebecca and shook his head. "These soldiers probably don't even know she's in here, Davie," he said grimly. "A man like Jett wouldn't have the courage to tell them that a woman rejected him."

"If we gave her to them, maybe they'd let us go," David said.

"They don't care about her," Booth insisted. "They want me."

"But couldn't we send her out?" Davie asked.

"I'm not sending a defenseless woman out into that pack of wolves, Herold. I'm the reason she's here—the least I can do is protect her."

"But they're going to kill us, Mr. Booth!"

"Be quiet!" Booth said. "Listen!"

Booth leaned against his crutch and tried to track the

sounds outside. From the old sofa, Becky could make out two strong, harsh voices drifting toward the front of the building, then a hard shuffling of boots in the trees, as a whole command of soldiers began scattering around the place. Her heart began to pound rapidly in her bosom.

A dozen torches lit up the open spaces in the siding of the barn as the marching drew closer and closer. Then the noise abruptly ceased; the front door rattled and crashed open, and a small, awkward form stumbled headlong into the barn.

"Don't shoot!" The boy blindly flung up his arms to protect his face. "It's me, Bill Garrett!"

While the boy was gaping about in the dark, a heavy, strong voice boomed through the open door. "Booth!" it called out. "This is Lieutenant Luther B. Baker. I am here with Colonel Conger and Captain Doherty of the 16th New York Cavalry. We represent Colonel Baker of the War Department."

Booth leveled his carbine at Garrett. "Don't move a muscle, boy," he said.

"No, please, listen to me, Mr. Boyd," he pleaded. "I didn't want to tell them you were in the barn. They made me. They were hurting Poppa."

"I remember you talking about the reward, Bill—and what you'd do if I came around."

"That was all; just talk. I didn't know who you were then."

"Booth!" Baker yelled. "Do you hear me in there!"

"I hear you," he answered.

"All right, we're asking you to turn your weapons over to the boy and give yourselves up. You have my word, no one will be hurt if you do what we say."

Davie Herold advanced anxiously. "Maybe we'd better do it, Mr. Booth," he offered weakly.

"I'll never do it."

"Booth! Do as we say or we'll burn you out. Do you understand me?"

The actor let out a sigh of disgust. "Why don't you get out of here, Garrett," he ordered the boy. "You little traitor. If you're not gone in ten seconds, I swear to God, I'll shoot you down where you stand."

Bill Garrett instantly wheeled toward the door. "Captain!" he hollered. "It's me! I'm coming out—don't shoot!"

Herold reached Booth's side the instant Garrett broke out. "Mr. Booth, I'm scared," he whimpered. "If they let Garrett out, wouldn't they do it for us, too?"

"Go back to your post, Davie."

"But there are too many of them out there. They're everywhere! And if they set fire to the barn—"

"They won't do that—now get back to your post, Herold!"

"Mr. Booth," he choked. "I can't . . . do it. I can't stand around and wait for them to kill us. I don't want to die."

Booth looked directly at Herold for a long time, then yelled out to the officer in a clear, powerful voice. "Baker! There's someone in here who wants to leave!"

"Send him out!"

"Mr. Booth—" Davie whined.

"Go on, Herold. Leave me, damn your soul!"

"I'll stay if you ask me to."

"Just get out of here! I don't want you to stay. Go ahead and desert me; everyone else has."

Herold swallowed hard, started to say something, then

turned toward the door. "This is Davie Herold," he shouted, banging on the wood with his fist. "I want to come out!"

"Throw out your weapons, Herold!" Baker commanded.

"I don't have any weapons," he declared. "He has them all!"

After a long pause, Baker spoke. "All right, Herold," he said finally. "You can come out; but do it just the way I say."

"I didn't kill anybody," he protested. "I swear, I hardly even know the man. We were just riding together. Ask Willie Jett—"

"I want you to stick your hands out the door," Baker told him. "I want to see what you're holding!"

"Look, here they are!" Herold complied. "See, I ain't holding a thing in them. Hurry up—I don't want to be in here anymore!"

All of a sudden, Herold's body was yanked out of the building and the door slammed behind him with a loud bang. Becky and Booth were surrounded by darkness again.

After a noisy scuffle out front, Baker spoke. "We've got your man, Booth," he announced. "Now it's your turn."

"I'm not going to give up that easily, Lieutenant," he asserted.

"Don't be stupid, man. You know you'll never get out of there alive. We have fifty armed soldiers out here. I'm going to give you one last chance. If you're not out here in five minutes, Colonel Conger will give the order to start the fire!"

Becky jumped to her feet as troops of soldiers began to bump against the outside walls. Through the spaces between the siding, she could see lighted lanterns swinging back and forth, then chunks of hay being stuffed between the cracks. It was terrifying. The instant someone laid a torch to that dry hay, the wind-swept old barn would go up like a stack of matches.

"Mr. Booth—" She stepped toward him.

"Not now, Miss Windfield," he chastised her. "I've got to brace myself for a gun battle with fifty men."

"They're not going to fight you," she told him. "Didn't you hear him—they're going to burn the barn!"

Ignoring her words, he limped over to the wall. When he got next to the door, he laid the barrel of his revolver into a crevice. "Baker!" he shouted.

"I'm listening."

"Lieutenant, I've got a bead on you," he said. "I'm aiming right at your hairline. I can kill you any time I want to."

"What do you want, Booth?"

"I want a fight. I don't want to die like a hunted animal. Back up your men and give me a hundred yards and I'll come out shooting."

"Sorry. I can't let you do that."

"Damn you, don't you realize that with one squeeze of this trigger I can end your life!"

"I don't care; I'm not risking any of my men in a shootout."

"You idiot!"

"Your time is up, sir. Are you coming out or not? What's your answer?"

"You can lay down a stretcher for me, boys, because my answer is no," he declared. Pulling away from the wall, he looked at Rebecca. "Looks like I'm to be one more stain on the glorious old banner, doesn't it?"

A second later, the raspy voice of Colonel Conger croaked out a command that chilled Rebecca to the bone. "You heard the man," he ordered the soldiers near the wall. "If that's the way he wants it, let's burn it down!"

The unpainted slats of the tobacco barn exploded into flames like strips of dried kindling as the crackling fire raced up three of the walls of the shed. In seconds they were caught in a trap of blazing light and searing heat.

"Mr. Booth!" Becky backed up to the center of the barn. "We have to get out of here!"

For a moment the actor stood dazed, hypnotized by the whooshing sound made by the scorching flames as they swallowed up the wood. But he snapped out of it when the front door swung open with a thud and a cloud of choking black smoke came rolling into the barn. Shielding his face in the haze, he staggered back to Rebecca.

A look of horror crossed his face. "I should have told them you were here," he said to her. "I didn't think they'd do this. I've got to get you out!"

"Mr. Booth, why don't you give up before it's too late? Tell them we're both coming out!"

"No!" His eyes followed a tuft of burning hay as it dropped out of the walls to a stack inside the shed. "I'm not going to give them a chance to laugh at me while they hang me from a tree. I won't let them demean what I have done."

"Is this any better?" she pressed excitedly. "Is there any dignity in dying like this—in burning to death?"

His lips quivered as he gazed at the rising flames. He nervously wiped the sweat off his forehead with his sleeve. "God in heaven, Rebecca," he said bitterly. "What am I doing here? What have I done? It's all become so ugly."

"But it's not too late," she answered, taking his arm. "We can go out together."

He wouldn't move. "I was wrong, wasn't I?" he cried

mournfully. "I killed a man and now I'm damned for it. I thought about it for so long—how could I have been so wrong about it?"

"Mr. Booth—" She yanked him away from a smoldering haymow and toward the door.

"Nobody will ever forgive me for what I've done, Rebecca." He let her move him slowly. "Not even God will forgive me. I know it—"

"We have to run through the smoke in the doorway."

"No, Rebecca—" He broke away from her. "If we're going out, I'll go first. They may be waiting to shoot."

"Mr. Booth—"

"I said I'm going first, Rebecca," he insisted and flung down the carbine. "And I'll do it on my own two feet." He lifted his shoulders off the crutch, drew himself up, and let it drop to the ground. Then, staggering into the smoke sweeping through the door, he strained to see out into the darkness. "Baker!" he called out. "Hold your fire. I'm coming out!"

At the precise moment Becky heard him say the lieutenant's name, her attention was drawn away from him to a bumping noise above their heads and to the rear of the barn. Her eyes quickly snagged on the ominous sight of a huge man in black, squatting in the hayloft of the barn, aiming a pistol down at Booth.

Before she could utter a sound, the man had squeezed off a single round from his navy Colt revolver. Everything seemed to happen at once—the powder exploded from the barrel in a white puff, a shot cracked, and the head of John Wilkes Booth snapped backwards as the bullet smashed into the top of his spine and knocked him instantly to the floor.

Becky stood paralyzed in shock as the man in black

scrambled back through an opening in the wall and out of
the barn. In the middle of the swirling flames, she stared at
Booth's fallen body, unable to move. She knew she wasn't
strong enough to drag him out of the burning barn. They
would both die of suffocation before she managed to budge
him a yard. And yet, she couldn't just leave him there to
die. She had to do something—

But then, all of a sudden, a tall, lithe figure in a gray
coat dashed in through the open door and materialized in
the smoke. "Becky!" he called out.

"Stephen!" she cried as he swept her into his arms.

"I just got here," he said. "Thank God, you're all
right." He looked down at the crumpled body of John
Wilkes Booth. "Which way did the killer go, Becky?"

"He was up there—" She indicated the loft, which was
now engulfed in flames and dripping fire to the floor
below.

"They'll be coming for Booth," he said as he picked
the actor's carbine off the floor. "I'm going after his
killer—I've got a score of my own to settle with him."

"Well, you're not going without me," Becky declared.

He looked around him. The way he'd entered was choked
with fire and smoke now, and most of the stacks of hay
inside the barn were burning now; the flames were reaching clear up to the rafters. They had to get out immediately
but there was no easy way.

"All right," he conceded. "We're going to have to
break out of here."

Through the smoke, Stephen spied an old mower practically covered with hay. "This ought to do it," he said,
handing Becky the carbine. He scraped the refuse off the
iron mower and, with a great surge of strength, rammed it
halfway through the thin wall of the barn with a thundering

crash. After ripping apart two of the splintered and burning boards, he quickly grabbed Rebecca's hand and led her over the mower and through the hole, just as Baker and Conger swept through the flames and into the shed after Booth.

Outside, Stephen and Becky almost bumped into two blue-coated soldiers, standing guard with rifles poised at the shoulders.

"Hold it!" one of them warned, peering at them through the swirling smoke. "Stop or I'll shoot!"

"Wait a minute, Corporal," the other exclaimed. "Hold your fire—it's a woman!"

Just then a shout was heard above the noise and confusion: "We've got him! We've got John Wilkes Booth!"

As the two soldiers quickly turned and raced toward the front of the barn, Stephen pulled Becky away from the burning building and into the woods nearby.

"Are you all right?" he asked her anxiously.

She nodded, coughing, struggling to catch her breath.

"Booth didn't hurt you, did he?"

"No," she replied and with bewilderment shook her head.

"Good." He took the carbine from her. "Becky, the man you saw in the hayloft was Mason Butler. He killed Paddy."

"Oh, Stephen, no! Why"

"I'll tell you about it later. Right now I want you to stay here. Will you do that? I'll be back as soon as I can."

"Stephen, don't leave me—"

"I have to go, Becky. Butler is getting away."

"Can't the federal troops go after him?"

"If we wait, we may never be able to prove anything. I have to find him now."

"Stephen—" She tried to hold him, but it was too late. He gave her a quick kiss on the cheek, broke toward the open field, and disappeared into the darkness.

On top of a hill just beyond the tobacco field, Stephen came to a stop. He had caught a glimpse of Butler only a moment ago, lumbering noisily through the trees and heading toward the river. Then he had lost him.

With his chest heaving, he stopped to scan the area from the flaming barn on his left, through the open pasture to the woods slowly becoming visible in the dawning light. He could see nothing. It was as if the man had vanished into the air.

He thought of Paddy. Was this how the big Irishman had died—by being gullible? Had Butler lured him into the woods and stabbed him from behind?

Inching his way north, he managed only a few steps before he froze at the sharp sound of a dry twig snapping behind him. With Booth's carbine pressed tight against his shoulder, Stephen turned slowly around, hesitated, then started to walk toward a clump of trees. At another breaking sound, he paused and listened. He could tell that someone was nearby, only a few feet away—

All of a sudden, a massive black shape shot out from behind a tree, swinging a club the size of a human arm. Immediately it came swishing through the air, straight at Stephen face. Ducking slightly, he went on down to his knees as the wood clunked squarely across his forehead.

The next thing he saw was the looming body of Mason Butler. He was aiming a Colt revolver at his head.

"Sorry, Captain Bedford," he said in a low voice. "I'm afraid this is as far as you go."

Stephen had only one chance—to find the carbine he had dropped on the ground. But where was it? He hadn't even seen it fall.

"It's almost morning, Bedford," Mason commented. "But you're not going to live to see another day. That's a shame, isn't it?"

He remembered now. It had fallen to his right. Extending his right arm as far as he could, he plowed through the damp leaves and wet dirt, groping, stretching until he finally felt the tips of his fingers touching the cool metal breech of the carbine rifle.

"Say hello to that stupid Irish friend of yours," Butler snorted, "wherever it is you go from here—"

"Stephen!" Becky suddenly screamed behind them.

Bedford had only a split second to act, but it was enough. As Butler reacted to the unexpected sound of Becky's voice, Stephen rolled sharply to his right. His fingers grasped the rifle breech and coiled around the trigger. Praying the gun was already cocked, he aimed it high at the chest of the body turning toward him.

Both weapons fired at once. Mason Butler's bullet went awry and thumped harmlessly into the ground, a half-dozen inches from Stephen's head. But Bedford's aim was true; his shot struck home and erupted with a spatter of blood into the other man's heart.

'Stephen—you're hurt!'' Becky came running to him.

"I'm all right," He raised himself groggily to his knees. He crawled over to Mason, lying flat on the ground, his breathing labored. "Butler—" Stephen panted, "can you hear me?"

After a long moment the clerk opened his eyes. "I should've seen to you in the beginning," he muttered. "That was . . . poor planning on my part."

"Butler, listen to me. You've been shot in the heart. You're not going to make it. Do you understand me?"

"I don't believe you, Bedford," he groaned.

"I want you to tell me about the assassination plot."

"What's that?" he rasped painfully.

"You're dying, man—there's no need to lie any more. Who planned it? What was your part in it?"

"I deserve better than this," he mumbled angrily. "Cameron promised me a political job, but thanks to Lincoln and Stanton—"

"Butler!" he cut him off. "Whose plan was it!"

"I could've been . . . President, instead of a lowly junior clerk—"

"For God's sake—"

"Go to hell, Bedford," he sneered, then began to choke and spit up blood. Then, with a scowl on his long face, he rolled back his eyes, let out a moan, and died.

Stephen stood up and put his arm around Rebecca. "He never even gave Paddy or Booth a thought," he said sadly. "All he could think about was his damned job!"

"Stephen—"

"God, it scares me, Rebecca, to think what one man like Mason Butler can do."

"Stephen, I want to see about Mr. Booth," she said.

He nodded, looked at the body one more time, and started with her back toward the barn.


They found the barn burnt to the ground and most of the soldiers packed tightly together around the porch of the Garrett farmhouse. Pulling Becky by the hand, Stephen nudged his way through them to the porch where Booth lay propped up on a straw mattress. Stephen was startled to find the once-magnificent actor nothing more than a ghostly image of what he had been. The man lay on his side, as stiff as a corpse. He was rolling his eyes wildly, yawning his mouth open and shut in silence, straining to speak to the dark-bearded officer kneeling beside him.

"What is it, Booth?" Colonel Conger asked him. "What do you want to say?"

"I . . ."

"Go ahead, man, say it; I'm listening."

"I . . . can't move my hands," he cried. "What's wrong with my hands?"

"I don't know; it looks to me like your whole body's paralyzed."

Booth's eyelids dropped at his words. "Then why don't you just kill me," he said quietly. "Please, kill me. I want to die."

"Our orders were to bring you in alive," Conger replied calmly.

"For God's sake, Colonel. I'm an actor. If my body is dead, I'm dead, too."

A few feet away, Stephen felt Rebecca's soft form at his side, then her hand unconsciously squeezing his. He glanced at her sad eyes, then looked back at Booth. The handsome face that had excited and disturbed thousands of women had now become a dark and bloody mask of itself. Twisted in pain, it was the only thing on his whole body that seemed to have any life left in it.

"I have to cough," Booth groaned. "Colonel—" He heaved silently in the air, then closed his mouth.

"Booth, listen to me," Conger pressed. "Do you want to make a statement before you die? Is there anything you wish to say?"

He managed a faint smile. "You're asking an actor

that?'' he said. He thought a minute, then said, ''I'm ready. Is there any blood in my mouth?''

''No, Booth.''

''My mouth feels wet,'' he complained. ''Are you sure there's no blood in it?''

''I swear to you, there's no blood.''

The actor nodded, tried to swallow, but couldn't. ''Would you . . .'' He choked then started again. ''Would you tell my mother . . . I died for my country? Just tell her . . . I did what I thought was best.''

''I'll tell her,'' Conger promised.

''Colonel—where are my hands! Did I lose my hands in the fire?''

''Your hands are by your side,'' he said.

''I don't believe you. I can't feel them. A man can feel his own hands.''

''Look at this, Booth—'' Conger raised the actor's right hand in front of his face. ''It's yours, isn't it? You still have them.''

Recognizing the palm, Booth wrenched his face into a hard, desperate smile. ''Yes,'' he acknowledged, ''but they're dead, aren't they? I wonder if I'll need them where I'm going?''

''Booth, is there anything I can do for you?''

''There's nothing anyone can do for me now, Colonel,'' he answered. ''Not after what I've done.'' He seemed to summon every ounce of his mortal strength for one last surveying look at all those around him. Then he muttered in a pitiful little voice, almost under his breath, ''It was all for nothing, wasn't it? Useless, useless.''

While Rebecca turned around and buried her head into his chest, Stephen watched the actor manage one last gasping cough before Conger eased his lifeless head down on the wooden porch.

The colonel lingered at the body for a while, then drew up as a soldier handed him a small calendar book he had rescued from the burning tobacco shed.

"It looks like a diary," Conger announced as he leafed through it. "The last entry is dated the twenty-first, six days ago." Stepping over to the bannister, he held the volume up in the golden light of the sunrise, paused a moment, then read aloud in a sombre, funereal voice:

> After being hunted like a dog through swamps, woods, and last night being chased by gunboats till I was forced to return, wet, cold, and starving, with every man's hand against me, I am here in despair. . . . I have given up all that makes life sweet and holy, brought misery upon my family, and am sure there is no pardon in Heaven for me. . . . I have never hated nor wronged anyone. This last was not a wrong, unless God deems it so. And it's with Him to damn or bless me . . .

"Amen," someone in the crowd responded. "Let God decide."

"The poor, misguided . . ." Conger began, but let the sentence trail off in the stony silence in front of the Garrett house.

"What else did he write, Colonel?" Baker asked after a minute.

Conger didn't seem to hear as he thumbed interestedly through the pages, skimming each entry. Then he looked around until his eyes found Becky. "Are you Rebecca Windfield?" he asked her.

"Yes," she replied expectantly.

He raised his eyebrows. "According to this diary, you have been with John Wilkes Booth for the past six days."

"Colonel Conger—" Stephen broke in.

"Stay out of this, sir. I'm speaking to the lady." He took a step toward Becky. "Is this true, Miss Windfield?" he demanded. "Have you actually been staying with him all this time?"

"I wasn't staying with him, Colonel," she protested. "Not the way you mean."

"I don't mean anything, ma'am," he said indignantly. "I'm just asking a question: were you with Booth the past six days?"

"Becky, don't answer him—"

"Yes, Colonel," she admitted. "I was with him."

"Then you are under arrest, ma'am," he said simply.

"Now just a minute, Colonel—" Stephen thrust his body in front of Rebecca as a soldier advanced. "Miss Windfield was taken as a hostage—"

"I don't care how she came to be there, sir," he declared. "All I know is, she was with him. That's enough for me to arrest her."

"Well, it's not enough for me to allow it."

"Sergeant!" Conger blurted to a soldier. "Restrain this man!"

Stephen felt hands snapping hold of his arms from four different directions. Straining against the powerful grip of the soldiers did no good; he was forced to stand and watch two other men in blue guide Rebecca sharply off the porch. "What's the matter with you, Colonel!" he said through clenched teeth, boiling inside. "You know she's not a criminal—"

Conger raised his chin up. "Anyone aiding the escape of John Wilkes Booth is automatically a criminal."

"She didn't aid him! He forced her to go with him!"

"The court will decide that, sir. But I may as well warn you. The governor is outraged over this murder. I would suspect that anyone even remotely connected to this conspiracy will wind up dangling at the end of a rope."

"Damn it—she's not connected!" Stephen insisted.

"Well, this says she is." Conger thumped the diary against his palm. "And I believe the testament of a man who knows he's about to die. Take them away men," he ordered.


At dusk that evening, April 27, the federal troops led by Conger and Baker arrived at the Potomac River. With his hands fettered behind his back, Stephen Bedford waited on the shore near Rebecca as the soldiers carefully loaded the body of the dead actor aboard the tugboat *John S. Idle*.

"Stephen," she asked as they laid the corpse into the waiting hull, "what do you think they're going to do to me?"

"I don't know," he admitted. "People go crazy at times like this."

"If John Wilkes Booth had lived . . ."

"Yes, but he didn't live. He died leaving a diary with your name in it—and an angry nation itching to punish somebody for the death of their president."

"Stephen, I'm scared."

"I am too."

"Can't somebody do something?"

"Somebody has to."

"Better step over to the boat, ma'am." Lieutenant Baker

swept up beside her and took her elbow. "You'll be sitting next to Davie Herold all the way back to Washington."

"Stephen—" She looked back at him.

"We've still got one chance, Becky," he told her. "Maybe if I told him the whole story—"

"If you told who?" she fumbled as Baker forced her into the boat.

Before he could answer, Stephen felt a steely hand ram into his shoulder blade and shove him forward. Boarding the tugboat a minute later, he gazed around at the grim-faced officers and soldiers settling down into their seats. All they wanted now was to do their duty and go home, he thought. But with a bit of luck, they might dutifully deliver them to the one man in the world who could save them.

But he wondered—would Edwin Stanton even bother listening to their story? Or would he do his duty, too, and let the bloodthirsty prosecutors send Rebecca to the gallows along with her fellow "co-conspirators"? They would present her to the jury, after all, as a woman deserving to be hanged—a woman who had spent a week of her life in the company of one of the greatest villains in American history: the man who shot Abraham Lincoln.

# Chapter 22

On the foredeck of the monitor *Saugus* in the Navy Yard in Washington City, Stephen sat with his wrists manacled to a long, heavy chain. Two hours earlier he had sent Edwin Stanton a letter explaining his part in the Booth-Lincoln affair. But, so far, the Secretary hadn't responded.

While he waited for an answer, he examined the solemn faces of the other captives shackled to the chain that stretched down the deck of the boat. At the end, Lewis Powell stared dully at the sun rising over the bow. Dr. Mudd and Samuel Arnold, a friend of Booth's, were whispering anxiously to each other about their impending fates. Dark-haired Mary Surratt sat with her knees drawn up to her chest, looking straight ahead with an expression of fear and confusion frozen on her face. The heavy sense of gloom hanging over the boat made Stephen's whole body shudder.

Where was Becky? he wondered. Had Conger and Baker taken her to the *Montauk* and huddled her with Davie Herold, George Atzerodt, Michael O'Laughlin, and Ned Spangler? Was she doomed to die with them?

Suddenly, a young, red-headed soldier clambered onto the gunboat and stomped noisily across the deck. When he came to a halt, he was looking straight down at Stephen.

"Are you Bedford?" he asked him.

"That's right."

"Then you're coming with me." He bent down and snapped off the cuffs.

"Where are we going?" Stephen asked, rubbing his wrists.

"Back to the Old Penitentiary," he replied. "Mr. Stanton's orders."


At the prison near the Arsenal, they were met by the pig-faced guard. "Well, I'll be . . ." He grinned at Stephen. "I knew you'd be coming back. They always do."

"It wasn't my idea," Stephen said.

"No, I reckon it wasn't," he chuckled. "But maybe this time you'll be staying longer, huh? Say about twenty years or so? If they don't hang you first."

With the guard's ominous words echoing in the halls behind him, he was led down a long, damp corridor, deeper and deeper into the dark maze of the cells. The farther they penetrated, the dimmer the place became.

"We're almost there," the soldier muttered after a while.

A minute later they passed through an open door of steel bars, into a huge chamber. When his eyes adjusted to the low torch light in the room, he saw two sentries in blue coats standing at parade rest behind a rectangular hole dug into the floor—a grave.

Then he heard the noise of footsteps behind him. He could make out the sounds of five or six people shuffling his way. The steps were sharp and cadenced—had a firing squad come to execute him? Had they dug the grave for him?

No—he could see now, emerging from the darkness, four soldiers carrying a corpse upon their massive shoulders. Behind them were Stanton and Becky. Before he could make a move toward her, the red-headed soldier shot his big fist forward, struck his chest with a thump, and pinned him back to the concrete wall.

"Be still," he whispered. "And listen."

He took a deep breath as the soldiers lowered the body into the ground and Edwin Stanton stepped toward the grave. Speaking in a deep, measured voice, he delivered a short eulogy for the dead man wrapped in a Union army blanket:

> *"In his time on earth, John Wilkes Booth possessed a bold and sensitive spirit that for some reason lost its way. We may never really know what it is that can drive a gentle man to such an act of violence as he committed. Perhaps we aren't even meant to know. The ways of God are mysterious.*
>
> *But we do know this: the body of John Wilkes Booth lies secretly and ignominiously below us now, in the bowels of an unholy place. And I for one do not believe this is wrong, for we are not here today to lay the man to an everlasting rest. It makes no difference what we say or do this day, or any day—his soul will*

*never have peace. He has destroyed a living great-*
*ness that can never be replaced. He has committed an*
*evil so extreme and so blasphemous that this country*
*and its people have been stained by it forever.*

*So let my final words be these: that for his crimes, let*
*John Wilkes Booth answer to no man, but to the Lord*
*God Almighty who created him.          Amen."*

The attendants shoveled in the damp black dirt, replaced the stones on the floor, and marched quietly out of the chamber. For a minute the room was silent. Then Stanton brought Rebecca over to Stephen.

"Here's your letter, Captain Bedford." He handed him the note Stephen had sent him.

"But every word of it is true," he protested.

"Maybe it is," he conceded. "But I have a feeling in this trial of the conspirators, the truth will become tangled enough without you adding to it."

Stephen took the letter. "But what about Mason Butler?" he asked. "If you ignore this, you'll be ignoring the fact than a man in the War Department was a key figure in the deaths of Lincoln and Booth."

"I know I will," he acknowledged. "But since Butler's part in the assassination of Lincoln doesn't change the guilt of the other conspirators, what good will it do to reveal it? It could destroy the credibility of the government. We can't have that—not now, with our country about to enter one of the most trying times of our history."

Stephen gazed over at Booth's grave. "Lincoln once said it was the duty of the living to draw strength from the dead. Maybe this is what he meant. Maybe in order to have one nation again, we have to suffer through the

agony of a terrible murder and the misery of a harsh
Reconstruction.''

"But we will be one nation again," Stanton vowed.
"And we will turn into what Lincoln predicted: the strong-
est nation in the world. It will be a country of the people
and for the people—rich and poor, black and white, North
and South. We'll be part of a great nation that will never
perish from the earth.''

"And what happens to us, Mr. Stanton?" Becky asked.

"You are to be part of it, Miss Windfield," he said.
"You and Captain Bedford here."

"Do you mean you're letting us go?"

"Yes, I'm letting you go. The soldiers who know you
were with Booth will be kept as quiet as those who helped
us bury the man today. Your secret is safe—as long as you
never breathe a word about Mason Butler."

Becky swallowed. "What about Mr. Booth's diary?"
she asked. "Some of the pages had my name in them—"

Anticipating her, the Secretary was pulling the diary out
of his coat pocket. "Seven pages, to be exact," he told
her. "Five entries, dated April 16 to April 20."

"Won't they be made public at the trial?" she asked.

"No, they won't, he said, ripping the leaves from the
spine. "If you keep my secret, I will keep yours." He
handed them to her.

"Mr. Stanton—" She received them with trembling
fingers.

"Read them to your grandchildren someday." He smiled
wistfully, then cleared his throat. "In the meantime, why
don't you two get out of here? Go on—prove me right.
Show me the North and the South can find a way to unite
together.''

*      *      *

Outside the Old Penitentiary, a few yards in front of th
waiting War Department carriage, Stephen watched Re
becca fold the diary pages carefully into a neat square
"You know, people are going to wonder what happened t
the missing pages of Booth's diary," he observed.

"Well, let them wonder," she said.

"What about me, Rebecca?" he ventured. "Aren't yo
at least going to tell me what's in them?"

"Why should I do that?"

"Because it just might put my mind at ease, that
why," he said.

"At ease about what?"

"About you and Booth, Rebecca," he said, trying n
to become angry. "About how you happened to be wi
him in the first place."

"I was forced to go, Stephen."

"That's not what Bell said. He told me he saw you g
with Herold willingly."

"Oh, for God's sakes, Stephen. You can't really belie
that!"

"I don't want to believe it. But I keep remembering, t
first time I ever saw you, you were going up to Booth
hotel room. Then you had breakfast with him. And yo
rode with him in his carriage—"

"And I lived in sin with him for a week in t
swamps—is that what you're thinking?"

"I don't know what I'm thinking, Rebecca. That's ju
it. I don't know."

"But you do know you want me to prove my innocenc
by letting you read his dairy?"

"I didn't say that."

"You didn't have to say it. It's written all over yo
face. Well, I'm not going to let you read them."

"God. Paddy was right. Massachusetts women are tough as nails."

"Well, I'm sorry, Stephen. What is it you want—an empty-headed Southern belle with a clapper for a brain?"

"Southern women are not like that, Rebecca."

She stared at him. "We just can't agree on anything, can we?" she said.

"No, we can't."

"And it's been that way since the first time we met, in Ford's Theatre. And it doesn't look as if it's going to change either."

"No," he agreed. "It doesn't."

She pressed her lips together to keep from crying, spun around, and bolted toward the carriage.


He wandered aimlessly through the streets of Washington after that. He knew Rebecca had gone to the Seward House to see Frances, but not knowing what to do about her, he simply walked. Eventually he found himself at Ford's Theatre. After hesitating a few minutes, he went in.

In the wake of Lincoln's violent death, he expected the dark, empty theatre to feel cold and dismal. But to his surprise, the atmosphere of the building was fresh and stimulating, like calm country air after a storm.

Stopping in the middle of the orchestra seats, he looked up at the black cloth draped over the railing of the President's box and considered how close he had come to preventing the assassination—to changing history. Then, somewhere in the theatre, he thought he heard the loud crack of a pistol, followed by the shocked and painful screams of a thousand people mourning. And finally, silence again.

A warm sensation washed over his body, almost taking

his breath away. As he stood facing the balcony, feelin
exhilarated and excited, a familiar voice drifted down t
him from the high ceiling.

*"It's all right, Captain,"* it said. *"This was the way
was meant to be."*

"Paddy?" he said aloud, then realized he had onl
imagined the voice. But the words, wherever they ha
come from, sent an idea jolting through him. What Lir
coln had said was true! Some things reach beyond th
grave. Some things are greater than we are. They reac
beyond all differences of politics or personality. Eve
beyond—

Instantly he sprang out of the seats, raced through th
theatre, and burst out the door. Before he had covere
twenty feet of Pennsylvania Avenue, he drew up. A beaut
ful blonde woman in a fresh, salmon-colored dress wa
driving an open carriage at full speed in his directio
When he realized she was stopping and climbing down
the walk, he broke into a run.

They fell into each other's arms and began kissin
passionately.

"Oh, Stephen, Stephen—"

"Becky, I love you."

"I love you, too."

"Then that's all that matters, isn't it?"

"Yes! Yes! Frances is all right, and you and I ar
together—"

"And we can get through whatever happens—no matte
how hard it is!"

She nodded eagerly. "No matter how differently we se
things."

He pulled her to his chest and held her close. Then h
felt compelled to ask her. "Becky, about Booth—"

"John Wilkes Booth is dead, Stephen." She pulled away. "Can't we just let it be?"

He paused, sighed, and nodded. "All right," he agreed, "we'll let it be. I trust you."

"Well, finally."

They walked together back to the open carriage. "Becky, would you come to Arlington with me?" he asked brightly, as he helped her up.

"I don't know," she settled into the seat. "That depends."

"On what?"

"On whether you'll come to Boston first—to meet my parents."

"I'm not sure your parents would welcome a former Confederate officer into their home," he said, climbing in.

"I can face that if you can," she offered.

He held out his hand. "May I have the reins?" he asked.

"I usually drive." She hesitated.

"Becky—"

"But today, why don't you drive?" She gave them to him.

"Thank you."

"You're welcome. Is there anything else you want?"

He sat looking at her for a long time. Then he smiled. "There is one thing I want you to do for me, Rebecca," he said.

"What's that?"

"Direct me to Boston."

"Just head north," she laughed. "Way up north."

"Well then, I guess we've got a long way to go then, haven't we, Becky?" he said.

"I guess we do. But I'm ready if you are."

Stephen Bedford glanced back at Ford's Theatre, then ahead again. "You know, I believe I am ready, Becky," he said and popped the reins on the horse's rump. "I do believe I am."

# *THE GAMBLERS*
## Lee Davis Willoughby

NEW ORLEANS: 1856—dashing Jason Lowell, uncrowned king of the riverboat gamblers, seems to have fulfilled his dream. In his own boat, *Argos*, bought with gold he'd won in California, he prepares for a series of trips up and down the mighty Mississippi that will bring him untold riches.

At first glance, the passenger list looks promising. There is the distinguished—and extremely wealthy—Senator Stephenson, who cannot resist a game of chance, along with his lovely and mysterious young ward, Melissa Wainwright. There is the well-heeled Duncan Sargent, who claims to be researching a book. And there is the picture-pretty Elizabeth Brigham and her wild brother Charlie, and incurable gambler.

But Jason and his loyal young brother Gus don't realize that there's a cargo of death in the hold, and that the *Argos* is headed toward their biggest gamble—in Bloody Kansas.

Be Sure To Read *THE GAMBLERS*—forty-fourth in the series, *The Making of America*, on sale how from Dell/Bryans.

At your local bookstore or use this handy coupon for ordering:

# THE ROBBER BARONS
## Lee Davis Willoughby

Tall, intense Clay Monroe, long isolated from his family, a dynasty of lumber merchants, was suddenly called home from abroad. Why did multi-millionaire speculator Harvel Packer want him as his assistant? What did Packer's seductive daughter, Eugenia, really want from him? Why had his brother, Cyrus, vowed to destroy him? Was the husband of his secret love actually his natural father?

Everyone seemed to know more about Clay Monroe than he did himself, and as he moved brilliantly ahead in the world of Harvel Packer, Philip Armour, J.P. Morgan, John D. Rockefeller, Jay Gould and Jim Fisk, the mystery deepened.

Only in the midst of a bloody battle for control of America's railroads—pitting Clay against the power of Jim Fisk, biggest, boldest Robber Baron—does the daring young man discover the key to his past, and to his true destiny.

Don't miss *THE ROBBER BARONS*—forty-fifth in the series, *The Making of America*, on sale how from Dell/Bryans.

At your local bookstore or use this handy coupon for ordering: